Dana Lost

Stephanie M Turner

Dana Lost

Stephanie M Turner

Sasmjadahoha Publishing

ISBN 978-0-9929881-2-8

Sasmjadahoha Publishing
Email: books@sasmjadahohapublishing.com
Tel: (+44) 7546856165
www.sasmjadahohapublishing.com

To my husband Stephen, and our children Jason, Damon, Holly and Harriet, for their support, encouragement and inspiration.

ACKNOWLEDGMENTS

Stephen Turner, my husband, just for always being there..

Chapter 1

It's so dark. Why is it so dark? I can't see anything. What's happened? Oh my God I think I've gone blind, or an accident of some sort. Maybe I'm paralysed. No phew, I can feel my hands, my fingers and wait, yes my face and the rest of my body. I'm blinking but the darkness is still there. It shouldn't be, not this dark, it's still summer, early evening in August when the nights are still light. So maybe I'm just sleeping. That's it I'm asleep and dreaming. I'll wake up soon I hope, I don't like this dream, it's too scary. I'm afraid but I don't know why.

It's still dark and so very quiet. I'm sure I'm not dreaming now, I'm sure I'm awake. I can feel my bed underneath me. The duvet is all squashed up and wrinkled. I haven't washed the cover in a long time, haven't got any washing powder. The sheets smell, actually no they don't. That's weird, they haven't been washed in like forever either. Oh well that's not so bad then.

I should get up. But it's still night, dark, I think... yes! That's it. There's no moon tonight. That's why it's so dark. Wow that dream I had really rattled me. Made me hold my breath so that when I realised it was a dream, I felt all the air just whoosh from me. I must have been holding it for a long time. Didn't know I could do that because it really did come out in one long sigh. I mean when we go swimming, me and the gang, I can't stay under water for long, just a few seconds really. Bet next time we go I can. I'll have to tell Penny later. She can swim right across the pool under water. Maybe I will have a go too now I know I can hold my breath. I bet before I was just scared.

So it must be morning now. I've been awake for ages but it still seems so dark. Or is it? I think I can see a little light. Just on the edge of my vision. Yes, it's not pitch dark now. At last the day is coming. That's a relief. I'm not usually afraid of the dark, but this night, what with the dream, seems to have lasted a very long time.

I should probably get up even though it's early. I have to do something. I just can't quite remember what it is though. If I can shake off the dream more maybe it will come to me. Hally! It has something to do with her. I've been horrible to Hally for like forever. Penny too but she does it because I tell her to. The others as well. Perhaps that's what I have to do, stop bullying her. She's never done anything to me. Yes, that's it, today I will stop bullying Hally.

Chapter 2

Hally woke, the scream that was about to erupt from her throat dying on her lips as she realised she was awake. A warm arm encircled, her drawing her close, soothing, Wes was there she was safe.

For a few moments she lay quietly, her eyes adjusting to the dark. The nightmare that had woken her hovered on the edge of her memory. She tried to grasp it, remember it, but as objects in the room began to take shape, the dream further escaped her. She sighed and Wes' arm gently tightened across her tummy protecting her and loving her.

They had been together now for over a year, yet it still felt so new to her. She was also still amazed that a boy as gorgeous as Wes loved her. He could have had anyone from school but he had chosen her. She smiled to herself and snuggled into him.

She closed her eyes and let her mind drift away from the nightmare to when they first met. It had been after her mock exams the year before. Not long after her birthday. She had only just turned fifteen and was shy and nervous. Wes had recently moved to Colingford, was eighteen and worked in the Hotspot, the most popular café

3

in the town. She had met him there. There was instantaneous mutual attraction and though there had been a rocky patch, here they were, still together and very much in love.

Hally sighed contentedly. Mum and dad let Wes stay over sometimes and tonight she was extremely glad they did. His mum and dad were cool too, but with Ellie there, it was often more relaxed here in her room.

Her breathing slowly took on a steady rhythm as sleep began to take her. The hand that had clasped Wes' arm when she awoke relaxed, her fingers slipping open. Her whole body settled into the bed and her head nestled comfortably against her pillow. A soft hoot from an owl in the trees outside was the last sound Hally heard before she fell into a deep dreamless sleep.

Hally felt soft lips on her cheek. She opened her eyes to sunshine streaming through the window and Wes sitting by her side, a cup of steaming tea in his hand.

"Morning sleepy head."
He said with a grin as he held out the mug. Hally eased herself up into a sitting position and plumped her pillow behind her back. She took the tea and sipped.

"Mmmm lovely. What time is it?"
Hally asked, cupping the mug in both hands.

"Just after eight."
Wes replied. Hally sighed.

"I'll see you at college tomorrow then."

Wes frowned. Hally was usually ok with his every other Sunday shift at the Hotspot café. But this morning she seemed cross that he would be working then going home. He was worried.

"Hally what's wrong?"
Hally shrugged.

"I don't know. I had a nightmare last night but I can't remember any of it."

"Was it like the ones you got last year, after you know, Dana?"
Hally sipped her tea and mulled over his words.

"I really don't know. I just know I woke up from something really terrible but I have no idea what it was. I don't think it was about Dana. Anyway, those went away quite quickly remember. I mean at first I blamed myself for her suicide. But deep down I knew it wasn't my fault, and talking it through with Mr Austin at school made me understand that, and they went away. Besides, that was a long time ago, so why would it be about Dana? No, maybe it's just something to do with college, you know it's only been a couple of weeks and it's so different from school."

"I can come over after work if you want."
Wes said very gently. Hally took one hand from her mug and laid it across his. He would do that if she asked but she wouldn't. Between college and his part time job at the café, Wes didn't get a lot of time to spend with Ellie his little daughter. Hally saw him often, most evenings and breaks at college. She wouldn't take him away from his little girl and spoil the precious time he shared with her.

"No Wes. Ellie needs her dad. I'm fine."

Wes kissed her softly and stood up. He was still worried, Hally could see it in his eyes. She leaned back against her pillow and grinned at him. She wanted him to leave feeling unperturbed.

"I really am fine Wes. A piddly dream isn't going to cause me any trouble, I promise. Go to work, have fun with Ellie, and I'll see you in the morning. The girls might come over, we can have a girlie evening. And if they don't, I will still be all right."

Wes reluctantly left her on a kiss and a little wave. After he was gone Hally drank her tea and desperately tried to force the dream to the front of her mind. But it was gone. Yet there was something niggling. Deep inside she felt the dream's intensity, the fear hovering close to the edge of memory, but hiding and shadowing the reason. No matter how hard she tried to remember the details, the dream evaded her.

Mum was in the kitchen and like any Sunday was sitting at the table drinking tea and flipping through the Sunday papers. Hally hid a giggle behind her hand as she heard her mother grumble something to herself about what was going wrong in the world. Mum sensed her presence and looked over her shoulder.

"Talking to yourself mum?"

Hally asked as she gave her mum a hug. Mum patted her hand and grinned bashfully.

"I know. It's just so much is happening out there and so much biased reporting, it makes me cross."

"That's why you read all the papers mum, balanced reporting."

Mum laughed and folded the pile of papers. She stood up and flipped the switch on the kettle.

"Talk about reporting."

She gave her daughter a sideways glance. Hally sighed as she sat in the chair her mother had vacated.

"Wes, the snitch. What did he say?"

"That you had a nightmare."

Hally fiddled with the corner of a newspaper, her eyes down.

"He's worried angel."

"Mum, I'm fine. Yes, I had a nightmare a pretty horrid one I think. I say that because I cannot remember one bit of it, only that I woke up scared. But as soon as I was awake, the fear went away and I went back to sleep. Wes worried that I might have been dreaming about what happened with Dana."

"Do you think that?"

Mum asked as she poured water into two mugs. Hally shook her head as mum placed a mug of coffee in front of her.

"No reason to. Those dreams stopped practically as soon as they started, and it was ages ago."

Mum sat next to her and lifted one of the newspapers. She tapped the top.

"A year ago, well just over a year by a couple of days Hally, that we found out Dana was dead."

Hally dropped her shoulders and head, her long blonde hair falling across her face. Mum lifted a finger and gently pushed the strands away from her cheek, exposing a frown and turned down lips.

"I still don't think the dream was about Dana. I mean, if you hadn't just reminded me, I wouldn't have even known the date of the anniversary."

Mum put her arm around her and pulled her into a hug.

"That's true. So I'll drop it. No more talk of nightmares or anniversaries of dead girls."

Hally burst out laughing, her coffee slopping over the rim of her mug.

"Well mum, that's sure to give me even more nightmares."

Mum patted her on the head and kissed her cheek. They were both laughing when dad came through the back door.

"Finally up Tink."

He stated, a cheeky grin on his face. Hally huffed.

"I've been up for ages. You weren't here."

"Always know how to ruffle your feathers."

He said as he flicked the switch on the kettle. Mum pushed back her chair and went to her husband's side. He gave her a peck on the cheek as she spooned coffee into a mug for him.

"Stop teasing her Colin. She had nightmare."

"Mum, it was just a dream."

7

Hally grumbled. May looked at her husband who raised his eyebrows.

"Dana?"

Mum shrugged.

Hally plonked her mug on the table, again sloshing coffee over the side. Both her parents looked around in concern. Hally stood, her hands planted firmly on the table top, her lips pressed together in irritation.

"Look, I didn't even realise it was so close to the date Dana died until mum showed me the paper. So I had a flipping nightmare. Nathan gets them sometimes but you two don't go all psychotherapy on him."

She stopped. The steam went out of her as quickly as it had come. In its place tears rolled over her lashes and down her cheeks. She dropped into the chair and sobbed. Her parents rushed to her side and dad scooped her into his arms.

"Angel I'm so sorry, we're sorry. We shouldn't have pushed you."

He soothed. Mum took one of her hands and stroked the back of it.

"We talked about this on Thursday, the anniversary. We wondered if you had remembered, but you didn't say anything, so neither did we. So when Wes told me you had that nightmare, I thought it might be connected, that you had remembered and I was worried. Your dad was out with Nathan, he dropped him off at Drake's, remember Drake's mum and dad are taking them to the Wildlife Park?"

Hally nodded into her dad's shoulder. She had remembered her little brother was going on an outing. But she hadn't thought about Dana in a very long time.

"Honestly I didn't know what day it was. I haven't thought about Dana since, oh I don't know, ages ago. The last year has been busy. So much has happened especially for Wes and me. There's been no time to think about her and what happened. Yes, I still feel sorry for her, wished I had helped her. I offered, she turned me down. So why would I start getting nightmares about her now? I think it's more likely the dream was about college. You know how I get at the start of a new term. Well this is a new place too. I'm not finding it difficult, just different."

"Ok angel we won't say any more about it. You know we're always here for you, so if anything worries you, come and talk to us."
Mum said. Hally sniffed and wiped the tears from her face.

"I know mum. I'm one of the lucky ones. Thank you."

"It's our job Tink."
Dad told her.

****

It's taking ages to get light. Maybe it's not morning or night. Maybe…aha didn't old fatty Cartwright, my science teacher, talk to us about that thing that happens to the sun every so often. What was it she said? Try and remember Dana. Got it, an ec…eclispth. No that doesn't sound right at all. Jesus why can't I get words right? Numbers too for that matter.

I'm just thick, I know. Mum always tells me that. Mum, my mum, mummy, huh not that I've used that word in years. Where is she anyway? I don't remember the last time we spoke actually. Suppose that's not unusual though. She's always off with some bloke or another, out all night. Days can go by and I won't see her, she doesn't care. No one does.

I wish someone did. Really did that is. Not the boys who say they love me so they can cop a feel under my top. They don't care. Penny, she's like a sister. But then I don't know what a sister is meant to be like because I haven't got one. And where is Penny? It feels like I haven't seen her all summer and we're supposed to be best mates.

So this weird half-light. The sun, yes it's got to be doing that thing fatty Cartwright said, where something blocks it out and it all goes dark for like hours. It's horrible though, I don't like it. Oh yeah, she said if you use these special glasses you can watch it happen. But that means going outside. I don't want to get up yet. I stayed up very late and I'm tired. Wait, no I'm not tired I've slept for ages, I think. I don't know what the time is. I don't even know where my phone is. Probably gone flat anyway since I don't have any money to put credit on it.

Penny was going to lend me some money she said. But she hasn't been 'round. At least I haven't heard the door knock. Perhaps she's out with the gang watching this sun thing. They wouldn't care about it, would just watch 'cos they think it would be cool. Huh none of them are cool, not without me there. They do what I tell them. I'm the leader.

But lately I haven't been interested in telling them to do anything. So maybe I'm not such a leader and none of them have been bothered with me really. Well that's how it seems. I mean, I haven't seen anyone in ages. No that can't be right. We were all in the Hotspot the other day. Hally was there and Penny just couldn't wait to start on her, but I wasn't in the mood, and I told her to cut it out. Is that why she hasn't been 'round? She's mad at me.

Am I ill? I don't feel sick or hot or anything. I just don't get why my mind keeps drifting from one subject to another. It sort of starts a trail of one thing, I remember conversations and places, then it gets lost and I start thinking of something else. I've heard people say that can happen when you're not well. But I don't remember feeling ill at all. No I'm fine, well not fine. I haven't eaten properly in what, weeks? I had some bread and a bit of butter left, that was, um…don't know. I have got water though. The letter said they can't cut us off like the gas and electric. Did mum show me the letters? I'm not sure.

Maybe I'm just going crazy now. No food only water. That will be it. So I have to get up and do something.

I haven't a friggin clue what that will be though. Perhaps if I'm nice the gang will help out. Penny, if I go to her and tell her I'm sorry, maybe she will lend me that money. Haha a first, Dana Edwards saying she's sorry.

****

Hally finished the bacon sandwich mum had made for her. She licked her fingers like a little girl and grinned at her dad.

"That was just what I needed. Yum. Why does a bacon sarny go down so well, especially on a Sunday?"
Dad bit into his own sandwich and chewed. He swallowed and replied.

"Maybe because the rest of the week is hectic and breakfast is usually a bit rushed. But on a Sunday you can take your time. Or…" He stuffed the last of the sandwich in his mouth and mumbled around it. "…bacon just hits the spot. Mmmm greasy and bad for you."

"Oi Mr Mackeller!" Mum poked him on the shoulder playfully. "I grill my bacon, it's on wholemeal bread and you have Flora instead of butter."
Dad rubbed the spot on his shoulder pretending it hurt. Hally creased up. She loved her parents and loved the way they were with each other. She hoped her and Wes would last as long and be the same.

As mum and dad continued their pretend spat, Hally mulled over her relationship with Wes. He was everything she could ever want. Yes, she was young, still only sixteen, but her mum had been too and she and her dad loved each other so much. But, and this little niggle at the back of her mind, the one she wanted so badly to lock away but kept escaping, worried her. The niggle was Ellie, Wes' toddler daughter.

Hally had found out about Ellie when the child had been rushed to hospital last March. To say she was shocked was an understatement, and for a short while she didn't think she would be able to forgive Wes. But miserably and in tears, he fully explained and she decided to give him a chance. Now they were still happy and strong. She loved the little girl and Ellie loved her. The niggle wasn't about that. It was though all about their future as a family. She was still young, that was what frightened her. Would her love for Wes last? She believed it would but could she be sure?

Hally almost asked her parents this question but bit it back before it slipped off her tongue. She didn't want to interrupt their happy Sunday. They were still playing, laughing and just having fun. To ask something so serious right then was not fair. No, she would go upstairs and text the girls. They would come around and then she could voice her concerns.

Mum watched Hally slide her chair under the table and head off out of the kitchen. She frowned, sure her daughter had something on her mind she wasn't imparting. Colin gave her a hug.

"She'll tell you in her own time."
He whispered. May leaned into her husband and sighed. Her child had been through too much in a year. She hoped it wouldn't scar her.

Hally texted her two best friends Corrinne and Clia. She knew the girls wouldn't be seeing their boyfriends today either, as the three had agreed alternate Sundays would be their time. Their boyfriends were friends of Wes, and as the group knew about his work schedule and time with Ellie, they had worked out the best times to see each other as couples, all together and just the girls.

Hally, Corrinne and Clia were so close they could have been sisters. They had supported each other for many years, long before any of the boys came along. They each loved the time they spent alone with their guy, but still held tight to their girlie get-togethers. Both girls replied quickly to Hally's text and between them arranged to be at Hally's the middle of the afternoon.

****

I think I fell asleep again. I feel so lazy. I don't want to get up. But I should. I can't stay in bed forever, I'll waste away. That sun thingy must be ending because it's definitely lighter now. I can see the end of my bed. So why am I in bed? I don't actually know. I mean I had a late night I think. Wait, he was here. Yes! I remember that. He gave me wine. It was nice wine, fizzy. And chocolates too, so I have eaten something. But not enough to soak up the wine. That's it, he gave me wine on an empty stomach, not supposed to do that.

So I wonder where he is now. He said he was going to stay with me. Or did I just make that up in my mind? I'm really fuzzy in the head. It must be a hangover. Alcohol, and I didn't have any water. I suppose I must have passed out from the booze. Maybe he did stay and has already left and I just don't remember because I was drunk.

If he did stay it was the first time. He doesn't usually come to my house but now mum's gone, hang on has she gone? I remember I haven't seen her in a while but gone completely? Oh God I hope not. The last time she did that I ended up in foster care and that was horrible. But if she has gone again, this time I can take care of myself, I think. I'm going to be sixteen very soon, not sure if that will actually make any difference.

I remember something else now. He said something about me being nearly sixteen but I don't know what it was. I think I was telling him about mum being gone. So yes she has gone, I just don't know where. So what was I saying? Oh yes, I told him she was gone and I'm sure he said he would come 'round then. He must have because I had the fizzy wine. I don't remember what happened after that.

Chapter 3

Corrinne and Clia arrived together bouncing through the back door like two six-year-olds instead of the sixteen they both were. Mum greeted them like they were her own.

"Hi. Kettle's on, coffee is in the mugs ready."
She said giving them a hug and kiss on the cheek.

"Hey, hi."
Beamed Hally coming into the kitchen.

The three hugged and gabbled as they waited for the kettle to boil, Hally feeling less out of sorts now her two best friends were with her. The kettle clicked off and mum made their drinks. She handed them out and the girls thanked her and set off for Hally's bedroom.

Mum stood leaning against the counter holding her own mug in two hands. She felt a little hitch in her breath as the girls disappeared through the door. They were growing so fast, young women, not really children anymore. She still had Nathan but it wouldn't be long before he didn't need her as much either. There was her dad. He would need her always, especially since her mum died back in January, just nine months ago, and it was still so raw. Of course Colin would be her rod to prop her up and support her through everything, as he had done since they met. She sighed, she would be ok.

Hally closed her bedroom door and turned to her friends. Corrinne dropped her big bag to the floor with a sigh and Hally giggled.

"What's in there today?"

She asked her friend. Corrinne carried numerous articles in her bag, her 'just in case' motto ever present. She shrugged her shoulders.

"It's not as warm out today and a bit cloudy. So extra jumper and umbrolley, undies and toothbrush, in case I don't go home. Oh and..." She blushed slightly. "...one of Gregg's T-shirts so if I do stay over anywhere I can wear it to bed."

Hally wrapped her arms around Corrinne.

"My very weird but absolutely darling friend."

She giggled, Clia joining in. Corrinne smiled knowing Hally meant no harm in her words. She lifted her shoulders in another shrug.

"Just me, the way I am."

They got themselves settled. Hally's room wasn't big but it could accommodate three plump beanbags on the floor under the window. Holding their mugs and sipping coffee the three chatted about nothing in particular. Then Clia turned the conversation to college.

"So how are you two finding it?"

She asked.

"It what?"

Hally replied. Corrinne was frowning questioningly.

"College of course."

Clia stated. Hally leaned back on her beanbag and nearly spilt her coffee.

"Oh I know I'm clever..." She laughed. "...but a mind reader I am not."

"Huh you think you're clever..."

Clia teased but with no malice and Hally nodded. It was all part of the way the girls interacted. Corrinne put her mug on the floor and held up her hands a palm facing each of them.

"Time out, time out."

She called.

"Actually, I think I might be finding it harder to adjust than I thought."

Hally said all joking aside. Clia leaned forward and covered Hally's hand with hers.

"What's up Hals?"

Hally stared into her mug swirling the contents slightly. She had wanted the girls to come over not just for company but to air her concerns. She could do that with the girls. She could tell mum anything too but she didn't want to worry her, not until she felt she had to. Mum had been through so much herself since the beginning of the year.

"Well, I had a nightmare but I can't remember anything about it."

Clia squeezed Hally's hand gently.

"So what makes you think it was to do with college?"

Hally sighed.

"I don't really know. It's just the only thing on my mind."

"Are you finding the work difficult?"

Corrinne asked. Hally shook her head.

"College itself then?"

Asked Clia. Hally nodded.

"I hated school. You know that. All the bullying from Dana and her gang. That's why I didn't want to go into sixth form. College was the best option, better than school, as there are far more courses not just A levels. The work is a doddle actually but I am enjoying it. I'm just scared. There's so many more people at college than school. There we would be the oldest, at college we're the youngest."

She stopped and drained her mug. She felt a bit stupid now saying all that to the girls. But both were nodding.

"Hals I know what you mean. It's a bit like starting secondary school again. And the campus is huge compared to school. We're taking different courses so we don't see each other like we did in school. It's weird. I mean, at the moment we're all in every day of the week but that will change later. Me and Corrinne, well we didn't see Rhys and Gregg at school 'cos they were already working but your Wes was at school and now he's at college. But I bet you don't see him like you did at school."

She paused finishing her own coffee. Hally looked up, her face creased in misery.

"No I don't. It's…um…not just that though. I mean all you have said is right but what I get most scared of…this is going to come out all wrong."

She stood up. Still holding her now empty mug she looked out of the window. The garden was busy, birds fighting and scrabbling at the bird table. It was a sight that always soothed her. She took a deep breath.

"Because there are so many people at college, um…boys…men…I'm scared I'm going to meet one and be…like…attracted to him."

She finished, a tiny sob catching her breath. Corrinne and Clia stood and came to her side.

"Have you Hals? Have you met someone?"

Clia asked in a quiet soft voice. Hally shook her head.

"No but what if I do. It would destroy Wes. And there's Ellie to think of and you two. Rhys and Gregg are Wes' best friends."

Tears flowed freely now as all of her worries flooded from her. Corrinne grabbed her big bag and pulled out a wad of tissues. She dabbed at Hally's eyes with one and stuffed the others into her hand. Clia took her other hand and rubbed the back of it.

"Hally sweetie don't cry. Even if you did meet someone else we would be fine. But I don't think you will." She looked at Corrinne who nodded in agreement.

"Because we know how much you love Wes, have done since you set eyes on him. You two are linked by your hearts like your mum and dad. But anyway, if it did happen it wouldn't make any difference to us or our boyfriends. We love you Hally, that wouldn't, couldn't change. As for Wes, I don't know how he would cope but like I said I don't think it will ever happen anyway."

Hally swiped at her tear stained face with the wad of tissues, Clia's words exorcising her fears. She knew how much she loved her Wes, knew there couldn't possibly be another man that she could love more. She gave herself a mental shake.

"I'm just being silly."

Corrinne shook her head.

"No Hally you're not. You are being sensible thinking about the future and its possibilities. None of us can say for sure how we're going to feel next week, in a month, a year. We all have to just hope that what we have now is what we want later."

"I know I still get scared."

Clia chimed in. Hally and Corrinne looked at her with a frown.

"Remember before, I told you I get insecure when I don't hear from Rhys, well that hasn't gone away. Even now, I know he loves me but I think sometimes he's getting older, more grown up. He goes to all these places to work, meets all sorts of women. What if he finds someone else? Someone more mature than me. I've asked him and he tells me it won't ever happen, that I'm the only girl for him, but I still wonder."

Hally took one of Clia's hands and one of Corrinne's and pulled them close. They all had their teenage fears. She suspected mum would be very helpful if she did go to her but still didn't want to bother her. After all she thought, if the girls were feeling some of what she felt then it must be natural. And for all she knew the boys could be mulling over the same problems too. She would see Wes tomorrow, talk to him and he would tell her exactly what the girls had told her.

****

It's much lighter now so the sun thingy must be passing. I can see more of my room the window too. But outside it looks foggy. Maybe that's what's making it seem weird. The sun thingy and fog, no wonder it's been so dark.

Well that was even more weird. I got up and don't remember doing it. But I must have because now I'm looking out of the window at the fog. It's really thick out there. Don't think I've ever seen it like that before, well not in summer. Hmm sometimes in winter it gets bad when you can't see anything, even your hand in front of you.

My head feels funny, sort of achy but not. And I'm stuffed up. Probably got a cold. Great, on top of the hangover I've got a frigging cold. They're worse in summer for some reason. Bet he gave it to me last night. Can you catch a cold that quick? Ohhh I don't know.

I wish I could see the street but the fog is too thick. I'm lonely. I wish he hadn't left last night. Did he even stay? My head is so unclear. I just can't think. I might as well go back to bed, sleep some more. Then when I wake up the fog might have cleared and I might feel a bit better. I should get a drink, but funny I'm not actually thirsty. Not hungry either. Those chocolates he gave me must have really filled me up. But I'm not even sure if he did give me any.

I hate this. I don't usually have trouble remembering stuff. Oh God, what if I've got something horrible wrong with me like a brain tumour or something? I've heard they can take away your memory, your speech. Can I speak? Let me try. La la la. That did come out loud, I heard it, my voice. So no can't be a tumour. Phew a relief so I suppose just the hangover.

Ah that's better. The bed is soft. I can't really even feel it under me. Odd though, again I didn't notice I was moving. It's like I just thought about my bed and there I was, on it. Crikey this is going to be a very strange day. That is if it is day, it's still not properly light. The sun thingy, the fog, no clock, no phone. Can't turn on the telly, no electric. Sleep just sleep.

Wait. Hally, I have to do something to do with Hally. She came here once, I remember that. What happened? What did she say? It was after her birthday. Yes, the booze! Oh God how rotten of me. I got some girls to plant booze at her party to get her parents in trouble with the police. Why? I don't remember that bit. Hang on, there was a burglary at, at...um, it's there almost... an off licence, yes got it. But now I can't remember what that's got to do with it.

Oh this is far too exhausting all this trying to recall stuff. My eyes feel heavy and the room is getting dark.

****

A light tap came on Hally's door and then mum poked her head in. She had a plate in her hand with an assortment of biscuits on it.

"Thought you might want a nibble."
She told the girls coming further into the room. Hally grinned at her mum and put her hand out for the plate. May looked at her daughter's eyes and instantly knew she had been crying.

"Angel what's up?"

She asked, a frown of concern on her face. Hally took the plate, a chocolate biscuit and bit into it.

"Mum I'm fine. Really."

"Hally you would tell me wouldn't you if something was wrong?"

Hally passed the plate to Clia and walked into her mother's arms snuggling against her chest.

"Yes mummy I would. But there is nothing to worry about. I got a bit teary over college, and no I'm not having any problems. Just like I said earlier, new term, new work and all that. The girls..." She glanced at her friends. "...they are feeling a bit the same."

Corrinne and Clia nodded to May to give her reassurance. She stroked Hally's back and kissed the top of her head.

"Well ok. But if any of you..." She waved her hand around the room. "...have concerns, I am here and will listen."

Hally stepped out of the circle of her mother's arms and playfully went to grab the plate of biscuits back. Clia held on and as they each tugged the biscuits began to slide. Corrinne leapt forward cupping her hands as the lot slipped from the plate. She caught all of them.

"Haha all mine now."

She giggled. Hally and Clia pounced.

"Not flipping likely Bryant."

Hally said trying to snatch a biscuit from her friend's grasp.

"Back off Mackeller. Corrinne you had better share."

Said Clia as she too tried to get a biscuit. Corrinne swivelled and lifted her hands, laughing so much she nearly dropped them all. May shook her head, smiled and backed out of the door leaving the girls to their play.

Corrinne finally relented and put the biscuits back on the plate. She had melted chocolate on her fingers and licked it off. The girls were all giggling as they plonked back onto the beanbags and tucked in. Some of the biscuits were broken but that didn't deter them. For a while they munched in silence.

"So you can't recall any of the dream then?"
Clia asked around a mouthful of shortbread. Hally shook her head catching crumbs in her hand as her biscuit broke apart. She mulled over the question.

"Um, no. I woke up and I was terrified. I think I might have screamed if I hadn't woken at that moment. All I know is something terrible was happening but the actual dream itself is just a fog. No words, people, nothing. Just fear. Like I was out in space or under water all alone and something was there too, it just didn't appear."

Clia shivered despite the warmth of the sun coming into the room. She looked at Corrinne whose face told her she was feeling just as creeped out.

"That's horrifying Hally. I don't think I've ever had a nightmare like that before."

"Do you remember when I was little?"
Corrinne said. Hally and Clia nodded. They had known each other since pre-school and even back then had sleepovers.

"I used to get nightmares quite a lot."
The other two again nodded.

"They were scary but I know what they were about. Because I don't have any brothers or sisters, I used to dream mum and dad would leave me. That they had other kids and left them, and I was the only one and they would get rid of me soon too. Stupid I know because I couldn't have more loving caring parents. Of course as I got older and realised they cherished me because I was their only child, that mum couldn't have any more, the dreams went away."
Hally gave Corrinne a questioning look.

"The point is, as terrifying as the nightmares were, I did know what was happening in them. Before, when you had those nightmares about Dana you knew what was going on in the dream and awoke with it in your memory. Last night was different wasn't it?"

Hally nodded and Clia leaned forward her elbows on her knees.

"So what do you think is going on then Corrinne?" Corrinne shrugged. She had a theory Clia guessed but was not confident enough to voice it. Hally reached for Corrinne's hand.

"Corrie please. If you've got an idea tell me." Corrinne sighed deeply. She was taking psychology as part of her course at college and had read quite a lot over the summer. She lowered her lashes and pressed her lips together.

"Well I'm reaching here. I mean, I'm not qualified or anything and it's well…just a guess I suppose. But…" She paused and Hally and Clia leaned forward even more.

"Well it could be something that's happened to you in the past and you've completely blocked it out because it's too painful to remember. And now for some reason, it's coming back a bit. You don't want it to but your subconscious does." She shrugged again and stuffed a biscuit into her mouth.

Hally slumped back against her beanbag. Crumbs dropped onto her lap but she left them. Could Corrinne be right? She thought. She shook her head without realising she was doing it.

"But there can't be anything." She murmured almost to herself. She blinked.

"I'm going to call mum up. She would know."

Before the girls could reply Hally jumped up and opened her door. She stepped out onto the landing and leaned over the banister. Taking a deep breath, she called out "Mum!"

Both her parents appeared at the bottom of the stairs frowning. Hally beckoned them up and they flew up the stairs, dad taking them two at a time.

"What's wrong?"

He said panting slightly as mum reached him.

"I need to ask you something."

Hally said turning back to her room, expecting them to follow. May looked at Colin. His expression told her he was as worried as she was. Taking her hand, he led his wife into Hally's room.

Corrinne and Clia sprang up giving Hally's parents the beanbags. Instead the girls plonked themselves on Hally's bed and waited expectantly. May sat down, Colin did too but kept a firm hold of her hand. Hally stood facing them.

"Hally you're scaring us."

Colin told his daughter. Hally took a deep breath.

"Oh, mum, dad I didn't mean to. But I have to ask you something."

May nodded as if to say go ahead. Hally kneeled in front of them.

"Has anything really bad ever happened to me?"

Both Colin and May looked perplexed. They had no idea what Hally meant.

"Tink, I think you had better explain."

Her dad said. Hally chewed her bottom lip.

"Um, like I said. In the past when I was little, did something happen to me? An accident, trauma or something?"

Mum and dad shook their heads.

"No Hally. I mean you had the usual kiddy falls and scrapes. You fell off your bike when you were four and cut your lip open. Um…Nathan kicked his football when he was little and his aim was way off, clobbered you in the face…but no nothing serious. Colin?"

Mum said. Dad shook his head.

"My angel your mum's right. Nothing serious. I mean, of course there was all the bullying, that upset you a lot, but you never got physically hurt. And even the name calling was mostly bitchiness. You never had anyone attack you, no internet stuff and as a family we made sure the school did everything to try and stop it. I know they couldn't, not all of it, but we think, hope you coped and it didn't affect you too much."

Hally slowly nodded.

"I did, I mean have. No the bullying hasn't had lasting effects. It was horrible and so pointless, that's why I think it hasn't scarred me. I could see, even years ago, Dana and her gang taking the mickey out of me, it was just a waste of their time. They didn't even know me and so much of it didn't make sense anyway. I think I just got the short stick. It could have been anyone, it just happened to be me. It wasn't really personal. Nothing they ever said was."

Dad put his hand on her head and stroked her hair. Hally turned slightly so her cheek rested in his palm. She closed her eyes as her dad's big, warm hand soothed the tension she felt. Everything was so confusing. With her eyes still closed she murmured.

"So if nothing happened to me, then what could the nightmare have been about?"

Dad sighed.

"So is this what all the questions are about?"

Corrinne sat up quickly.

"Oh no that's all my fault."

Mum sat up straight, a frown on her face.

"I think someone had better tell us exactly what's going on."

Corrinne's face began to flush and she took a steadying breath before explaining, but Hally jumped in.

"No Corrinne it's not your fault at all. You just offered a possible cause."

"To what Hally?"

Mum said exasperation in her voice. Hally took a deep breath and let it out very slowly whilst she gathered her thoughts.

"The nightmare. We were trying to work out what it might have been about. So Corrinne had the idea that it might be something to do with a trauma or something that happened a long time ago. But you said there's nothing. I'm sure it wasn't about Dana, or college, or even Wes, so...well," She shrugged. "...maybe I'm just being dramatic and it wasn't about anything at all."

Mum nodded but didn't look convinced. Colin took her hand and squeezed it reassuringly. Hally smiled at them both.

"Probably some stupid film or programme I watched on TV."

She said lightly, finishing with a little giggle.

Colin pulled his wife to her feet and put an arm around her shoulder. He steered her towards the bedroom door and out onto the landing. Then he looked back over his own shoulder to Hally.

"For now we will accept what you say. But..." He held up a finger. "If it happens again, I think we need to explore a bit further."

Hally nodded to her dad as he left the room and closed the door.

"God, now they think I'm nuts."

She sighed, sprawling across the bed between her friends.

"Course they don't Hals, they just care."

Clia said pushing Hally's hair from her face. Hally knew her friend was right and closed her eyes for a moment. She was scared but wouldn't show it, not yet. She hoped the nightmare wouldn't recur. Hoped it was a one off. But she had a nasty suspicion it wasn't, that it had some significance that she couldn't put her finger on at that moment.

Chapter 4

Mum made Hally her favourite hot chocolate as she prepared for bed. May thought it would help relax her daughter before sleep, encourage a restful nightmare free night. She sat on the side of the bed and tucked the duvet around Hally, waiting with her as she sipped the creamy beverage. She deliberately avoided any mention of dreams and kept the conversation light.

"Nathan so enjoyed his outing today."

Hally giggled. Her little brother had bounced through the back door around five o'clock. He was full of his day out and didn't stop chatting about it until it was time for his bath. For once mum had no trouble getting him into it. But as she washed his hair he suddenly stopped talking and realised where he was. He tried to sulk and object but his enthusiasm over the day got in the way and then it was time to get out.

Hally came up the stairs just as mum was leading Nathan from the bathroom to his room wrapped in a bath sheet. Her little brother was grumbling about the bath one second, then remembering something else about his day out. His little face switching from fury to excitement as he plodded to his room. Hally saw her mum hide a giggle behind him, winking at her daughter on the way.

Now Nathan was fully tucked up and probably sound asleep as she sat against her pillows sipping hot chocolate. She envied her little brother's uncomplicated life, remembered when she was little. There was nothing but play and happiness. The tree house Granddad had built, hours spent there with Corrinne and Clia. The only decisions that had to be made were which outfit their dolls would wear, and whether to have tea or orange squash in the tiny tea set they played with. She sighed.

"That sounded very deep."
Mum said. Hally closed her eyes.

"I was just thinking about being little. No worries or anything. I was remembering my tea set in the tree house."

Mum shifted forward a little and covered Hally's hands around the mug. She would willingly take away her daughter's angst if it were possible. But she knew it was all about growing up.

"Angel, it is very hard being a teenager. Your body and mind are in turmoil at times. Problems appear bigger than they really are. On top of that you have to make all these decisions about your future. At least it seems you do. There's so much pressure from everywhere. College, assignments, even everyday stuff like what you wear and your makeup. But I promise you it doesn't have to be like that. You have a whole lifetime to make decisions not just a couple of years. Take your time, don't rush anything. If college gets too much right now it's fine to take some time out, same with uni, if that's what you are considering. Like you said, the last year has been crazy. So if a break is what you need, dad and me will support you."

Hally smiled at her mum. She always gave her sound advice.

"Thanks mum. What you say makes sense. I have been worrying that everything has to be crammed into the next two years. Even this early our tutors are plugging on about university and what grades we will need and so on. Maybe it is just too much too soon."

Mum released her hands so she could finish her drink. She then took the mug and gave her daughter a kiss. Hally slid down under the duvet as her mother stood up.

"Could you please tilt the blinds so I can see the sky?"

Mum did as she asked then left the room closing the door behind her.

Hally turned to face the window. She could see stars sparkling in the early autumn sky. Her window was open slightly and she could hear the odd car pass along the street and the rustle of leaves from a little breeze. They were all normal sounds, soothing and safe. She lay for some time just listening and watching. The room gradually darkened as her eyes closed and sleep overtook her.

A whisper close to her ear brought Hally quickly out of a deep sleep. She opened her eyes. The room was dark, clouds racing across the sky blotting out the starlight. She held her breath for a moment, waiting for the whisper to come again, but there was silence. The blinds flapped as the wind coming in through the slightly open window caught them. The sound was hollow and more like a tap than a whisper, so Hally was sure that wasn't the sound that had awoken her.

For a while she gripped the duvet under her chin. She was cold and shivered. Still she waited for any sound other than the wind and blinds. But there was nothing. She took a breath and let it out. Slowly she pushed the duvet away and sat up. The room was warmer than she expected. She swung her feet over the edge of the bed and tested the carpet with her toes. It wasn't cold. She slipped fully from under the duvet and padded to the window.

The wind had whipped up through the night. She turned back to her bedside table and pressed the unlock key on her phone. The time was two thirty in the morning. Rubbing her bare arms, she went back to the window and closed it. As she reached out the wind touched her hand. It wasn't cold, yet she still shivered, a cold chill running down her spine. A tiny prickle of fear made her turn and look over her shoulder. The room was empty but for herself.

Hally stood at the window for several minutes watching the trees sway and the clouds run riot. The sight eased the tension in her heart and she began to feel warmer. A few leaves smacked against the glass but again they didn't make the sound that had awoken her. She scrunched up her face and pondered. A dream maybe, she thought. She nodded her head and in a hushed voice spoke to the night.

"That's it. I had a dream and it woke me."

Hally quietly padded back to her bed, the carpet cushioning her footsteps. She was very glad of that. Mum was a very light sleeper and Hally knew she worried about her. If she heard her wandering about her room this late she would be up to find out why.

Without making a sound, Hally slipped back under the duvet and lay down. She was no longer cold. She wondered about that. She had been tucked up in bed, cocooned in her bedcover, yet she had awoken freezing. But getting up and standing in front of an open window had warmed her up. She shook her head from side to side, confused and a little afraid. She closed her eyes and tried to sleep but the memory of the whisper kept invading her mind.

Hally tried to relax. She practised contracting her muscles and relaxing them. First her fingers then her toes. Next her arms and legs. Finally, her whole body. It was a technique she had been taught at school during drama and it usually worked. Tonight it failed her. She sighed and sat up. She reached for her phone automatically then paused. She had been about to call Wes. That's what she always did when she was stressed. Had done that last year when she was frightened. But tonight she wouldn't call him. It wasn't fair to wake him for no real reason. He had to get up for college too. She would deal with this herself.

Hally lay back down and pulled the cover back over her. She let her arms rest by her sides not gripping the quilt. She pictured Wes in her mind, flipped through the photo album of memory. She saw him smiling, hugging her. She caught the gleam in his eyes as he kissed her. Wes, her man, the only one who could truly ease her fears. Those were the thoughts that finally rested her active mind and tipped her over into sleep.

****

Ahhh that's so much better. He's here by my side holding me. He cares, he said so. He loves me. At last someone loves me. Mum doesn't love me. I know that now. She left me again. I remember that so clearly now. She found an American guy, went to live with him in the states. What was it she said, oh yes. 'Dana, it's time you stood on your own two feet. Jesus you're not a little kid anymore. I've put my life on hold for too damn long. I've made so many sacrifices. No life, no man, just bringing you up. Well now I've found my Mr Perfect and I'm not letting him go. He wants me to go and live with him in New York. So I'm going.' All a load of rubbish really. She's always had different blokes, always gone out and left me by myself.

I did cry though, sobbed really, if I'm honest. I begged to go as well. But all she said was 'No no no. I need this Dana, just for me. A new fresh start. You will spoil that. My guy doesn't want ties. We're planning on travelling around the good old US of A. we're going to see it all. You're almost sixteen, old enough to take care of yourself. The rent's paid until the end of June so go and get a job. How many girls your age can say they have got their own place to live, are totally independent. I bet your mates will be really jealous of you.'

Humph I do not think so. Jealous of what? A stack of bills, no food and no money. How the hell am I supposed to get a job? Even grown-ups and people with qualifications are struggling to do that. Who's going to give a fifteen-year-old still in school a job? No one that's who. I mean as soon as I'm sixteen I can try but I'm not legally allowed to leave school until next year, even though I will be sixteen quite soon now.

But for now I can push all that aside. He's here. He's warm and safe. He might even look after me. Yes, I bet that's what will happen. He will take me out of this horrible house and I'll be his princess. Yes, that's what he calls me, Princess. He strokes my hair, cuddles me and so much more. He loves me I know. He's told me so many times and I love him. He asks me to say it all of the time and I do because it's true, real.

Chapter 5

Hally felt drained as she showered and prepared herself for college. She hadn't slept well after being woken by the whisper. At first she had drifted into a restful sleep but something woke her again shortly after. That time she kept her eyes tightly closed and managed to doze off. But soft rustlings and what seemed to be murmurs intruded so frequently, she found herself trying to keep her eyes open scanning the room. She would drop into sleep as tiredness took over, only to be awoken by the next series of sounds.

Standing in front of the bathroom mirror Hally examined her image. Her eyes looked darker than normal and she hoped her mum wouldn't notice. She wasn't one to wear makeup to college, didn't feel the need and would probably smudge it anyway. So she left her clear, tanned skin free of cosmetics. Today she was tempted but guessed that would alert her mum straight away.

With a big sigh and a shrug, Hally trotted back to her bedroom and dressed. As she pulled on her jeans her eyes swept the room in search of the sleep intruder. Of course the room was empty. She glanced up at the picture above her bed, the baby in a crib being watched over by a pair of angels. A christening gift from her grandparents.

Last May on her birthday she had believed she had seen one of the angels lean over and kiss the baby. She hadn't been afraid. Her grandmother had died in January and Hally felt sure she was now one of the angels in the picture watching over her. That thought brought comfort to her, eased the stress she felt as she readied herself for college. If Gran was close she wouldn't let any harm come to her.

Mum was sitting at the kitchen table with Nathan. He was gabbling away about football as he shovelled cereal into his mouth. Hally strolled over to the kettle and flicked the switch. She leaned against the counter and smiled as Nathan tried to explain something that had happened on the pitch around a mouthful of cornflakes.

"Nathan, don't talk with your mouth full."
Mum said. Hally hid a giggle behind her hand as her little brother chewed furiously, swallowed and hurriedly gave the explanation, a spoonful of cereal and milk already on its way to his mouth.

Hally made her tea and stood sipping it. Mum glanced over her shoulder at her and frowned. Hally inwardly sighed. She had hoped Nathan would keep their mother occupied but mum was far too sharp.

"You all right?"
She asked with a frown. Hally turned sideways and dropped two slices of bread into the toaster, thereby keeping her eyes from mum's.

"I'm fine."
She said lightly. Mum slid around on her chair to face her.

"Hmmm you look peaky."
Hally couldn't help but laugh and that in itself made her feel a lot better.

"Honestly mum I am ok. The wind kept waking me up last night but it was too warm to close the window."
She lied turning fully away to butter her toast so mum couldn't see her face at all.

"Well ok. Just don't overdo it today."

Hally bit into her toast and wondered exactly how she would accomplish that. Monday at college was her fullest day. She would only get lunch and two breaks, one in the morning, the other in the afternoon. But she kept that to herself.

Just as they had in school, Hally met her two best friends at the junction where their roads met. Corrinne was as usual loaded down with her big bag, containing not only her college materials but everything she would need in the event of a small war. Hally was so used to her friend's quirkiness the bag went unnoticed. Clia flicked her thick brown hair behind her ear and smiled warmly at Hally.

"How are you this morning?"
Hally pressed her lips together. She knew she would and could tell her friends anything.

"I had a very weird night. So I'm knackered."

Corrinne linked her arm through Hally's and led her in the direction of Colingford's College of Further and Higher Education. As they walked Hally told them all about being woken in the night and the fear that came with it. By the time they reached the college gates, the three were deep in discussion about what could have caused Hally's broken night.

"I still think you're blocking something out that is trying to break free."
Corrinne stated with a shrug.

"But there isn't anything."
Hally replied dropping her shoulders in frustration.

"Morning beautiful."
Hally jumped then grinned, her face lighting up as Wes put his arms around her. She leaned back into him and sighed, feeling completely safe and loved.

"So what are you three chatting about?"
He asked. Hally shook her head just the tiniest bit, enough for Corrinne and Clia to notice and be warned not to spill to Wes.

"Nothing in particular. Just day to day stuff."
Hally told him. He nuzzled her neck and accepted her
words without question.

The four stood and chatted for a while until it was
time for them to depart to their own departments. Wes was
taking an accountancy course. His mother was an
accountant and they planned to start up their own business.
Corrinne was aiming for a career working with children,
Clia journalism and Hally wanted to be a social worker.

Hally's first session didn't go well. She couldn't
concentrate. Her mind kept drifting off, first to the
nightmare, then her restless night. By the end of the lesson
she was furious with herself. Her tutor gave her a little
frown as she shoved her notebook and pen into her bag but
made no comment. Hally threw the strap of her bag over
her shoulder and stomped from the room. She dived for the
ladies and stood in front of the mirror staring at her image.
She clenched her fists and pressed her lips hard together.
She would not let the weekend get in the way of her
studies. She ran cold water over her wrists, and with a very
deep breath resolved to push her worries away and
concentrate on her next lesson.

By lunchtime Hally was in a much better mood. She
had enjoyed the rest of the morning and participated well in
her lessons. She had a new assignment which she was
determined to start on that evening before Wes came
around, and as she walked into The Food Hall she spotted
Corrinne already seated at a table. She joined her and just
after Clia came in too. They chatted about their morning,
Hally avoiding the disastrous first lesson, and ate their
lunch. It was very relaxing and pleasant.

Hally was relieved the rest of the day improved. So
that by the time she met up with the girls for the walk home
she was feeling on top of the world. They parted at their
usual spot knowing they would text each other later. Hally
strolled down her own road. The weather had picked up

again, warm and sunny. Before she reached her house she had decided she would start her work sitting in the garden and catch a few autumn rays whilst she could.

Sitting with her feet up on a sun lounger Hally rested her laptop on her knees. She had made an excellent start on her assignment and was very pleased with her accomplishment. Her mind was fully engaged and she felt completely at ease with herself. Mum had brought her a jug of her special homemade lemonade and had left it on a small garden table by her side. She was relieved to see her daughter back to her bright bubbly self.

Taking a short breather, Hally leaned back to sip the refreshing, cool beverage. There was nothing quite like mum's lemonade to quench a thirsty palate. She gazed up at the sky for a moment. It was clear blue, not a cloud in sight. Warm and perfect. She loved the sun, the warmth it gave. It was comforting, soothing. Her gaze turned towards her bedroom window. For a tiny moment Hally thought she saw a shadow pass across the open blinds. She blinked and it was gone. She sat upright and took a long swallow from her glass. She would not let her imagination spoil this gorgeous late afternoon. She put her drink aside and purposefully read through her work, making small adjustments, concentrating fully, not letting her mind drift. By the time mum called her in for dinner Hally was a long way into her assignment, and not once had she looked up at her bedroom window again.

Hally was helping mum clear the kitchen after dinner when a light tap came on the back door. She knew it was Wes before she looked over. He was opening the door as she put the last plate in the dishwasher. Her heart skipped a beat at the sight of him. Even after a year and a bit together he still made her feel that way. He slipped a hand under her hair and gave her a gentle kiss on the lips.

Mum was used to this so simply carried on with the clearing up.

"You two go through. I'll finish up here."
She said. Wes shook his head.

"No you go and sit down. Hally and I can do it."

Mum dried her hands on a towel and left them to it. As soon as she exited the kitchen Wes pulled Hally into his arms for a fuller kiss. She sighed against him.

"Urgh!"
Hally pulled back from the kiss. Nathan was just coming in from the garden and was glaring at them. Wes grinned and scruffed the child's hair.

"Oi!"
Nathan moaned. Wes laughed and did it again.

"You wait. When you're older and kissing your girlfriend I'm going to say urgh to you. See how you like it."
Nathan shook his head.

"I'm not ever gonna kiss any girl."
He stated.

"Mum! Can I have some crisps?"
He then yelled. Hally covered her ears with her hands. Their mother came through the door with her hand held up, palm out.

"Nathan. There is no need to shout I'm only in the next room."
She told him firmly. Nathan dropped his head almost to his chin. He pushed his bottom lip right out and scrunched up his face preparing to cry. Hally had to hide her face in Wes' shoulder to stop herself from giggling. It was a true Nathan ploy to avert a telling off. But mum was ready for it.

"Won't work my boy. Now try again. Speak quietly and ask politely."
Nathan gave his mother his best *I'm a good boy really* look, but mum wise to his charms just waited. Nathan frowned and crossed his arms. Hally actually did giggle then. Her

little brother was cute and would try anything to get out of being told off. Mum waited, her brows raised. Nathan gave in. He stepped toward her and wrapped his arms around her waist.

"May I please have some crisps?"

He asked so sweetly. Mum kissed the top of his head and smiled at Hally.

"One packet. But that means no more snacks tonight."

Hally knew Nathan was about to protest as he backed out of mum's cuddle. Mum predicting this too held up her forefinger. With a big sigh Nathan conceded and with his head still down strolled to the cupboard.

Hally took Wes' hand and led him from the kitchen up the stairs to her bedroom. She plonked down on a beanbag and Wes sat opposite her. The sun was still bright and shone through the open window. Hally let her eyes wander around the room trying to locate the source of the shadow. But there was nothing.

"Babe, you ok?"

Wes asked. Hally brought her eyes back to his. A worried frown creased his face. She nodded.

"I think so."

His frown deepened.

"No, I am."

She stated trying to alleviate his concern. It didn't work. Wes knelt in front of her and took her hands in his. He was warm, his big hands engulfing her small ones.

"Hally what's wrong. Something was up yesterday morning and now today, well you're scaring me. Have I done something to upset you?"

Without knowing why tears trickled from her eyes and rolled down her cheeks. Her breath hitched and before she could get control the floodgates opened and she began to sob. Wes kneeled up and pulled her into his arms. He let her cry without question knowing she would open up once the flood subsided. With Wes gently rubbing her back Hally gradually managed to get her emotions under control.

Taking deep breaths, Hally pulled away a little wiping her face with her palms. Wes leaned around her and grabbed a wad of tissues from a box on the bedside table. He dabbed at her face.

"I'm sorry."
Hally mumbled.

"What for?"
Wes asked shakily. He was afraid now. He loved her so much, couldn't bear the thought of not being with her. Hally saw the misery in his eyes and inwardly scolded herself. She covered his hands with her own and rested her cheek against his palm.

"Oh Wes. I'm not breaking up with you or anything bad like that."

Wes' tensed shoulders relaxed and he tried a smile. It worked. But he couldn't hold back the tears that had choked him. As they spilled down his cheeks it was Hally's turn to give comfort. She wrapped her arms around him and kissed away his tears making him laugh.

"What a pair we are."
She said. Wes nodded and held her tight. Speaking into his shoulder she murmured.

"I don't know quite what's going on."
Wes leaned back and looked into her eyes. He could see worry and confusion.

"Babe I'm here. You can tell me anything you know that."

Hally nodded and re-settled herself on the beanbag. Still holding his hands, she lifted her eyes to the ceiling, took a moment to gather her thoughts, then spoke.

"That nightmare. I think there was more to it but I don't have a clue what. Me and the girls tried to work it out yesterday but nothing came of that. Then last night I woke up really scared, no nightmare but...oh this is going to sound nuts…something else…a whisper, like someone was in the room with me. It was creepy. Then before dinner I was out in the garden and I swear I saw a shadow here in my room. Crazy huh?"

She dropped her eyes. Wes would think she was going mad, would probably want to break up with her.

"Why didn't you call me?"

He said placing the tip of his finger under her chin and tilting it up.

"I nearly did. Then I thought it wasn't fair to. You had to be up for college too."

Wes sighed in exasperation.

"Hally Mackeller. It's my job to keep you safe and happy. You're my world. So if something is bothering you then I have to know about it, no matter what the time of day it is."

Hally knew he was right. Ever since they had met he had been there for her through everything. When she had been told about Dana's death he had been by her side. When her grandmother died it was Wes that had helped her through it. He had supported her during her exams, been her rock, always there anytime.

"I know. But like I said, it just didn't seem fair. Anyway, I went back to bed and slept ok, no nightmares."

"But it's still playing on your mind isn't it?"

Hally took a deep breath and puffed it out between her lips. She felt a bit stupid now. Maybe she was just being a complete drama queen she thought. One nightmare and she was turning it into a first class issue. She felt a little giggle bubble up and pop out. Wes looked perplexed.

"I should get Clia to write a piece, you know practise her journalism on me. I can just see the headline." She held her hands up. "Girl Goes Crazy After Nightmare." Wes laughed and dragged her onto his lap. They both sank into the beanbag and nearly rolled off.

"You are my crazy, gorgeous, beautiful girlfriend."

Wes said punctuating each word with a kiss on her face. Hally giggled, delighting in his attention. As his lips found hers the kisses became one long deep one, his hands finding places that made her sigh and lean in closer.

****

I can hear something. I'm not sure what it is. I swear the walls of our house are made of paper because a lot of the time what goes on next door is so clear. But this isn't coming from next door. It's like um…it's in the room with me. If I hold my breath I can hear it better. Someone crying. That's what it sounds like. Maybe it's me. No my face is dry. If I was crying there would be tears on my cheeks. Anyway I don't cry, not anymore, it doesn't do any good.

I can definitely hear someone crying now. A girl properly sobbing. She sounds ever so upset. But where is she? I mean I am alone. My room is empty. Oh God, it actually is empty. There's nothing in it. Where's my furniture gone? I know I don't have much, just a bed and an old tatty wardrobe with a squeaky door, but it is all mine. Not many clothes either and they've gone too. How cruel, those debt collecting people. They've come in and taken everything whilst I was asleep.

If I had my phone I could call him. He would come and take me away like he said he would, I think. Ah, there it is again, the crying. It's easing off now. Wait, voices, I can hear speaking. A girl and a man. Maybe he's here, come for me. Maybe Penny's with him. But why would Penny be crying? And for that matter why would he be with Penny? He doesn't like her, he told me. He said I was his girl, just me. That's why he gave me the booze, wine was it? For a moment I thought it was vodka.

So I'm drifting again like before. I'm sure I'm not sick. Just finding it hard to keep my concentration just like in school. Hang on it's still the summer holidays so don't think about school. That's a couple of days away yet thank God. Although actually it might be better than hanging around here in my room all day with nothing to do.

The crying, no not anymore. It has stopped but the voices are clearer. I'm going mad. I'm hearing people who aren't here. Best not tell anyone that, they'll lock me up for sure and he won't want me then.

Funny, I don't remember moving but here I am standing at the window again. No it's not the window. What is happening to me? There's nothing around me but blue. I can't feel the floor and I can see the voices now. It is a girl and a man. They're blurred but I don't wear glasses. Has something happened to my eyes? Can that happen if you're really hungry?

The couple, yes that's what they are. The way he's holding her. His lips are moving, he's speaking. Concentrate Dana. Yes, I can hear his voice. He's worried. She's telling him not to be. She's pretty, I've always known that. Always been jealous of her. Not because she's pretty, I know I am, but because she has a nice home and parents who love her. That's pathetic I know. It's not her fault. I should be nicer to her. That's it I remember. I'm going to stop bullying her.

Ah the voices. They're Hally and her boyfriend. The new guy. He's only just come to our town. She's so lucky. He is gorgeous. All the girls think so. I've seen them flirt and try to get him to notice them, I did a bit too if I'm honest. But none of them got anywhere. Penny, that was funny. She properly shoved her boobs out at him in the Hotspot the other day. Well I think it was anyway. He didn't even bat an eyelid, just handed over her change and turned away. She was fuming, mumbling under her breath something nasty about Hally.

Hally and what's his name? um…do I even know it? Doesn't matter. The voices are fading in and out and I can't see them so well now. Wait, if I concentrate. Yes, that's better, their faces are clearer so are their voices. Just not enough to work out exactly what they're saying. I'm closer now too. It's like…um…like I'm standing outside the window looking in now. But no it can't be. I don't like this. Something is very wrong. There's nothing around me but the blue. There's no glass and no walls and nothing below my feet. I can see them sitting on beanbags. I can see the room, it's pretty, very girlie, not like mine. But it's like everything is floating, I'm floating.

No I don't like this. Their voices are clear. They're talking, saying something about a nightmare. Perhaps that's it. This is my nightmare and Hally and what's-his-name are in it. But it doesn't feel like a dream. Hally just looked up. Can she see me? She's not taking any notice of me waving, but if I can see her surely she can see me. She's frowning like she's working something out. Concentrate Dana.

There, I'm in the room, her room. I can see the floor, the blinds, Hally and her boyfriend. I'm near the door. Hally is looking right at me. Why? What the hell am I doing in Hally's bedroom and exactly how did I get here? Oh I don't like this, not one bit. Please stop, please let me go back to my room.

Chapter 6

Hally snuggled against Wes on the beanbag, all her woes forgotten for a while. It felt so right, so comfortable. He was her whole world. He could and would keep her safe. This was exactly where she was meant to be. All the confusion and fear she had spilled to the girls the night before were just imagination. Right then she couldn't ever see herself loving or wanting to love another man.

Wes stroked her hair and nestled her in his lap. He was relieved to see his girlfriend was back to her usual loving self. She was more important to him than anyone else, that is except Ellie. His toddler daughter was a part of him. What he felt for her couldn't ever be measured or compared to the love he had for Hally. He would gladly give his life to protect both of them.

"So how was your day at college?"
Hally asked, breaking into Wes' thoughts.

"It was good actually. We went over quite a lot of stuff that I sort of knew already but couldn't quite get. Mum was well chuffed. We're going to start on the software next, which I can then teach to mum. We have the program at home but she's never known how to use it."

Hally grinned at him. She could feel the enthusiasm emanating from him.

"She's very proud of you Wes. Deciding to be an accountant and working towards having a business with her is brilliant. That way you can both still be a part of looking after Ellie without having to send her to someone else."

Wes nodded. His mother had been there for him right from the start. When Ellie's sixteen-year-old mother had up and left for a life in Australia with her parents, relinquishing all rights to the child, Wes' parents had taken her in. Wes had only been sixteen too and completely naïve about how to raise a child. His parents had moved them all from Oxford to Colingford to begin a new life, his mother giving up her job as an accountant to look after the baby. As a way of repaying her and supporting his daughter as well, Wes chose to train in accountancy with the aim of working with his mum. So far the plan was going well.

Hally had been very relieved to know her boyfriend wasn't intending to head off to university. She felt a little selfish at times about this but still it was a comfort to know he would always be close. She had pushed her own future far to the back of her mind. She didn't want to make plans, didn't want things to change even though she knew they inevitably would. For her, life was the here and now.

"Hally babe. You still with me?"

Hally jumped. She had been so far into her own thoughts she hadn't heard him.

"Oh sorry I was miles away."

She said twisting strands of his hair between her fingers.

"Which planet?"

Wes asked playfully. Hally pushed her lips to one side, mulling over the question. It was a frequent game of theirs.

"Um...let me see."

Wes tickled her under the ribs. She wiggled and giggled.

"Stop it, don't, you're spoiling my planet."

She pretended to whine.

"You're jetting me off to outer space wiggling like that."

Hally laughed and batted him gently on the arms.

"Your own fault Wesley."

Then she deliberately wriggled a bit more. Wes wrapped his arms around her and pulled her into an embracing kiss. Hally relaxed into him and enjoyed all of the feelings he gave her, giving back just as many. Even though they spent some nights together they still thoroughly enjoyed the teenage over the clothes intimacy too.

****

It's still foggy outside. That's weird because it wasn't a little while ago when I could see all the blue and Hally and her gorgeous boyfriend. He is, gorgeous I mean. Wish I had someone like that loving me. Because I'm sure he does love her. The way he was holding her, the boyfriend that is. He doesn't hold me like that. He says things to me, tells me he loves me but only if I ask. I remember that now. I have to say it to him and when I do I have to kneel in front of him and look up at him. He's so tall, big, strong and hard. A bloke like that should look after me. But where is he now?

I closed my eyes and opened them and here I am back in Hally's room. This is the strangest dream I've ever had. It is just going on and on. I mean it has to be a dream because things keep flipping. One moment I'm in bed. Then my room's empty again. Then I'm by my window. Then in Hally's room. That's the best bit about this dream, if it is that. Don't know what it would be if it isn't.

Never mind. In Hally's room it's nice. Quiet and pretty. It should smell fresh and clean, not like my room, but I can't smell anything actually like with my bedding. So yes, got to be a dream.

Oh it feels a bit wrong like I'm spying. Hally's on her boyfriend's lap. Those beanbags look wickedly comfy. They're kissing. Really kissing and their hands are all over each other. Uh Oh, I shouldn't be watching this. But I can't turn away. For some reason it's like I'm glued to the spot.

Of course if this is a dream then it doesn't matter, no one will know. But what if it's not a dream? They might see me. Jesus I'll be in a heap of trouble then. Can just see it. The cops will haul me down to the station and ask loads of questions again, like after the booze thing. I had to tell then. It wasn't fair on Hally really, trying to get her mum and dad in trouble. I did need the money, but actually in the end it wasn't enough, so not worth the trouble it got me and others in. It was obvious it was me who dobbed them in even though I did it anony…something, that thing where you don't give your name, and I expected to get a wallop for it, but for some reason I didn't.

My mind's rambling again. Can't seem to get a fix on any one thing. Maybe I had an accident. I heard a kid from school once got slammed into a lorry on his motorbike. He didn't die, not exactly. They said he could hear and see and everything, but couldn't talk back or move. The kids in school said it was horrible for his family because he was something like locked in his own brain. God I hope that's not what's happened to me.

But surely if I'd had an accident I would remember that. So no, something strange is going on but I didn't have an accident. Anyway he was with me last night. I spoke to him. He held me, talked to me, did more to me than Hally and her boyfriend are doing right now. It was so nice. He made me feel so nice inside, all over really. So yes he does love me. He wouldn't do that if he didn't. He loved every moment too, I think.

Maybe if I close my eyes, because I can't move away from Hally's room, then I at least won't see them. La la la. It's not keeping out the sound. I can hear them, all the sounds of love. LA LA LA, it's not working. Even with my hands over my ears I can still hear them.

Ah, they've stopped. Oh, someone is knocking on the door. I'm going to be in the way if they come in. Hally and her boyfriend are looking up. They must see me. The door is opening behind me. I have to get out but how? A voice, a soft motherly voice. She's asking them if they want a cup of tea. She's coming in the room. She's right next to me. Can't they see me? I'm waving, jumping up and down. Why are they pretending? I'm right here. Hey look, I'm in Hally's room. I shouldn't be. See me, hear me. Don't, please please don't ignore me. Mum does that. He does too sometimes especially when others are around. Hally! Help me. I don't know what's going on. Please just don't ignore me.

****

Mum popped her head around Hally's bedroom door. Her daughter was sitting on Wes' lap and they looked happy. Mum sighed inwardly. She was worried about Hally, but didn't want to show it. At that moment though it didn't look like there was anything to be worried about. Hally was beaming and mum knew it had everything to do with the young man that held her.

Hally glanced at Wes for his answer to mum's offer of tea. He nodded so Hally smiled at her mother and accepted as well. May left the room closing the door behind her. As she did Hally thought she saw a shadow shimmer in the draft from the closing door. She blinked and it was gone.

Determined not to let anything else bother her, Hally ignored the inner feeling that she had seen something strange and pushed it to the very back of her mind.

"So back to my planet."
She stated and Wes burst out laughing. It was so nice and normal to be playing. To be just a normal teenager doing

teenager stuff. Sometimes she felt life was far too serious for her, for both of them. She wasn't ready to grow up, be an adult and take on adult responsibilities. Then it hit her, she already had taken on at least one, Ellie was most definitely a grown up responsibility. She felt her face begin to flush, feelings of guilt flooding through her veins.

"What's that for?"

Wes asked touching her flaming cheeks with a fingertip. Hally lowered her eyelashes masking her true feelings.

"Uh...just had a thought."

"And?"

Wes coaxed. Hally took a breath giving herself time to come up with a reply.

"Just um...that if mum had come in a couple of seconds earlier she would have seen us."

She lied.

Wes frowned. May had never once walked in on them in a compromising situation. She always knocked and gave them plenty of time before opening the door. He was sure something else had caused Hally's flush but he wouldn't push her. He was certain she would tell him in her own time.

Hally buried her face into Wes' shoulder. She felt terrible lying to him. At the same time, she knew she couldn't tell him the real reason for her red face, he would be devastated. His little girl was so important to him. If she gave even a tiny hint of the way she was feeling, walls would be erected between them and nothing would ever be the same again.

"Let's go out."

Hally suddenly spurted out. Wes jumped a little, startled.

"Um, ok. Where do you want to go?"

They usually stayed in on week days. College was exhausting especially for Wes, who had his part time job at the Hotspot and his daughter to give his attention to. But right then Hally felt a need to get out of the house. She felt penned in. It was like something was sucking all the air from her room making it difficult to breathe. Her thoughts were crashing together, rocks on a beach being tossed up by a turbulent sea.

"Anywhere. The park."

Hally gabbled as she jumped from his lap tugging at his hand.

Wes came to his feet frowning in confusion. Not many minutes before his girlfriend had been accepting a cup of tea from her mum, now she was pulling him towards the bedroom door.

"Hally, hold up a bit."

He said. Hally kept a grip on his fingers, not immediately realising Wes wasn't moving. When she finally did feel resistance she turned, her eyes wild.

"What? Come on. It's too nice out to be sitting here in a stuffy room."

"What about tea?"

Hally frowned.

"You know, your mum's bringing up tea."

It took a moment for his words to click. When they did she shrugged.

"Oh, yes. Well we'll just...um...drink it in the kitchen then go. Come on."

Hally gave a final tug and Wes gave in.

Mum was in the kitchen pouring water into mugs. She was surprised to see Hally and Wes.

"I was about to bring it up."

"No it's fine mum. We'll have it here then we're going to the park."

May gave Wes an enquiring look. He raised his brows but said nothing. Hally didn't notice. She was too busy lifting her mug and taking a sip of the hot tea. Mum passed him a mug too and leaned against the counter watching Hally.

"Careful angel, you're going to scald yourself."

She warned. Hally put her cup down.

"Hmm yes too hot. Sorry mum I'll have to leave it. Come on Wes. It's getting late."

"Hally! Let the man finish his tea."

Mum gasped, totally confused. Wes put his mug down.

"No it's ok May."

He told her. Hally grinned and spun around towards the door.

"Have you got your phone?"

Mum called as they were leaving.

"In my pocket. See you in a bit mum. Love you."

Hally was practically running down the garden path towards the back gate. She held onto Wes' hand tightly her nails digging into his flesh. He let her pull him along hoping she would calm down before she drew his blood. As soon as the gate closed behind them Hally felt a sense of relief and eased her pace. Wes was very glad. Slipping an arm around her shoulders he walked by her side in the warm evening air.

The stroll to the park calmed Hally even more. So that by the time they entered the gates she was feeling relaxed and happy. Wes noticed the difference but kept his thoughts to himself. Taking his arm from around her he linked his fingers through hers leading her towards the pond.

The park was quite busy. Families, teenagers and old couples enjoying as much of the fine weather that they could before it disappeared into winter. Hally was in no hurry, was happy to dawdle along the path that edged the pond. She swung her arm holding Wes' hand in a far more relaxed grip. She looked up at him and smiled, her eyes gleaming. Wes' heart nearly exploded. He loved her so much and was relieved to see her face bright and cheerful.

"Feeling better now?"

He asked keeping his voice light. Hally nodded.

"Much. Sorry about back at home. I…"

She paused, not sure how to explain the overwhelming sense of suffocation she had felt. Wes stayed silent as they walked. Hally breathed in and tried again.

"I think...it was like I couldn't breathe and needed to get outside."

She felt a little squeeze on her fingers.

"Oh Wes. Nothing to do with you."

She exclaimed, stopping and standing in front of him. Wes looked down into her beautiful blue eyes.

"I promise. Look, let's go over there and sit down."

She pointed to an empty bench under a tree. It was surrounded by red and gold leaves, a true sign autumn was definitely here.

Hally sat slightly sideways, taking both of Wes' hands in her own. She raised them to her lips and kissed them lightly. She might be feeling confused about Ellie but she knew she was very much in love with the man before her.

"This time last year we hadn't been going out together for very long. It seems such a long time ago. I couldn't believe you wanted me, kept expecting you to break up with me because I was so much younger. I was sure an older girl, or prettier one would come along and catch your eye. But it never happened."

Wes turned her hands over and kissed her palms.

"No one is prettier than you Hally. I used to get scared you would get bored with me and finish it."

Hally giggled. What a pair they were. Now though, over a year on she had different fears. She no longer worried Wes would find someone else. She sighed.

"Last night when I asked the girls to come 'round I told them something."

She felt her cheeks begin to flame again. Wes frowned worriedly.

"This is what bothered you in your room?"

Hally began to shake her head then remembering exactly what she had been thinking, stopped.

"Uh yes."

Wes felt a shiver of fear creep up his spine. He almost couldn't breathe. Not wanting to know but sure he had to, he bit his lip.

"And…"

His voice cracked a little. Hally saw the misery in his eyes and shook her head, trying to formulate a way to tell him how she felt without hurting him.

"Wes I love you. I'm absolutely sure about that so please don't take what I'm going to say the wrong way."

Hally covered his cheek with the palm of her hand. She could feel soft bristle under her fingertips and stroked it with her thumb. A tear trickled down and landed softly on her skin. She was hurting him and hated herself for doing it. But she knew she had to get her worries off her chest. They would only grow and get to her even more. At least if she shared them with Wes, her boyfriend, the man she loved with all her heart, he could reassure her as he had done so many times before.

"Don't cry. Please."

She whispered. Wes closed his eyes trying to shut off the flow.

"Just tell me."

He said his voice husky with emotion.

"It's being at college."

Wes opened his eyes, confused as to where her words were leading.

"It's so different from school. Bigger, more people. Not just kids like school but grown-ups and all different ages. I've never met so many people before. At least never noticed. It's always just been us, you know people our own age."

She paused unable to put into words what she had so easily told Corrinne and Clia. Wes was staring at her bemused. She looked up into the tree, watched it shed a few more red and gold leaves and hoped for inspiration. She sucked in her breath and let it out slowly.

"Have you?"

Wes asked tentatively. Hally frowned.

"Have I what?"

"Met someone else?"

His said, his voice barely above a whisper. Hally's shoulders slumped as she realised what she was doing to him. She slid forward and wrapped her arms around him.

"No oh God no Wes. I love you, only you."

Wes pulled back from the embrace and looked into her turbulent eyes.

"Then what Hally? You're freaking me out. I'm scared and I don't even know why."

"This has not gone how I wanted it to. I've made a right pig's ear out of this. It was so easy telling the girls but I've just upset you."

"Well then tell me what you told them. I won't get angry or upset. So long as you're not planning on breaking up, then I can handle anything."

Hally gave him a light peck on the lips.

"It's still going to sound bad. But well...like I said, there's so many different people at college. Every time I go into the Food Hall there are faces that I don't recognise. I just got scared that one of us would meet one of those people and..."

She left the sentence unsaid having changed it to we instead of I, believing that small lie would give Wes comfort. It seemed to have worked.

"Oh babe. I can see how you would feel like that. But I promise you there is no other girl for me anywhere. And I can only hope that you feel the same way about me. But I have to accept that you are still so young and it could happen. I just hope and pray it doesn't."

Hally saw in his eyes the truth of his words. She felt relieved and her heart swelled. She was confident in her feelings for him, sure that she wouldn't be attracted to anyone else.

"Oh Wes it won't. I know that. Back when we first got together, I kept asking mum how I would know this was it, the real thing. She told me I would feel it and I do. I might be young, and these days it's not seen to be the right thing to get serious at my age, but I think we are doing it the right way. It's not like we've moved in together and given up everything. We're both studying, have ambitions. Mum always said, no one can tell you how things will work out, you just have to believe in yourself. Well I do and I believe in you. So I believe we have a great future together. There, crazy girlfriend has spoken."

Wes burst out laughing. He was very relieved. His own mother had often voiced her concerns over his relationship with Hally which he didn't agree with. He had never told Hally about those conversations. She and his mum got on very well and he didn't want to do or say anything that would change that. Besides, he had made it clear to his mother that he knew what he was doing, what he had got into with such a young girlfriend, and now his convictions in their relationship were confirmed.

For a moment his thoughts took him back to when he was sixteen. He had been immature and very naïve. His then girlfriend had been far more forward. She had been the one to take their relationship to the next level, the result being Ellie. But she wasn't mature where Hally was.

He hated comparing the two girls, but the times he did he knew Hally far outweighed Sophie in every aspect. In fact, it was difficult to think of Hally as being sixteen most of the time. Right at that moment was an exception. She was usually so level headed and composed, her brief outburst at home and here in the park such a rarity, Wes was surprised. Still he told himself, she had every right to act like a sixteen-year-old teenager now and then. He couldn't and wouldn't fault her for that.

"What planet are you on Wes?"

Hally broke into his thoughts. He grinned.

"Planet Hally and all the glorious sunshine and love that it possesses."

Hally giggled and slid closer on the bench. Wes slipped one arm around her waist and his other hand on the back of her neck. She came willingly into the kiss he offered. She closed her eyes and kissed him back. It was wonderful. Everything was fine, all back to normal.

★★★★

They've gone. I don't know where and I wonder, will they come back? I heard some of it. Hally wanted tea then they were gone. The nice lady I suppose is Hally's mum, she left and closed the door. Hally looked at me, I'm sure she did when the door closed. She frowned. I wonder why? Probably I look a right mess. I've had to shower in cold water. It's not very nice but because it's still so warm out it's not so bad. I don't have any shampoo though, and I have to let my hair dry naturally so it sort of frizzes up quite a lot. But even washing in just water is better than not washing at all.

Hally's room is really nice. Wish my room was like this. She has pretty things. Pink and purple bedding and a lovely white wardrobe and dressing table. She has a really cute laptop too. He brings his laptop 'round sometimes. He takes photos of me, says I can be a model if I just pose the right way. So he gets me to practice. It's ok, sometimes.

Hally's got a sweet picture on her wall. It's, hang on what is it? Oh, it's angels watching over a baby. If I had a baby, I would watch over her too. My baby would be a girl, they're cute. I would be a good mum, better than mine. I wouldn't leave my little girl by herself with nothing.

Mmmm Hally's bed is soft, better than mine. If I rest my hand on the cover, I can feel...no I can't. Oh God not that again. I can see things but I can't feel them. Am I even touching the bed? I don't remember walking across the room to the bed. I was by the door now I'm on the bed. I bent my knees to sit, I think, but it's like there's nothing but air under me. My tummy feels a bit wobbly like when you go on a ride at the fair and get a bit dizzy. I hope I'm not going to be sick. I'd hate to mess up Hally's room. That would be awful and really unfair. I've been horrible enough to Hally for so long, being sick all over her bed would just be cruel.

No I'm not going to be sick. The feeling has gone. But I still feel a bit floaty. There's her school bag on her desk. She's lucky she has somewhere to do her homework. Bet she can ask her mum or dad to help if she gets stuck too. I do try and do mine at the kitchen table but I find it ever so hard. I've got no one to help me, mum can't be bothered and anyway she's gone now. School starts back in...one, two, um, what day is it today? I think it's Tuesday but I can't be sure. So that means less than a week left before school.

I think I'll try hard at school this year. I've stopped bullying Hally, I just can't be bothered anymore it's so pointless. We're all growing up. Hang on, I'm supposed to be trying to get a job as soon as I'm sixteen. I need money, far more than a few hours after school can give me. Oh hell. Just as I frigging decide to put some effort into school I remember I have to get a job. This is so unfair. But I'm not going to find a job like overnight. So I might as well try a bit at school. I know it won't look cool to Penny and the rest of them but I just don't care anymore.

I've spent years being the cutesy curvy bossy Dana. I'm sick of it now. The boys, even the older ones are a bunch of losers. I know it's been a bit of a laugh and all that but the booze thing went too far. I could have ended up in gaol over that. Penny and the other girls keep on nagging me all of the time. Let's see if we can get in the pub, let's nick that mascara from Chandlers, on and on. I've had enough.

The boys, they just think I'm easy. But I'm not. I make out I am but I haven't gone all the way with any of them. They wouldn't dare tell their mates though that I turned them down. That wouldn't look cool at all and I do have a reputation for being the coolest girl in school. No they tell each other how good I was and I just smile and wink and flirt, oh and pretend. Penny thinks I'm great because of that, huh what does she know? She's done it with a couple of the boys but the others they don't really like her much. I don't think I do anymore either. The other day was it? In the Hotspot when she started on Hally. I just got so mad, nearly thumped her. There's my life falling apart around me, and all Penny can do is start on the one girl I've decided to stop bullying. So that's probably why she hasn't been 'round. Maybe I even told her not to bother me anymore, I don't remember.

So yes I'm going to put some effort into school. Mr Haines keeps telling me I can do better if I just try. He's my English teacher. Well, actually was, we're going into year eleven now so different teachers. I think the set I was in, bottom actually, might have either Mrs Creeley or Mr Shah. Hope it's Mr Shah, he's nice. He took us once when Mr Haines was off.

There's some papers on Hally's desk. Wonder what they are? We don't get homework in the summer. But Hally's so clever, she gets high grades all of the time, maybe she's doing something to show when she goes back. There's no one here so I think I'll have a little peek. It's all piled neatly into a plastic folder.

Wait, this can't be Hally's. I bet it belongs to that gorgeous hunk of hers. No it's got her name on the top. And, what the frig is going on? We don't get assignment notes like this and why does it say Colingford College of Further and Higher Education? Hally's too young to go to college. I know she's intelligent but even she's not that good. I don't like this not at all. I can't breathe. Where is the edge of the room? The walls are wobbling. I think I'm going to faint.

Chapter 7

Hally and Wes stayed in the park on the bench even after the light began to fade. They chatted and shared more about their day at college, the previous subject avoided. Hally was very glad. She was happy. She had Wes and she would cope with whatever was thrown at her regarding Ellie. After all, even though she hadn't known about the toddler when they first started going out, it had been her choice to stay with Wes once she did know.

A little breeze brought a slight chill to the air and Hally shivered. She had all but run from her house forgetting to pick up her jacket. Wes spotted she was cold and took off his hoody.

"Here you go. Put this on. That top isn't meant for autumn evenings."

Hally slipped it on and snuggled into its large folds. She could smell Wes, and breathed in his scent. Instantly she felt warm.

"I didn't think about it getting cold. It's been so warm lately."

"Then maybe I should see about getting you home."

Hally shivered again. This time it had nothing to do with the physical temperature. She didn't know exactly what it was, just something.

"Oh let's go to the Hotspot. It's still early."

Wes pulled his phone from his pocket and checked the time. It was just after half eight. The Hotspot would be open for another hour and a half. Although he worked there he didn't mind socialising there too. It was the most popular café in the town with teenagers. The only place open until that time other than fast food outlets and licensed premises.

"Ok. I don't mind."

He said standing up and offering his hand. Hally grinned and bounced to her feet. The Hotspot was more than special to her, it was where she had met Wes.

Even though it was Monday the Hotspot was busy. Where a year ago Hally wouldn't have dreamed of coming in during the evening, now she walked into the café confidently, her hand wrapped around Wes'. There were several people they both knew. Hally said hello to a group of girls from her old school who had chosen sixth form. They smiled cheerily and gave Wes flirtatious looks. Hally giggled inside, it always happened but Wes never took any notice.

Wes went behind the counter and poured them both cokes. His boss permitted this but only for Wes and one other employee, Raj. They were his two most trusted workers. They could be left in charge of the café, the office, safe and the keys, so he willingly allowed them little perks like free drinks. Neither of them took advantage.

Wes carried their glasses to a vacant table. A few lads he knew joked and teased with him on the way. Hally smiled and felt happy. Even when the door opened and Penny Cuthbert came in, her arm linked with Martin Cob, Hally didn't feel threatened. She was surprised to see the two so close though. Rumour had it that Martin had been madly in love with Dana Edwards and couldn't stand Penny. She shrugged to herself and thought, oh well people do grow up.

Wes sat opposite her and slid her drink towards her. He leaned in close and in a hushed voice said.

"Those two have been seen together a lot lately. A couple of the lads reckon Martin's turned over a new leaf. You know he got sent down last October?" Hally nodded. "Well he got out in April on good behaviour. He was supposed to do twelve months. I heard that this time inside he barely spoke to anyone, did as he was told and even did some training."

Hally mused over this information. She had purposely taken no interest in what any of the gang, who used to bully her, had been doing over the last year. With Dana gone the bullying had stopped, and as far as Hally was concerned that was the end of any contact or interest in any of them. Martin Cob had not been involved in the bullying, he was older and just trouble. But it had been his influence that had pushed Dana and the others to plant alcohol at her party to try and get her parents into trouble.

"Well at least that's something maybe for all the bad stuff he's done over the years. I am surprised though that him and Penny are so cosy. Maybe he feels closer to Dana because Penny was her best friend. Well I say that but I don't think Penny really knows what a best friend is. I mean, remember she didn't even turn up to Dana's funeral. Martin must have been locked up by then because he wasn't there either."

"Yes I think he was. Apparently he was in a state after Dana died."
Wes whispered. Hally leaned in closer lowering her voice too.

"It's actually really sad I think. If she hadn't done, you know what she did, maybe they could have both turned their lives around." She shrugged. "It can happen I suppose.

I'm not so sure Penny will be good for him if he is trying to steer clear of crime though. She's more of a bitch than Dana was.

I know Dana was horrid to me and led the others too. But when I saw what she was going through at home, I could sort of understand. But Penny, she's got a family. She's always got money and the latest gadgets and clothes. Maybe that's why she used to hang out with Dana, she was so spoilt no one else would be her friend. You'd think she would have tried to help her wouldn't you?"
Hally glanced over at Penny. Even though Martin had his arm around her waist, she was batting her lashes at one of the boys talking to them. Hally frowned.

"But looking at her now, I think she just wanted the attention Dana used to get. I mean, she's got Dana's man. He might not be into all the gang stuff anymore but I bet she still feels he's the tough guy. Soon as he doesn't live up to that she'll be onto the next bloke." She sighed. "I'm just glad our little group are not a part of that."

Wes covered her hand with his. He knew she had gone through some very difficult times before he met her. The bullying by Dana and her gang had been hard to cope with. He was just thankful he had met her, had helped raise her confidence and show her that she didn't have to hide away and avoid the places other teenagers went to.

"We're the lucky ones. We have families who actually care and we all look out for each other. This might sound really uncool and soppy, but I think you and the girls and me and the boys are going to be close for life."

Hally gave him a tiny sideways glance. Wes blushed a little. Hally grinned.

"What are you saying Wes?"
She coaxed. Wes could never deny her anything, especially when she smiled at him and flashed her big blue eyes. Feeling a little flustered he tried to put his feelings into words.

"Um, uh…only that…well. I can't imagine life without you by my side. And Rhys and Gregg, they're serious about Clia and Corrinne. So well…that's what I meant."

Hally felt warm inside. Wes told her daily that he loved her. Her two best friends said the same about their boyfriends. But hearing him say outright that he expected their relationships to be lasting, it was simply comforting.

The door to the café opened and a few more teenagers came in. Hally vaguely recognised one of the girls from college and waved a greeting. The girl waved back but it was the look she gave Wes that had Hally's nerves on edge. She glanced at Wes, his cheeks had gone pink. Despite Wes' words minutes before Hally felt irrational jealousy.

"Do you know her?"

She asked Wes, a frown creasing her brows. Wes nodded.

"Sort of."

Hally twisted her glass and waited.

"She waits outside one of my classes."

Hally's mouth opened slightly ready to give an angry retort. Wes held his hand up.

"Not for me. One of the lads in my group."

Hally relaxed only a tiny bit, certain there was more to it.

"And?"

She said. Wes' blush deepened.

"But I sort of get the impression she fancies me."

Hally looked over at the girl. She was still staring at Wes until she saw Hally watching her. Then she quickly turned away.

"Hally babe it's totally one sided I promise."

Wes said drawing her attention back to him. Hally felt raw inside. She knew other girls found Wes very attractive. Usually she brushed it off, proud he was hers. For some reason this one girl, who was obviously after her boyfriend, felt like a threat.

"I…I'm just going to the ladies."

She muttered. She needed a minute by herself to get her feelings under control. She hated being jealous.

Hally ran cold water over her wrists trying to calm the pounding in her heart. Wes would never cheat on her. Wes would never let another girl come between them. Wes loved her. Wes was hers for life, he had said so. The thoughts raced through her mind. She took long deep breaths and gradually as the water flowed, her pulse began to settle.

Feeling more composed, Hally jumped when the door opened. She half expected it to be the girl but it was Penny. Hally sighed inwardly. She no longer feared her but she didn't relish being in the same room either. Penny smirked as she came and stood next to her.

"Looks like your boyfriend has a thing for someone else."

She said gleefully whilst applying a fresh layer of makeup.

"Get lost Penny."

Hally replied turning to the hand dryer. Pouting at her reflection and smoothing on bright red lip gloss Penny shrugged.

"Looks mean more than words. Just saying."

Hally finished drying her hands and stood facing Penny.

"Look, I don't care what you say, it doesn't bother me. That girl out there, she might fancy Wes but he doesn't fancy her. Get it."

She went to walk away then changed her mind.

"I'm surprised she's not one of your mates since you don't seem to mind going after someone else's fella."

Hally had reached the door when she felt a hand on her shoulder gripping her skin.

"What is that supposed to mean?"

Penny said through gritted teeth. Hally turned and faced her. Her eyes were thunder and Penny quickly relinquished her hold and stepped back. She had seen Hally lose her temper once before, had felt the sharp slap from Hally's hand after she had goaded her.

"Martin Cob that's what I mean. He was Dana's boyfriend wasn't he? Now he's yours. Why's that Penny? You were always glued to her, did everything she did. Yet you didn't even bother turning up to her funeral. Some friend you were. You just take, take, take. Spoilt little brat. I saw you out there flirting whilst Martin had his arm around you. I don't think you care about anyone but yourself."

"How dare you."
Penny said her voice threatening. Hally didn't move.

"I'm not scared of you anymore Penny. So don't try the old how dare you stuff, it won't work. You're nothing. In fact, I feel sorry for you. Martin probably goes out with you because you're his only link to Dana."

Penny physically deflated in front of Hally. One moment her eyes were hard and aggressive, next she simply crumpled. Tears spilled onto her cheeks, black mascara streaks making paths through her foundation. Hally didn't know what to do. Normally she would offer comfort, but Penny was so hateful, Hally couldn't bring herself to do that.

"I'm so...sorry Hally. I...um...I found her. It was horrible. I've never been so scared in my life."
Hally wasn't expecting to hear that. Sympathy for Penny overtook her anger.

"Penny have you spoken to anyone about it?"
Penny swiped at her tears, smudging her makeup even more. She shrugged not really understanding what Hally meant.

"I told the police. Well, the neighbours did actually."

"I mean have you seen a counsellor?"
Penny shook her head.

"I'm not crazy."

Hally took a breath.

"I know that. Look, you're still at school. Mr Austin is a trained counsellor. Talk to him he'll understand."
Penny swung around to the basin and began to repair her tear stained face.

"Not friggin likely. I'm fine. Me and Martin, we're together because he wants me. He never even mentions Dana and neither do I. It happened over a year ago, we're over it."

Hally shrugged. She knew Penny wouldn't take her advice. As she exited the ladies she wondered if the tears had been a ruse. She decided not to dwell on it. Wes was looking towards the ladies, a worried frown on his face. He smiled when he saw her coming out. The girl who fancied him was sitting at another table facing theirs still staring at him. But Hally could see he only had eyes for her.

"Are you ok?"
He asked as she reached the table. She nodded.

"I'm fine. Just one moment."
She said holding up a finger and turning around. She put a bright smile on her face and strolled over to the girl's table. She was sitting with another girl Hally didn't recognise.

"Hi. I hope you're having a good evening."
The girl nodded, a slightly confused look on her face. Hally placed her palms flat on the table and leaned forward lowering her voice but keeping the smile.

"Wes is my boyfriend. He's not interested in you. So stop trying to get his attention by waiting outside his class, or any other way. You're embarrassing yourself staring at him all of the time. If I've noticed, then so have others. Find someone else because Wes won't ever be yours."
The girl's mouth dropped open and she blushed to the roots of her hair. Hally didn't give her a chance to respond. She straightened up, flipped her hair over her shoulder and sauntered back to her Wes.

"Hally?"

Wes said as she retook her seat and lifted her near empty glass of coke.

"Just staking my claim."

Hally said and Wes burst out laughing.

"And Penny?

Hally shrugged.

"We had words. But I'm ok. Don't think she is though. She tried the tears, not sure they were real. I offered her advice, she ignored it."

Wes looked puzzled.

"She brought up finding Dana."

Wes sucked in a breath.

"Jesus Hally. That was low of her."

Hally lowered her lashes.

"I sort of started it. I was pissed off at that girl gooey eyeing you, so when Penny tried bitching, I had a go back. Told her she had taken Dana's bloke. So she gets all teary but when I suggest she talks to a counsellor she goes on the defensive. So well, nothing I can do. I'm not even sure she needs counselling. It was probably all put on."

Wes reached for her hand and clasped it tightly. She looked up at him and was relieved to see his eyes were warm and loving. She always tried her hardest to be grown up and mature. To ignore nasty remarks or goads from others. Sometimes she couldn't quite manage it.

"Babe it's ok to get stroppy now and then. It doesn't make you like them and it definitely doesn't make you childish."

Hally was relieved Wes understood her so well and could sense her feelings. She hated the thought of acting like a kid especially since the age gap between them was over three years.

"Do you want another drink?"

He asked. Hally nodded.

"A chocolate muffin too please."

Wes laughed and stood up. Hally followed him with her eyes and as he passed the girl who fancied him watched for any reaction. She grinned when Wes completely ignored the girl as she smiled and batted her lashes at him. Hally knew she would have to have further words with the girl.

Wes and Hally shared the muffin and sipped their cokes as other teenagers came and went around them. Penny emerged from the ladies, makeup perfect and wrapped herself around Martin. He didn't seem to be that interested from what Hally could see. Yes, he kissed her back, kept his arm about her waist, but it was Penny that made all the moves. Not long after, Martin headed for the door, Penny trotting after him.

Wes and Hally stayed back after the Hotspot closed to help Raj clear up. As the three wiped tables and cleaned they chatted.

"It's weird seeing Martin Cob so quiet."

Raj said. He was a year younger than Wes and was training to be a chef so the Hotspot was his ideal part time job.

"Well Penny seems happy to be with him."

Hally replied. Raj grinned.

"Think that's pretty one-sided."

"Come on Raj, dish."

Hally coaxed twirling a cloth in her hands. Raj straightened the condiment caddy on the table he was cleaning.

"Did you and Penny have words tonight?"

Hally's look of surprise gave away the answer.

"So you dish first."

Raj said. Wes paused in his task too.

"I just told her she was a spoilt brat, that Martin was only interested because he missed Dana."

She said with a shrug. Raj bent over laughing.

"That explains it."

"What?"

Raj still chuckling replied.

70

"Penny came out of the loo and went all mushy on Martin. She was rabbiting on about how gorgeous he is and how she's so lucky he chose her. Martin stared at her for a moment then, and get this, it was so funny. He goes 'I didn't. You just latched onto me and I really can't be bothered so I go along with it.' Then he puts his glass down and walks out. Penny went scarlet, 'cos a few others heard too, and raced after him."

Hally felt a smirk start at the corners of her mouth and tried to contain it. She couldn't. It spread into a wide grin and then a full on laugh. Wes was smiling too.

"About time that little cow got put in her place."

He said. Raj nodded.

"I bet she stays away from here for a bit."

Hally shook her head.

"Probably not. She'll just hook some other poor guy and come in with him. Then she'll tell anyone in earshot that she dumped Martin."

"Well we know different. That looks like everything Raj. Just locking up left."

Wes said. Hally gave him a quizzical look.

"She's not worth our time or attention."

Hally leaned up and gave him a peck on the lips.

"Totally agree."

Raj walked part of the way home with Hally and Wes, the three chatting about nothing in particular. His road was nearer than Hally's so they stopped briefly to say goodnight. Wes and Hally then strolled on to her home.

They walked through the back door into the kitchen. As Hally flipped the light on her mum poked her head around the door.

"Everything all right?"

She asked warily. Hally let go of Wes' hand and threw her arms around her mother's neck.

"Perfectly mummy. I'm fine."

May raised her eyebrows at Wes over Hally's shoulder and he gave her a tiny nod back. She felt relieved.

With Wes following, Hally made her way into the lounge where her father was stretched out on the sofa watching television.

"Hi you two. Have a good evening?"

He asked without turning from the programme. Hally plonked herself next to him.

"Yeah, we went to the park then the Hotspot."

She yawned widely.

"I should get going babe. You're tired."

Wes said. Hally pouted. She was worn out but she was also reluctant for him to leave. It was always the same, she simply loved him being with her. Wes grinned and held out his hand.

"Come on walk me to the door. We've both got a busy day tomorrow."

With a huff Hally let Wes pull her up. He said goodnight to her dad and with his arm around her waist led her back into the kitchen. Mum was nowhere to be seen. Wes wrapped his arms about her and drew her close. She wound her fingers through his hair and waited for what she knew would be a lingering kiss goodnight. She might hate his departures but his kisses were the bonus.

After quite some time Wes pulled back and insisted he get off home. Hally held his hand letting his fingers slide through hers slowly. Wes laughed and finally disentangled himself. It was a routine they were happy to go through. Wes walked backwards down the path, Hally waiting at the open door. She waved as he passed through the back gate. She only closed the door once Wes was out of sight.

Hally went into the lounge to say goodnight to her parents. She was exhausted now. Dad was still watching his programme but mum wasn't there. Hally leaned down and gave her dad a kiss goodnight.

"Where's mum?"

"Probably upstairs."

Dad said giving her a quick hug. Hally left him to the drama he was watching and headed for the stairs.

Her mum was coming out of her own bedroom as Hally reached the top. She was carrying a pile of washing.

"Bit late for that isn't it?"

Hally said in a low voice. Nathan would be sound asleep and she didn't want to disturb her little brother. Mum shook her head.

"It's going to be dry tomorrow so if I get it in the machine now it will be ready to go out first thing."

Mum said also keeping her voice hushed. Hally put her arms around her mum and gave her a hug and kiss on the cheek.

"Night night mummy."

"Night angel. Sleep well."

May watched her daughter until she closed her bedroom door. She hoped Hally would sleep well. She sighed and clasped the bundle of laundry. She knew it was her job to worry for life about her children. Her own mother had done the same, right up until the moment she had died. May felt the prickle of tears in her eyes and lowered her head into the clothes she carried. It still hurt so much. She missed her mum more than words could say. Taking a breath, she composed herself. At least she still had her father. He was raw from the death of his wife but he was also strong and healthy. With a little sigh she plodded down the stairs.

Hally flipped on the main light in her room only long enough to flick the switch on her lamp. Usually she would walk straight into the darkness then turn on the lamp. Tonight she felt a little nervous of the dark. She began to prepare for bed, slipping out of the room to brush her teeth. As she returned she shivered. Her window was open, not wide, just enough to let in a little fresh air.

Hally padded across the carpet to close it. But when she got there the air coming in didn't feel particularly cold, so she changed her mind. She would snuggle under the covers and get warm. If it got too chilly, then she would shut it. She laid her phone on the bedside table, slipped into bed and flicked off the lamp. She knew she wouldn't sleep until she heard the beep of an incoming message from Wes. He always texted her once he got home to say a final goodnight.

The message came in as expected and she quickly tapped a reply. She smiled to herself, full of love for Wes as she settled down into the pillows. Her blinds let in ribbons of light, casting stripy shadows across the room. They swayed and danced as the light breeze moved the slats. It was soothing, almost mesmerising. Hally's tired eyes gradually began to close.

A darker shadow in the corner grew, moving steadily closer towards her bed. It stopped and hovered over her as she drifted off to sleep. The light from outside shimmered around its edges giving it form. As Hally lay sleeping the apparition watched and waited.

Chapter 8

****

It's dark again. It only just got light and now it's dark again. Where am I? Oh I can see, even though it is dark. I'm still in Hally's room. Did I faint? I think I did, it felt like that. Or that's what I think since I've never fainted before. Hally, she's in bed asleep. Ah that's why it's dark, it's night. It must be late if Hally's asleep.

She went out. I remember. Her and hunky boyfriend suddenly went out. They were going to have tea. Mmmm I'd like a nice hot cup of tea. I think I'm cold but I can't be sure. So Hally's mum was going to bring up tea. So why didn't they see me? I was standing right by the door. Then they were gone.

Hang on, what did I do then? Oh yeah, I looked at Hally's homework. Wonder if I can see it again in the dark. I daren't put the light on, that would wake Hally. She's got a little smile on her face. She's so pretty and lucky. I bet she's smiling because she's dreaming about hunky boyfriend. I'm sure I know what his name is. I mean I should know. He works in the Hotspot and I go there all the time. I know everyone who works there and goes in there. So why can't I remember his name?

Can't see the homework very clearly. I must be getting really good at moving quietly because I'm here at the desk and I didn't even notice myself walking. If I can have a peek, maybe it will give me some idea of what to write for my own homework. But wait, it's the summer holidays. We don't have homework in the summer.

Friggin hell, I'm going 'round in circles. That's what I said to myself earlier. I looked at Hally's papers. Jesus Dana, think you idiot. Remember what you saw. Nope, it won't come, nothing, blank. It's too dark to see the writing. Oh well forget it Dana, it's not worth the hassle.

The darkness is weird though. It's sort of waving. What? no that can't be the right word. The dark can't wave. It's um, like when it's foggy and one minute you can't see your hand in front of you then it clears a bit. That's not right either. Wish I could describe stuff better. I'd get good grades at school then. Hang on, got it. The dark is fading in and out. One moment it's pitch black and I can't see a frigging thing then shapes and objects sort of appear.

But now I don't know what I'm seeing. This is scary. I'm in my own room again but so is Hally. She can't be. She's in her bed because I know for sure it's not mine. No I'm in her room by her bed. She's asleep. But the room looks like mine. Now there's two rooms. I can see mine inside hers. The walls are see through and they're wobbling like jelly. If I put my hand out I can touch Hally's bed but I can't feel it.

****

Something was tickling Hally's nose. She was having a lovely dream about Wes but now something was annoying her. She didn't want to leave the dream but it was fading as her eyes opened just a tiny bit. She lifted her hand and rubbed her fingers across her face. She expected to grasp a spider, or flick away a moth but there was nothing. Sighing, she closed her eyes and slipped back into sleep.

She was lying in bed flat on her back. She had her eyes open. She could see her room. Everything was normal at first then it wasn't. She frowned. Her furniture was blurred and seemed to be floating. She turned her head to one side and gasped. There was another bed next to hers. It was transparent. She closed her eyes and opened them. The bed was still there, it was empty. She blinked a few times hoping her vision would clear. It worked. The bed was gone and her room was as it should be, the furniture stable.

Hally sighed deeply. She tried thinking about Wes but her mind kept drifting. She heard a whisper and looked about. The room was empty. The blinds were still, no breeze, night light finding its way in through the slats. She felt her bed give a little as though someone had pressed down on it. It would be Wes, he was with her. She smiled, his face coming towards her, his lips ready for a kiss.

****

My bed, I'm on it. He's here with me. He's holding me. He's stroking my hair, kissing my lips. But I can't move. He's saying something. He's pressing down on me. This is all so wrong. I'm on my bed with him right next to Hally who is sleeping in hers. The things he's doing to me, it's embarrassing in front of Hally even though she's asleep. Where he's touching me, it's nice, but this should be private. It's like being in a room with glass walls. Everyone can see.

He's talking to me. Sh, Hally will hear and wake. He's telling me I'm too old for him. I don't understand, how can I be too old for him, he's older than me. It's because I'm nearly sixteen he says. No you can't leave me. I have no one else. I'm crying but I can't feel my tears. He's angry that I'm crying. His face is all screwed up, but I can't really see it, it's blurred. His hands aren't gentle anymore. He's hurting me. He's pouring something into my mouth. It's wine and there's too much, it's filling my mouth, making me cough.

His hands are holding my head, no, they're either side of my cheeks. He's telling me to shut up. I can't move, he's still on top of me too heavy. There's something pressing on my neck under my chin. I think it's his thumbs. I can't swallow anymore and there's still wine in my mouth. Oh God, I can't breathe. I can't take in any air and my throat, it's hurting. I can feel my eyes closing but I don't want to go to sleep. I want to breathe. His voice is going away and darkness is coming. Hally please hear me. Help me Hally. I'm lost, alone and very afraid.

****

Deep in sleep Hally's dream took her exactly where she wanted to go, with Wes. It was perfect. Wes laid down next to her. He ran his fingers through her hair gently massaging her head. She felt so relaxed, so light, almost like she was floating. Then she was. She could no longer feel her bed beneath her.

Her eyes roamed the room. Everything shimmered, blurred around the edges. She could still feel Wes' hand in her hair but she couldn't see him. Her heart raced as panic began to grip like a claw around it. She wanted to wake up. She didn't like this dream.

The fingers were now gripping her hair pulling her head backwards. And she knew they didn't belong to Wes, but a stranger. It hurt. Whipping her head from side to side she tried to break free. The hold was too tight. There was pressure too, on her throat, cutting off her air. She struggled but there was nothing to resist against. The invisible hands held her firm. She lifted her hands to drag at the fingers but felt nothing.

The pain on her throat was becoming unbearable. Inside she told herself over and over to wake up, silently chanting it's just a dream. From the corner of her eye she saw a figure. At first it was little more than a shadow. She stretched her hand out, begging it for help, but no words came out. The figure began to take form, a girl.

Hally struggled and fought against the impalpable hands choking her. All the time the figure was becoming clearer. Its mouth was moving but Hally couldn't hear the words. It came closer, more solid, more real. The face leaned towards her, grey and cold. Hally recognised her. It was Dana.

Hally had no more breath inside. The hands on her throat were too tight. Dana came even closer and opened her mouth wide.

"Help me Hally, please!"
The words coming on a gasping plea. The pressure on Hally's throat eased a tiny bit, enough for her to suck in air. She took a large gulp and released it on a piercing scream. It broke through the nightmare and with shuddering relief Hally awoke, tears flooding down her cheeks.

Hally's bedroom door was flung open and both her parents rushed to her side. Hally sat up her arms outstretched. Mum dragged her into her own arms and held her, rocking her like she would a baby. Dad more slowly, sat on the edge of the bed and waited for his wife to calm their daughter.

"Sh. It's all right angel. Sh."
Mum said her voice soft and soothing. Hally sobbed, too afraid still to speak. Mum rubbed her back gentling her.

"It…it was horr…horrible mummy."
Hally stammered as mum shushed and consoled her. Hally felt her dad's hand close around her own and finally the trembling began to subside.

Slowly the tears dried on Hally's cheeks. Her parents stayed by her side protecting her from they knew not what.

"A horrible nightmare. That's all."
Hally whispered to no one.

"Do you want to tell us about it?"
Dad asked. Hally looked at her father, her eyes still full of fear. She nodded.

"But can we go downstairs? I don't even know what time it is."

Huddled in a soft teddy throw, Hally leaned into her father whilst her mum made hot chocolate. Gently he stroked her hair. She glanced at the clock on the wall, it was two thirty in the morning.

"Here you go."
Mum said handing her a mug of frothy hot chocolate. Hally momentarily closed her eyes breathing in the aroma.

"Mmmm lovely."
She whispered taking a sip from the cup. May passed a mug to her husband and for a while the three sat in silence.

"Most of it is fuzzy now."
Hally finally broke the silence. Her parents waited, she would say more when she was ready. Hugging the mug Hally sipped. Half way down the beverage she paused.

"My room was weird, like it was floating. I think someone was there with me but I don't remember. And I, I couldn't breathe. Then I saw a girl, Dana. She...um...she said something to me. Damn, I can't get it. I know I was scared. I suppose then I woke up."

"Angel, you screamed so loud I'm surprised the whole street didn't wake up."
Dad said trying to make the situation a little lighter. Hally frowned.

"Oh did I disturb Nathan?"
She asked worriedly. Dad rubbed her shoulder and shook his head.

"He's flat out. I looked in before I followed you and your mum down."

Hally let out a huge sigh. Waking her parents so early was one thing, to upset her little brother, another entirely. She lifted her mug and finished her chocolate.

"I wish I could remember the rest of the dream."

"But it was Dana?"

Her mum said, worry in her voice. Hally nodded.

"I just don't know why though."

Dad leaned down and put his empty cup on the floor. Then he turned sideways and looked directly at his daughter.

"Something's been on your mind this last few days. Maybe if you told us what we could help."

His voice was gentle, not probing or cross and Hally felt tears well up. She swiped at them with the back of her hand determined to control the flow.

"I...I don't really know. Well, I sort of worried about me and Wes but after talking to the girls and then tonight out, that's all gone away."

"In what way were you worried?"

Mum asked. Hally lowered her lashes. She was used to telling her parents private things and never found it embarrassing. But for some reason she was nervous about sharing the thoughts she had readily shared with Corrinne and Clia, and more recently Wes.

"Hally."

Mum prompted. Hally sighed.

"It had nothing to do with Dana though."

She replied, stalling. Dad enclosed her delicate hand with his large one and smiled. Hally relented. Taking a deep breath, she quickly and briefly told them what she had taken her time telling her friends and boyfriend. She didn't go into too much detail, it was over and done with. She didn't want it to grate on her nerves again and she was sure it had nothing to do with Dana.

"Well...I don't see how there's any connection to Dana."

Mum said when Hally finished. Hally nodded, glad her mum was seeing it the same way she was.

"But something triggered the nightmare."

Dad said a thoughtful frown crossing his brows.

"Look, it's really late, or should I say early. Why don't I call the school later and see if Mr Austin can have a chat with you at lunchtime? He helped you last time and he knows more about you than the college counsellors."

Mum suggested. Hally wasn't sure, but speaking to Mr Austin was far more preferable than the more austere counsellors they had all been introduced to on induction day.

"Ok, if he's not too busy."

Hally replied resignedly.

Mum took the empty cups out to the kitchen whilst dad cuddled Hally. She felt so safe in her father's arms. Leaning into him she closed her eyes relaxing. Colin still worried about his daughter gently rubbed her back, just like he had done when she was tiny. May came back into the room and smiled. Hally was asleep.

"She looks so peaceful now."

May said to her husband, her voice hushed. Colin nodded and whispered back.

"You go on up. I'll stay with her, let her sleep here on the sofa."

May frowned.

"No you have to go to work, I'll stay. You can't hold her for the rest of the night and the chair will make your back ache."

May protested. Colin grinned at his wife as he gently laid Hally down on the sofa and stood up. He pulled her into a hug and kissed her.

"You put everyone in this family ahead of you. This time, I'm putting you first. Go and get some rest. I'll be fine. Let me do this please."

He murmured. Reluctantly May gave in and kissed him back. She handed him the other throw from the back of the sofa and left him to it. Before she went into her own room she looked in on Nathan. He was fast asleep clutching one of his favourite action figures. She sighed. At least one of her children was getting a restful night.

****

It's all clear now. I remember. Everything has gone, my room, him. I'm just here standing next to Hally's bed. I'm dead. I know that now. I remember it all. It must have been a long time ago, over a year, that's why Hally's essay has the college name on it. She's not at school now.

I don't know why it's taken so long. Maybe I've been trying all this time to come here, to Hally, and have just forgotten. I don't know. It doesn't matter. I'm here now. She left her number once and offered to help me. Maybe that's why I've come to her. I don't think anyone else will help. It should be Penny but since I'm in Hally's room I suppose I can't reach her. But how do I tell Hally? I don't think she will be able to see or hear me.

I scared the living daylights out of her. I didn't mean to do that. I've done enough of that over the years when I was alive. I don't want her dead too. I don't want to harm her at all. There she was, all peaceful. Her face looked like she was having a lovely dream, expect about her gorgeous boyfriend. Then I go and shake it up. I don't know how I did it but I did.

I remembered everything and I can still feel his hands on my throat even though I know he's gone, alive and me left dead. Somehow I gave Hally that same feeling, like she was being choked. For a while I was inside her body, could see everything she could see and feel everything she could feel. So I know she was dreaming then about not being able to breathe. But it was hurting her and I really don't want to do that. So I left her.

It was so weird and I have no idea how I did it. One minute I was there in her head. Then when I realised how bad it was for her I slipped out and I was next to her. She was in her bed and I could see she was still gasping for breath. I had to wake her up, make her see me. I had to let her know what had happened.

I tried. I really tried. I don't ever try to do anything. I never put any effort into anything, that's why I'm thick. But I did this time. I stood by her side and pleaded for help. She woke up screaming. I thought she looked at me, could see me, but when her parents came rushing into her room they ran right through me and Hally reached for her mum not me.

I have to try and re-connect somehow. Not when she's asleep though, because that just gives her nightmares. But I have to find out what happened after I died, was murdered actually. He must have got away with it. I say that because I don't think I would be here trying to reach out to Hally if they knew what really happened to me. I wonder what they all thought? I wonder if they all came to my funeral? They must have, I was so popular. Bet they all cried and talked about me for ages.

It's so lonely here. I know I'm used to being alone but this is different. There's not even anyone to talk to. At least when I was alive I could speak to people and they would talk back. Now it's empty and quiet, solitary.

She didn't come back to bed. That was horrible. I feel isolated. I thought maybe I could try again, but now here I am still in her room all alone. At least it's not my dull bedroom anymore. At least all the fogginess has gone. Bright in here. I can move about properly too. Instead of just suddenly flipping from the window to the door I can sort of float across the carpet. I can't feel it but I can decide how to move, slow or fast, I can choose.

It is very nice in Hally's room. But if I can't make her see me or maybe even hear me, then it's going to be very weird and I suppose embarrassing stuck here. Because I am stuck here. I know that. I can't leave this room. I can look out of the window at Hally's garden. My garden was never like hers. It was just a patch of very overgrown grass that occasionally got cut by one of mum's boyfriends. The garden I can look down on is neat, full of flowers and birds.

I can go to the open door of her bedroom too. I can't go beyond it though. I have tried, thinking I might be able to see the rest of the house. Now that wouldn't be so bad if I could do that. Then if Hally never sees or hears me I could at least exist, because I can't live, but exist here. I can hear all that goes on, be sort of part of her family. She has a great family. It could be good, better than my life had been actually. I mean I wouldn't be able to talk to anyone, but hell, who did I talk to when I was alive? Can't happen though. When I try and go onto the landing everything disappears. The thick fog comes swirling back then I end up back in Hally's room again.

I have to think, really think about how I can talk to Hally. That's the only way I will be able to make her see what happened to me. Then if she will, help me to show the world that I was murdered. I hope he's feeling like hell, he should be. I hope he's miserable and full of guilt for what he's done. I pray and I've never done that before, that he's lonely and scared, just like I am. Ooh pray, what a laugh. I'm laughing, not making any sound, but inside I can feel it. I am actually giggling. God, oh that's hilarious too saying that. I can't remember the last time I had anything to giggle about.

Phew that feels like it was exhausting, laughing so much, even though I know it can't be. It does make me wonder though what will happen to me if I can find a way to communicate, hmm big word, with Hally and she does find out everything. Suppose though I put her in danger. That would be awful. I don't want that to happen. He might try and kill Hally too. No she's not stupid like me. She would make sure she had hunky with her, would never be alone with him for him to hurt her. So back to thinking, find a way Dana you have to. He has to be stopped before he does it again.

Chapter 9

Hally stood under the shower letting the hot water soothe her cramped muscles. The sofa was comfortable but she had woken in a tight ball, her fists clenched close to her chest. She didn't feel fully rested but at least there had been no more nightmares.

Mum was making tea and listening to Nathan's usual morning chatter over his breakfast when Hally walked into the kitchen. May gave her daughter a concerned look.

"I'm fine mum."

She said. Nathan stopped talking, his spoon half way to his mouth. As the milk dripped off he muttered.

"You in a mood again Hally?"

Hally looked at her little brother in surprise.

"I'm not in a mood. When was I in a mood?"

She said trying to fathom what Nathan meant. Her brother deliberately took his time, taking the spoonful of cereal, chewing and swallowing before speaking again. Hally frowned.

"Yesterday. You were all sort of…um…well you just looked cross when I saw you. And just now, you were frowning again."

Hally was shocked at how sensitive Nathan was. She was also annoyed with herself. It was unfair to burden her nine-year-old brother with her problems. Putting a smile on her face she sat down next to him ruffling his hair, an act that was sure to wind him up.

"Hey, don't."

He whined. Hally grinned and did it again. Nathan swiped at her hand which she rapidly moved to tickle his ribs. Trying to sound annoyed but giggling at the same time Nathan called out.

"Mu…mum. Tell her to…to…stop."

"I'm not moody. You are."

Hally teased whilst May watched her children play.

"Not me, you, you, you."

Nathan said enunciating each word with a wriggle and a jab at Hally with one finger. Hally laughed. It seemed Nathan was appeased.

"You two finished?"

Mum finally interjected. With one last jab at Hally, Nathan turned back to his breakfast.

Hally, feeling a lot better than when she first got up grinned up at her mum. May placed a plate of toast in front of her and handed her a jar of marmite.

"Mmmm thank you mum, my favourite."

She said as she applied the spread liberally to her toast and bit into it with relish.

After breakfast Hally planted a kiss on the top of Nathan's head, much to his chagrin, gave her mum a kiss and hug and left for college. She met up with the girls at the usual place and immediately gave them a complete run down of the previous evening, and the terrifying nightmare.

"I bet after Penny's little drama act your thoughts were on Dana and you didn't realise."

Corrinne announced. Hally tapped her own forehead.

"Jeez I'm thick. I didn't even think about that. She was prattling on about how horrible it was finding Dana. I suggested she get some help, but then after she bit my head off, I just put it out of my mind. I was more concerned with that girl who was staring at Wes. So yeah, I bet that's what triggered the damn dream."

"So Penny didn't go into detail about how…um…you know, Dana looked?" Clia asked. Hally shook her head.

"Just that it was horrible. When I woke up I'd forgotten most of the dream. I know it was really scary, that something dreadful was happening. The only thing that is clear is Dana. She was in the dream coming towards me, and she looked…um…" Hally took a deep breath. "…grey, cold…dead." Clia and Corrinne each took one of her hands as she shivered at the memory.

"Mum's going to call the school and see if I can speak to Mr Austin at lunchtime."

"That is a very good idea. Even if you have worked out that Penny sort of caused the nightmare. But…I'm not sure that it was her because you had one the other night too." Corrinne stated. Hally sighed deeply.

"I know. Just hoping I suppose that it was that simple."

Mum texted Hally mid-morning to tell her Mr Austin could see her at lunchtime. She messaged Wes and he said he would go with her but she decided to go alone. So as soon as her last morning class finished, she headed across the short distance between the college and school.

At the gates Hally paused. It seemed a very long time ago since she had last walked through them. But once inside the grounds everything was so familiar. She saw several students she knew, and was amazed at how tiny the year sevens looked, all in their brand new uniforms looking weighed down with their backpacks.

Hally made her way across the courtyard to the reception entrance. As she placed her hand on the door to push it open she felt a moment of trepidation and almost turned away. She wasn't comfortable in this place. The reception was a painful reminder of all the times she and her parents had sat waiting to see the head teacher about Dana's bullying. Forcing herself to move forward, Hally took a breath and pushed open the door.

The reception area was exactly the same. Mrs Durant sat behind her desk tapping away on a key board, her hair pulled tight into a knot at the back of her head. She had been there long before Hally even started at the school. She glanced up from her computer and smiled.

"Hello Hally."

"Hello Mrs Durant. I've got an appointment with Mr Austin."

Mrs Durant nodded and checked a diary to the side of her.

"Ah yes. Here you go. You know where to go?"

She said as she handed Hally a visitor's badge asking the question at the same time. Hally clipped the badge to her jacket and nodded.

"Thanks and yes."

She said turning for the door. Mrs Durant smiled back, her attention already back to her screen.

Hally made her way towards the English department where Mr Austin's office was housed. Students of all years milled about chatting or on their phones. It brought back memories of her and the girls during their lunch breaks. She kept her head down as she slipped inside the building and approached the office. She knocked. Mr Austin opened the door and stood back to let her enter, a welcoming smile on his face.

This office was the same too. The only difference Hally could determine was a new photo of Mr Austin's family on his desk. He indicated a chair and Hally sat down. He took his seat behind his desk and leaned forward, his hands crossed on a notepad in front of him.

"Hello Hally. Your mum was brief on the phone so why don't you tell me why you're here."

Hally fidgeted with the clasp on her bag, not sure how to start and not sure she even wanted to. Mr Austin sat waiting patiently. Finally, Hally decided she didn't want to waste his time.

"What happened to Dana?"

The look on his face told her he hadn't expected that and Hally was surprised herself. She hadn't meant to say that at all. It just seemed to pop out of nowhere. Mr Austin blinked, recovering quickly.

"She committed suicide Hally. You know that."

Hally sighed. This was not going well. She had formulated a plan in her head on the way here. She was going to tell Mr Austin about the dreams, just that and he was going to tell her she was normal. He would say college was causing her stress and that was all there was to it. Now suddenly Penny's words from the night before intruded on her thoughts and brought forward questions she didn't really want answered. She swallowed nervously.

"Um…I know. What I meant was how?"

Mr Austin sat back in his chair. He picked up his pen and twiddled it in his fingers. His frown told Hally he wasn't comfortable with her question. Hally looked down at her own fingers clasped tightly on her bag.

"I'm sorry. I shouldn't have asked that."

Mr Austin sighed and leaned forward again. He tapped his pen gently on the notepad. So far he had made no notes at all.

"No it's all right. Can I ask why you want to know?"

Hally looked up. She felt miserable.

"I don't really know. I came here to tell you about a couple of nightmares I've had. The one last night had Dana

in it. I…um…sort of had words with Penny last night at the Hotspot, Dana was mentioned. And I…well thought…"
She had no idea what she thought or what to say. Mr Austin placed his elbows on the desk.

"Ok Hally. Let's start from the beginning."
Hally lifted her hand and swept her hair away from her face. She took a very deep breath and nervously told Mr Austin everything from the first nightmare.

"So do you think if you know how Dana did it you will get her out of your mind?"
Mr Austin asked once Hally was finished. She shrugged.

"I have no idea. I mean, what's the connection between her and the other stuff I was worried about?"

Mr Austin flipped the edges of his notepad. Hally could feel the tiny breeze across the desk. He still hadn't made any notes.

"I don't think there is."
He said. Hally frowned, confused. He was quick to pick up on that, continuing.

"The first nightmare, Saturday into Sunday?" Hally nodded. "You can't remember any of that. Your parents and your boyfriend suggested it might have been about Dana, because it was close to the date she was found dead, and were worried you would remember too. So in their desire to protect you they inadvertently planted that seed in your mind. Then you had strong words with Penny. She told you she had found Dana and that it was horrible. You feel guilty that you didn't help Dana, even now, so your subconscious twisted it all up and there you have it, the dream, nightmare."
Hally swallowed, close to tears.

"I do feel guilty. I knew what she was going through. I should have said something to someone, you perhaps. I know she begged me not to but I should have."

The tears flowed swiftly down her cheeks. She sat with her head down and let them fall. She felt wretched inside. The guilt, it was more than just about Dana. How could she be so blissfully happy with her boyfriend? be so lucky to have friends and parents who loved her? have a happy secure home? Mr Austin passed her a box of tissues as she blurted all the feelings out.

"The reason you feel so guilty is because you are naturally an empathetic person Hally. You got through all of it last year, again when your gran died. You can get past it again. If it will help I'll tell you what I can about Dana." Hally dabbed at her eyes and nodded.

"The school knew about Dana's family life, to a degree. We knew her mother often left her and about the time she spent in care. We didn't know her mum had completely abandoned her, she wouldn't talk to any of us. As you know she spent a lot of time with Martin Cob and only just managed to stay out of real trouble with the police.

Dana made many bad choices. None of them you could have changed by telling us what she told you. She often drank alcohol, played truant frequently, and generally went against the rules as much as she could without getting suspended. She rebelled. Adults were her enemy, we were her enemy.

When Dana found herself in too deep, she did what she decided was the only thing she could do, take her own life. I can't be certain, as she never spoke to anyone about her intentions, but from experience I would say she felt she had nowhere else to go, no choice or control over her future.

So one night she drank nearly a whole bottle of wine, tied her school tie around her throat, attached it to the light fitting in her room and hung herself. The light fitting held long enough for her to choke. When it gave way she landed on her bed. It was there Penny found her."

Hally was stunned at the information, understanding how traumatic it must have been for Penny. But she didn't know if knowing the circumstances was going to be any help to her.

"Do you think what I've told you will make a difference?"
Mr Austin asked kindly. Hally shrugged.

"I can't see that it will. Maybe you're right. Dana is not the problem. Maybe it is just the changes, going to college and all that."

"Well Hally, see how things go over the next few days. Take some time over the weekend and relax. Don't push yourself so hard. And any time you want to talk to me I will be here. You might not be a student here anymore, but I do work closely with the college, so I can still be a counsellor to you. Like before, I have to make a report, but it's completely confidential. Ok?"

Hally gathered her bag and jacket and stood up. She thanked Mr Austin and turned for the door.

"Sorry for taking up your lunchtime."
She said looking back over her shoulder. Mr Austin smiled.

"I'll live. Besides, you'd be surprised at how fast I can munch a sandwich."
She giggled, feeling quite a lot better as she left his office.

Hally took her time crossing the school grounds. Now she no longer attended she didn't feel the need to rush away. It was strange she thought, as she watched the students milling about, that the familiarity of the place wasn't hostile anymore. When she was a student here she would bolt from it as soon as possible. Those fears had disappeared.

As her steps slowed but took her closer to the gates, her thoughts changed. She smiled inside, an inner light snapping on like a bulb. She had come to a conclusion. School had been a terrible place when she was there. Dana had bullied her all the way through. She hadn't ever struggled academically but her social life had taken a battering because of Dana. Now she was at college. A new place of learning. Dana wasn't there but some of her old gang were. She was projecting all her fears and emotions from school to college.

"That's it."

She whispered under her breath as the gates came into view.

"Oi what are you doing here?"

Hally jumped and then sighed as the voice she recognised became a face she would like to have avoided, Penny.

"Hello Penny."

She said softly, trying for polite but uninterested.

Penny was not going to let her get away with that as she stood blocking Hally's exit. A little of the old fear spiked Hally's heart but she lifted her chin and made herself breathe. It helped. Penny no longer frightened her, she was strong, the timid little teenager gone.

"Excuse me please."

Hally said again as politely as she could manage. Inside she really wanted to shove Penny out of the way. Ignoring her Penny asked again.

"I said what are you doing here?"

Her voice was gritty. A few of the old gang stood just behind her smirking. Outside the gates but within listening distance Martin Cob was chatting to a group of boys, some ex-students, others still at school. They turned when they heard Penny. Hally felt a tiny tremble in her limbs as memories flooded back. Memories of having her hair tugged, her bag knocked from her hands, the vicious remarks about her figure and many more. She took a deep breath and let it out slowly. She would not be intimidated by these immature girls and boys.

"Get out of my way Penny. It's none of your business why I'm here. Remember the Hotspot last night?" Penny's face went pale but she wasn't ready to give in.

"If you've come here to prattle on about that, forget it."

It took Hally a moment to register that Penny thought she was here to tell someone about her crying over finding Dana. Hally wanted to laugh but held it in.

"Jesus Penny. You really are egotistical aren't you."
Penny looked confused, obviously not knowing what Hally meant, so tried to cover it up.

"I am not. If you've said that I am to anyone…"
Hally did laugh then, she couldn't help herself. Penny's brows almost met in the middle as anger spots appeared on her cheeks. A long time ago that would have worried Hally, now she simply sidestepped around her.

"Self-centred Penny, that's what it means. Not everything is about you. I have no interest in discussing your…problems…with anyone. I'm here visiting. It's not your business but that's why I'm here. So run along and play with your little friends."
She held out her hand waggling her fingers towards Penny as she headed for the gate, a smile on her face. Behind her she heard a few oohs and ahs from other students who had witnessed the scene but she didn't look back.

He stood near the gates, the conversation he was having a diversion. He watched the little altercation between Hally and Penny and grinned inside. Penny really was a pain in the arse but a nice distraction. Older than his usual choice, but hey not by much. Now Hally, she would be a very nice exception to his usual rules. He sighed. But how to make that happen? That would take some thought.

He dimmed out the voices around him. He could do that, had practised it for years. Yet the talkers never knew. He could appear to be engrossed in what they said, could respond when needed, answer questions even. He was brilliant. He nodded at something someone said but his mind was really elsewhere.

He watched Hally as she flipped her long blonde hair, held her head up and purposely crossed the road. How he would like to follow her, that would be fun. But he couldn't do that. It would draw attention to himself. He had to keep below the radar, that's how he could do what he so enjoyed doing.

Dana was the exception. She had become too needy. They didn't usually act like that. A real shame. She had been one of the best. He had been able to help her become exactly what he wanted. It didn't take much but then it never did. He was so good at what he did and no one would ever suspect, not him.

But Hally, she was way out of reach, well to anyone else that is, but not to him, he was far too clever, could do whatever he wanted and keep it secret. Hally, she should have been vulnerable what with all the bullying. That was a bit of a conundrum, he felt like laughing then, but kept it in. Dana on the one hand, all tough and leading the bullying, but putty in his hands, Hally, shy, quiet and lacking confidence, yet totally unavailable.

He responded to something someone said, keeping up the front, his thoughts still on Hally as she disappeared from view. Maybe sometime soon he would find a way to just take her. That might be fun. He hadn't done that before, they were always so pliant, so keen to please. Of course them being young helped.

He would have to think carefully about Hally. She wouldn't be easy, she would fight. A shudder of pleasure swept through him, that would be exciting, but it would also be messy. Dana had been simple. Making it look like suicide had been a doddle, a shame, but in the end necessary. So would it be for Hally because she would tell and he couldn't have that.

People were beginning to move, the conversation coming to an end. He would have to move too. It would look odd if he just stayed here mulling. Never mind, he had time, so much time. He could do just what he wanted.

Chapter 10

Hally caught the last fifteen minutes of lunch. As she hoped, Wes had bought her a sandwich and handed it to her with a kiss on the lips too. She longed to lean into him, take her time to kiss him back, but her tummy growled again telling her to eat.

Quickly unwrapping the sandwich, she took a bite and sighed, it was good. In between bites she managed to give Wes a brief outline of her meeting with Mr Austin.

"I'll tell you properly tonight."

She said as lunchtime was over. Wes pulled her into his arms and gave her a loving squeeze.

"Ok. See you about seven."

Hally headed for her first class of the afternoon with a spring in her step. The meeting with Mr Austin was pushed firmly to the back of her mind and the clash with Penny not forgotten, but not a worry either. She would enjoy telling the girls and Wes about it and knew they would be proud of her.

The afternoon flew by. Hally found herself so completely absorbed in her work that she was surprised when it was time to go home. She spotted Corrinne across the campus and strolled towards her.

"Hi, where's Clia?"

Hally asked.

"Didn't you get her text?"

Hally pulled her phone from her bag.

"Oh I forgot. I put it on silent when I went to the school. Ah yes." She smiled. "Lucky Clia, she had a short afternoon."

"So how did it go, you know with Mr Austin?"

Corrinne asked.

Hally looked about her, she didn't want to be overheard. Corrinne immediately spotted her discomfort.

"Tonight?"

Hally nodded.

"Best to. Hey aren't you seeing Gregg tonight?"

Corrinne gave her a sly smile.

"Well…we…that is Clia the boys and me, sort of sneakily arranged to come to yours tonight and have a get together. I know we usually keep them to the weekend but we all just wanted to cheer you up."

She waited for Hally's response.

"Who's bringing chocolate?"

Was Hally's reply. Corrinne burst into giggles and linked her arm through Hally's.

"Actually the boys are."

She stated. Hally's mouth dropped open for a few seconds then she laughed too.

"You lot know me far too well. But hey, I'm not complaining."

As they walked home clouds began to thicken across the sky and the temperature dropped. It looked like the spell of hot weather was coming to an end. Hally tugged her jacket closer and felt chilly. She felt a little sad. She loved the summer, hot days even more. The autumn was beautiful, full of colour, but just a leap around the corner was winter. Crisp frosty days were something to look forward to, but more often than not an English winter meant mild wet days, little sunshine and lots of cloud. Hally sighed.

"What was that for?"

Corrinne questioned. Hally shrugged.

"Nothing really. Just the year is on its way out. The days are getting shorter and now colder."

Corrinne gave Hally a playful nudge with her shoulder, knocking her ever so slightly off balance.

"Oh come on Mackeller, cheer up."

"Oi."

Hally mock moaned. Corrinne giggled and did it again. Hally, expecting it braced herself so it was Corrinne who wobbled. The girls creased up as they continued their dallying, Corrinne making a little dance out of it. Gracefully she swung her hips from side to side rhythmically.

"Frosty the snowman, I'm dreaming of a white Christmas, jingle bells."

She sang out in time to her steps pulling Hally along with her. Hally couldn't help but laugh.

"Ok, ok I get it. Winter is good, lots to look forward to."

Corrinne nodded adding more snippets of lyrics to her song.

The girls came to the juncture where their roads met. Corrinne stopped dancing and gave Hally a quick hug. She then spun around and pranced off towards her own home. Hally watched for a few seconds, smiling at her friend's jaunty departure, Corrinne's big bag swinging dangerously close to a man she passed on the street.

Hally felt happy and alive. She was sitting on her bedroom floor with her back resting against Wes' knees. Corrinne and Clia were doing the same, the three boys having pounced on the bean bags as soon as they piled into Hally's bedroom. The girls didn't mind, they had better access to the chocolates in between them. Wes tried to lean around Hally to snag one but she got there first.

"Your own fault for nicking the comfy seats."

She told him, snatching the chocolates away with a giggle. Wes tickled her making her squirm but she kept a hold on the confectionary.

"Come on share. We bought it."

Rhys whined. Clia grinned and picked up a chocolate. She held it up in the air. Rhys leaned forward, his mouth open, but Clia waggled the chocolate about teasing, keeping it just out of reach. The others laughed as Rhys tried to grab it. Finally, he clasped Clia's hand and snagged the chocolate with his teeth. Corrinne simply picked up a sweet and tossed it over her shoulder.

"Catch!"

She called out to Gregg, the boys doing air punches when he did.

Hally was having so much fun with her boyfriend and friends that she didn't want to spoil it with talk of Dana. Corrinne though was not going to let her get away with it.

"So spill Hally."

No one needed an explanation. With a sigh she popped in another chocolate to give her time. Then she launched into a detailed account of her meeting with Mr Austin and the brief confrontation with Penny after. There were a few murmurs whilst she talked, but mostly the other five let her tell all.

"So Cobby's still hanging around the school then?"

Clia asked and Hally nodded.

"You'd think he would find something better to do."

Corrinne said her voice full of contempt.

"Well um, he is."

Rhys said a little warily. Clia stretched her neck back to look up at him.

"What do you know?"

Rhys, always much shyer than the rest of the group blushed. Bright red spots appeared on his cheeks standing out against his dark curly hair and brown eyes. Clia swivelled around, concerned she had put her boyfriend on the spot.

"Hey, we're not mad at you."

She said soothingly, taking his hand and resting her cheek in his palm. Rhys smiled and gave a tiny shrug.

"All I know is, he's started a course at college to do with plumbing."

"Well I heard he did some sort of training when he was inside. So maybe he's finally buckling down, given up the life of crime."

Wes added.

"Hmm suppose it's never too late. I think what Dana did got to him. I bet he feels really guilty missing her funeral."

Hally said. Corrinne nodded.

"Probably more than just the funeral. Not knowing how she felt and stopping her. He was sort of her boyfriend, at least that's the impression everyone got."

"I think it was more one sided you know. Martin thought that but not Dana. There was lots of chat about which boys she'd been with."

Hally replied then let out a big long sigh.

"But did anyone really know Dana?" She shrugged. "Penny didn't and she was supposed to be her best friend."

****

So Hally went to see Mr Austin today and by the sound of it she had a run in with Penny too, not the first either. It's very weird standing here listening to them all discussing me. A hell of a shock too. They think I killed myself. He must have made it look like that. But worst of it all, Hally's having nightmares about me. I don't like that. It's not fair on her. I don't want to frighten her.

They're all still convinced I took my own life. I mean, it was a pretty frigged up life, but I could have lived with it. That sounded funny to me and I think I'm laughing again, it sort of feels like it. But none of this is really funny. I must have come across as really sad to them all for them to believe it. So, he has got away with it. I wonder how? Now that is very damned unfair.

They all look very happy and carefree. Wish I was with them like that. Well I am with them, they just can't see, hear or feel me. I can't feel me. Not on the outside. I can feel me inside though and it's not a happy feeling. Being murdered does that to you.

Oh I missed some of that, something about my funeral. Damn, can't rewind. I wonder what it was like? Were all the gang there? I expect so. I bet it was a really big deal with all the girls crying and hanging onto the boys. Pity I wasn't there to see it. Ha ha Dana, you were there. Was mum? Maybe if I can get through to Hally properly she can tell me all about it.

Dana get a grip. Oh that one is hilarious. I've just been prattling on about not being able to feel. But no seriously girl, get a grip. It's quite interesting here listening to them. Being invisible has its...um...what's the word? Ad...something...vent, vant...that's it, advantages. Cripes, I'm getting better at using big words. Odd, very odd, how I'm remembering what the teachers taught me now. Why couldn't it have been like that when I was alive? I might have had a better life. Shi...no, no swear words Dana. I mean you're dead, yeah, but now you're using better words why be mouthy? So yeah, no one can hear me, but I can.

Weird though. When I was alive I didn't care what anyone thought of me. In fact, the more swear words I used the tougher everyone thought I was, I thought I was. It gave me street cred. Now I'm dead and it doesn't matter, except to me. Why oh why couldn't I have been like that alive? Why couldn't I remember the good words the teachers taught me then, like I can now? Funny I'm remembering words, how to use them, how to describe things, like when I died. But what is very fuzzy is faces. Those I can't see because I can't leave Hally's room, are like shadows. Penny, I remember her, but I don't know what she looks like. The gang, same with them and oh my God, him. I can't see his face. I can only remember his voice, can hear it in my mind and his touch. I can't even remember his name.

Whoa I'm rambling, drifting into a little world of my own. Ha ha, funny Dana, this is your own little world unless you can get through to Hally.

What was I doing? Oh yeah, watching and listening to Hally and her friends. They're all real friends. They look out for each other, are there when needed. They can tell each other anything and everything. I used to be able to do that with him but I suppose now I think about it, he wasn't really interested.

Anyhow back to now. Oh look they're laughing, mmmm chocolate, and having fun. Can't remember that one, fun that is. I remember chocolate. He gave me some that night, that last horrible night. Chocolate, smooth, sweet and romantic. Then, cold, dark and choking. Hell, what a difference.

★★★★

Wes leaned forward and wrapped his arms around her shoulders crossing them in front and drawing her close to him. He could tell the conversation had turned in the direction Hally was hoping to avoid. Hally put her hands on his arms and held him tight. She was afraid the topic would reignite her fears and tap into her subconscious, bringing back the nightmares.

"Too heavy guys. Come on let's talk about something else. What shall we do at the weekend? I'm off and mum and dad have all sorts of stuff planned for Ellie so…"
Wes said injecting buoyancy into his voice. Hally let out a grateful breath as they all began to chip in with ideas for the end of the week.

The rest of the evening was light and enjoyable. Silent mutual agreement had halted any further discussion about Dana, and Hally was relieved. Between them they arranged a shopping trip to Exeter on Saturday and the cinema on Sunday. Hally was pleased. She was up to date with her college work, having completed her latest assignment after dinner, and Clia assured her she was too. Corrinne told them she only had reading to do, which for Corrinne meant bedtime reading.

After Corrinne, Gregg, Clia and Rhys had gone home, Hally and Wes were left alone to curl up on her bed. Laid in his arms Hally twiddled his hair between her fingers. They were comfortable cuddling.

Hally had her eyes closed as Wes rubbed her back lovingly. Her mind was nowhere, her thoughts on nothing. She was completely relaxed. Her fingers began to slip from Wes' hair as she drifted into a doze. Sight and sound disappeared, yet she could still feel her boyfriend's gentle hands around her, so soothing.

A little glimmer of light poked under her lashes. She tried to close her eyes tighter, keep it out, but it glowed more brightly. She turned her head into Wes' chest, avoiding it, but it seemed to be attached. It was annoying her but she didn't want to move, she was so comfortable. She opened her eyes, blinked and closed them again, hoping it would go away, it didn't. She sighed.

"You ok?"
She heard Wes' voice, distant but there. She nodded and felt him draw her even closer his lips finding hers.

"Are you going to sleep on me?"
He murmured between feathery kisses. She shook her head and took his lips for a fuller kiss. The glowing light vanished as his hands pulled her head towards him.

****

Jesus Dana, rambling again. Hold it together, I missed that bit. Oh...looks like Hally's upset, her fella Wes, someone said his name, so that's what he's called, has put a stop to talking about me. Ah well probably best, I don't want to hurt Hally.

Sounds like their weekend is going to be awesome. Hellishly quiet and lonely for me though. I'll be all by myself in this room. Lovely as it is, not a happy thought. But Hally will be here at night when she sleeps, so not completely alone.

Hey they're leaving. Well her two girlfriends and their guys are. Hally and Wes, I like saying it now I know it, they're snuggling up on her bed. Yipes, cover your eyes Dana, looks a bit cosy to me. Hang on no, they're just having a cuddle. Hally looks so sweet and peaceful. She's got her eyes closed. Is she going to sleep?

What's that? I can feel something strange. A sort of pulling, as though someone is tugging my hand. I don't like it. It's like I'm being stretched, thinned, it's weird. Hang on, it's stopped. Phew, thought I was going to be taken away from Hally, away from this room, and that just cannot happen. Looks like she's dozing. Um...maybe I can try and speak to her. Hally hey Hally. Can you hear me? She's opening her eyes, yay, maybe she can hear me. Hally look at me, please, please hear me. Oh no...she's shut them again.

The floor, it's soft, or so it seems that way. I am shaking, crying, that's what I'm doing. But only inside, there are no tears. I feel so alone, no one to hug or comfort me. I can wrap my own arms around my knees and curl up in a tight ball on the carpet. That's all I can do, console myself. Ha ha, another big word, not funny at all this time though. I really thought she heard me, so hoped she had. I have to keep trying. I cannot give up.

****

Even though she didn't want to move Hally knew she had to. It was time for Wes to go home. It wasn't late but it was a week night. Grumpily she shifted into a sitting position. School might be over but college was just as demanding, meaning up early in the morning. She shrugged her shoulders and sighed.

"What was that for?"
Wes asked. Hally swung her legs over the edge of the bed.
"Nothing really."
Wes raised one eyebrow.
"I just wish it was the weekend already."
She said with a frown.
"Don't you like college? Or are you really finding it difficult and hard to cope with?"
Wes asked her gently. Hally swivelled around to face him, her eyes wide open.
"Oh no Wes. I love college and it's actually too easy. It would be better if it was more challenging. It's…" she shrugged "…so far this week has been totally freaky and I feel a bit drained."
Wes put his hands on her shoulders turning her until she had her back to him. He then massaged deep, relaxing her.
"Nightmares stop you from getting a full rest. It's not surprising you're done in."
Hally closed her eyes and let him ease the tense muscles in her neck. She knew he was right, hoped tonight she would sleep peacefully, probably would if he was with her. She would willingly have let him stay exactly where he was all night but he had college too and a walk across town home.

107

"I don't want to move but you have to get going."
She told him, forcing herself to stand up. Wes patted her
shoulders and laughed.

"Get some rest Hally. That is an order."

"Humph I don't like taking orders."

Wes kissed her and tickled her ribs. She giggled,
her mood instantly changing, the way any teenager's did.
She didn't mind taking orders really and Wes was only
playing. What she wouldn't admit to him was her fear. She
barely wanted to admit it to herself. She was afraid to go to
sleep. Despite what she felt had been resolved at her
meeting with Mr Austin, night time was like a different
world. Where during the day fears could be brushed off and
dimmed by sunlight, the night changed everything.

Putting on a bright smile Hally tugged Wes' hand
and led him downstairs. He called goodnight to her parents
and then spent several minutes kissing and cuddling Hally
before he departed for home. Hally watched him as he
slipped through the back gate, sighed and closed the door,
but not before glancing at the cloud thickening in the sky.

Her parents were in the study skyping friends across
the world. Hally waved to the couple they were chatting to
and kissed her mum and dad goodnight.

"Sleep well angel."
Dad said, mum nodding too. Hally gave a tiny smile.

"Hope so."

"Would you like me to make some hot chocolate?"
Mum asked. Hally laughed.

"I think I've had enough chocolate tonight already
but thank you anyway."
She replied giving her mum a hug. Her parents' friends
called goodnight as she turned for the door.

In her room Hally readied herself for bed. It was
much cooler tonight but she kept the window open, just not
so wide. Wrapped in her dressing gown she gazed out at the
night. Thick dark clouds charged across the sky, huge

goliaths battling for territory. Thunder rumbled as they collided, lightning flashing from their unseen weapons. It was an awesome sight and one which took Hally's breath. The wind picked up and rattled the blinds at her window but there was no fear in her. Forces of nature filled her with wonderment not dread.

The storm increased in intensity as Hally stood transfixed. A buzz from her pocket made her jump. She grabbed her phone and opened the message from Wes.

Home safely got in just in time, a few raindrops caught me. Night night babe sleep well love you very much. Xxxx

Hally smiled as she tapped back a reply.

Goody good just watching the storm from my window. It's amazing. Night night back. Love you lots. Xxxx

A flash of bright white lightning lit the room at the same time she hit the send button. Thunder boomed right overhead sending a tiny jolt of fear through her. Hally gasped and turned away from the window. In the dying light of the flash Hally froze, unsure and unbelieving of what she saw. She gave herself a mental shake.

"Just a reaction to the storm."

She whispered to herself as the outline of a figure disappeared as rapidly as it had come. Hally blinked and determinedly marched across her room to the spot where she had imagined, so she believed, the figure to have been. Lightning flashed behind her again lighting the whole room, her whole empty room. The thunder came again a count of two from the lightning. Hally giggled at her own nervousness.

"Idiot girl. Letting the storm give you the heebie-jeebies. You love thunder and lightning."

She said giggling again at talking aloud to herself.

Hally hung her dressing gown on the hook on her door and climbed into bed. She snuggled under the duvet and turned facing the window, watching the blinds sway in the breeze, their rhythmic flapping a lullaby singing her to sleep.

Hally relaxed, her fingers grasping the edge of the cover losing purchase. She stretched a little, her arms and legs unfurling from the tight ball she had curled into. Her breathing deepened, steadied, a sign of peaceful sleep. Her dreams began as usual with Wes, varying only by situation but always full of hugs and kisses and laughter. She was really very happy.

The dream changed, subtly at first. She was sitting on Wes' lap on the beanbag in her room. They were kissing and giggling, alone. Then someone was there only Hally didn't know who. The person didn't bother her, didn't make her feel embarrassed. The person simply stood by the window watching. Another change, Wes was at the door waving goodbye. Still she felt happy and safe. He was only going out for a short while so she could talk to the person in her room.

In her dream, Hally sat on the beanbag and leaned on her elbows bringing her closer to the person, a girl. But the girl had no definable face and no name. Hally could see her but she couldn't quite focus in on her enough to identify her. Hally wasn't even sure she knew who the girl was.

The girl's shimmery, frayed image smiled at Hally. She smiled back. The girl's lips moved but Hally couldn't make out any sound. Deep in the dream Hally spoke.

"Hi, do I know you?"

She asked in a friendly manner. The girl nodded, her smile widening, long hair fanning out about her. To Hally the situation was completely normal, real. The girl held out her hand and Hally reached for it. As their fingers touched, Hally felt ice. Still she was unafraid. The girl's cold hand wrapped itself around Hally's pulling her up out of the beanbag.

Rain and hail lashed against Hally's bedroom window yanking her out of sleep and out of her dream. She was sitting up in bed. The duvet was pooled between her legs. Her hand was stretched out in front of her. She opened her eyes and in that split second felt something slipping from her fingers. A rattling noise distracted her, her gaze turning towards the window. The blinds were fighting the wind that whipped them into a frenzy.

Hally dived from bed, the dream wiped from her mind by the raging storm. Rain water puddled on her window ledge and dripped onto the floor. The window was wide open, dragged by the wind. She reached out, her arm getting instantly soaked and jerked on it. For a few seconds she battled with the wind, finally won, and slammed the window shut. She giggled and again spoke to herself.

"Phew what a night."

Hally picked up her phone from the bedside table and pressed the home button. The screen lit up. It was just after two thirty in the morning. She was surprised it was still so early. She felt like she had slept all night, felt alive and refreshed. A niggle of the dream tickled her memory but wouldn't come. She sat on the edge of her bed twirling her phone between her fingers trying to recall it. It remained elusive. The only scene she could recreate was her bedroom. She huffed out a breath of frustration, wishing she could remember the whole thing, because she was sure this time it wasn't a dream to be afraid of.

Hally climbed back into bed and laid down. She fidgeted, tried to get comfortable but she wasn't tired. Her body did not want to go back to sleep. She thought about texting Wes, discarded the idea, then changed her mind. Before she could convince herself not to, she tapped out a message.

Had a dream don't worry not bad got woken by rain. Now not tired. Wish you were here. Love you xxxxx

She hit send before guilt could stop her then felt really bad knowing she would wake him.

Laying on her back looking up at the ceiling, Hally waited. Her phone chirped, the tone recognisable as the one she had set for Wes. Gleefully she opened the message.

It's ok. The storm woke Ellie. I went to her but mum was already there. Do you want me to come over? Love you too xxxx

A tiny flicker of irritation pricked her heart. She shoved it out of the way. If Ellie needed her dad because she had been afraid of the storm, who was she to get ratty about it? Hally silently berated herself. Wes loved her, she was completely secure in that love. She wouldn't let her teenage hormones damage that by being jealous of a toddler. She twiddled with her phone. All she had to do was say yes and he would be here. He would risk getting soaking wet to be by her side. She shook her head. She wouldn't be that selfish.

No I'm fine. Go back to sleep and I will too. See you in the morning. Thank you anyway. I really do love you very much my Wes. Xxxxx

She pressed send before she could change her mind.

Sliding further under the duvet Hally opened one of the apps on her phone. It was a word game. She had just started the game when Wes' text tone chirped.

Ok if you're sure. Try and sleep. Meet you at the gates. Love you more. Xxxx

Hally felt warmth spread through her. She really couldn't have a more loving and considerate boyfriend. The prickle of guilt became a jab, one she could not ignore. Sighing, she laid her phone on the bedside table and concentrated on her thoughts.

I'm sixteen, she told herself. Life is just beginning but that doesn't mean I have to be selfish about it. But that's the point isn't it. Sixteen year olds are selfish most of the time. Oh I know it's a hormone thing, all that confusion about the future and so on. But you know what you want. Do I? Do I really know? Yes, Hally you do. You want to get good grades at college. You want to keep your wonderful boyfriend and he has his little Ellie.

So when has she ever got in the way? Never, that's when. But what about as she gets older? She will want a lot more of his time and what will happen to you? Wes won't push me aside, he won't, he loves me too much.

Without realising, tears had seeped under her lashes and down her cheeks. It was the taste of salt on her lips that alerted her. She swiped at her face, angry with her thoughts and doubts. As she had told herself so many times, she chose to stay with Wes after she found out about his daughter. She pursed her lips and frowned into the darkened room.

"Stop this. You're making yourself miserable. No wonder you are having nightmares you dippy cow."
She whispered to the night realising how quiet it was. The storm had finally died leaving a soft patter of rain against the window.

Determined to quash her niggles over Ellie, Hally closed her eyes and pulled the cover to her chin. She had to go back to sleep. It was already Wednesday and she would be exhausted at college again. That she didn't want. At least today was a shorter one. She would finish at two, Wes lunchtime, then she would walk over to his house and spend the evening there.

Planning the coming evening with her boyfriend in her head, Hally finally drifted back to sleep. Her dreams began to take shape and like most dreams were snatches of everyday events. Wes kissing her, touching her in all the right places, flipping to writing notes in class, then to a brief snapshot of the school gates, only Clia and Corrinne were with her. Then the change began.

The girl was standing at the foot of her bed. Hally was sure she was in bed tucked up snugly, warm and safe.

The girl, her face still unclear was holding out her hand. Her lips were moving and Hally strained to hear the words she knew were being uttered. She sat up to get closer. The girl, her hair falling across her face drifted nearer. Hally wasn't afraid, it seemed perfectly normal that the girl would float. Hally asked the girl to speak louder.

"I can't hear you."

She murmured. The girl reached for her, took her hand. She smiled, her mouth forming words that Hally still could not hear.

"Who are you?"

Hally asked. The girl's face was still fuzzy like an out of focus movie. Hally felt frustration.

Hally's phone chirped. Opening her eyes, she huffed out a sigh. First the storm had disturbed the dream now her phone. She leaned over and picked it up not realising at first she was in a sitting position. When she did she shrugged, not caring. She was in a hurry to check the message, wanting to get back to sleep, back to the dream. The message was from Wes. She opened it.

Are you ok? Bad dream? Love you xxxx

She frowned, cross with the interruption, cross with Wes. She was about to reply with a snappy retort when something caught the corner of her eye. A shimmer of light, a glow with no defined form hovered at the edge of her bed. The phone slipped from her fingers before she tapped her message and slid to the floor with a gentle thud.

Hally ignored the phone and concentrated on the light. A face began to take shape then a torso, arms and legs. Hair hung from the face, still not clear. Hally held out her hand, reached. The form did the same. Their fingers connected, Hally's warm the other's ice. Hally shuddered, not from fear but from the cold. The lips on the face moved, this time a tiny whisper came from between them. Hally strained to hear, leaned even closer.

"Help me."

The words though like a breath of wind were clear. Hally held tight to the icy fingers.

"Who are you?"

She whispered back. The form opened its lips again, silent words like mime. Hally desperately tried to understand, tried to lip read to no avail.

"I can't hear you. Please speak up."

Hally begged. The figure became a fraction more solid but still unrecognisable. Hally waited, hoping, sure she was about to know who it was. The figure opened its mouth.

Hally awoke suddenly, the sound of her alarm trilling loudly in the morning light flooding through her blinds. She leapt to a sitting position her eyes flicking around the room, expecting to see the figure from her dream. She remembered every detail of it now, especially the tiny plea for help. She looked about for her phone, expecting it to be on the floor, but it was where it should be on her bedside cabinet. It was still playing her alarm call. She grabbed it and switched it off.

For a moment she pondered over the dream. She checked her messages. The last one from Wes arranging to meet. So every part had been the dream. It felt so real she thought and was relieved. She didn't like the idea of being angry with Wes, and she knew in the dream she had been for disturbing her. Feeling reassured that she hadn't actually been annoyed with Wes, Hally tried to analyse the dream.

The girl, she really could not work out who she was. If only she had been clear enough to identify and why did she need help? That much was apparent. The girl was in trouble, had reached out to her Hally. She sighed and slipped from bed. There was no way she was going to work it out. At least it hadn't been a nightmare. Shrugging, she made her way to the bathroom, thinking her imagination was probably just overworking.

Chapter 11

The girls were at the usual meeting place. Clia had her hood up tight around her face and Corrinne held an umbrella over both of them. It was drizzling. Hally jogged up to them when she saw them waiting, greeting each girl with a cheerful hi. She would wait until they were in the dry to talk about her latest dream.

Wes was at the gates and swung her into a big hug and kiss. His hair was wet and his jacket damp but Hally didn't mind.

"Morning gorgeous."

He said setting her back on her feet. Hally tucked her arm through his and tugged him towards the entrance with the girls. The lobby was crowded as everyone tried to cram in out of the rain. It was no longer a drizzle but a steady downpour. It simply dropped from the sky with no breeze to push it sideways.

Hally shook her hair, a few wet strands sticking to her cheek. Her hair was long, nearly to her waist and blonde. An idea lurked at the back of her mind. It tried to force its way through but Clia spoke sending it tumbling backwards.

"Hope it dries up before Saturday."

"Uh what?"

Hally replied.

"You know, the weekend, Exeter. Wakey wakey Mackeller."

It took a moment for Hally to remember the plans for the weekend then she grinned.

"Oh yeah shopping, cool."

"Come on. Let's go to the cafeteria, get a hot drink before classes."

Clia said taking her arm and pulling her towards a corridor. Hally went willingly, Wes and Corrinne following.

The cafeteria was crowded. It seemed everyone had the same idea. As one, they squeezed their way to the counter and managed to order coffees. Then holding their polystyrene cups closely, they jostled their way to the edge of the room. Wes being so tall, spotted a free table and grabbed it before anyone else could, the girls following.

"Wow it's manic."

Hally said as she flopped into a chair.

"The weather's been so good so the other students have done like we have and stayed outside."

Corrinne replied.

"Well maybe we should start getting here a bit earlier then. If it's nice we can stay out if not…"

Clia said with a shrug. Hally nudged her.

"Urgh great idea Clia, just means even less sleep."

"I bet you're up and ready long before you need to be anyway."

Clia said nudging her back. Hally giggled and nodded.

"Got me there Haywood."

"Talking of sleep. What dream woke you?"

Wes asked. Hally sipped her coffee before replying. The idea she'd had before fluttered in her mind. She lowered her cup.

"Um, not really sure. It wasn't bad, that much I do know. And it was weird."

Wes frowned.

"Well the first part before the storm woke me and I texted you, there was a girl..." Corrinne sat up straight. "...don't know who." Hally said quickly.

"I couldn't make out her face but she was smiling and just standing near the window in my bedroom."

Hally scrunched her brows for a second. That wasn't quite all she thought. The girl had held her hand.

"She um...took my hand and hers was icy cold."

Clia gasped making Hally jump. Coffee slopped over the edge of her cup and onto her hand. Luckily it had cooled and didn't scald her. Hally wiped her hand across her jeans frowning at Clia.

"Sorry Hally. I didn't mean to startle you. Is your hand ok?"

Hally nodded the frown staying put.

"Sorry. It's just...you saying your dream girl had icy fingers was well just creepy. It made me shudder."

"Girls."

Wes said lightening the mood. All three looked across at him.

"Let's not get carried away with this. Hally said the dream didn't scare her."

Hally took a deep breath and leaned her head on his shoulder.

"It didn't. Yes, the girl had cold hands, but listen, the storm woke me not the dream. Then when I did go back to sleep I started having the same dream again."

Hally quickly explained how the dream had developed, leaving out the part where she thought she had been woken by Wes and being cross with him. Clia gave her another wary look when she told them the girl had asked for help. Hally reached for her friend's hand and covered it with her own.

"Hey Clia. Don't worry. In fact, I think I worked it out."

"You did?"

Corrinne interjected. Hally nodded.

"It sort of came to me after we got here. I was pushing my wet hair out of my face and I realised. The girl in my dream was me."

"What?"

"Eh?"

"Huh?"

Three shocked voices bombarded Hally from three sides of the table. Then Wes leaned close and whispered.

"Babe what do you mean?"

Hally finished her coffee. It was tepid but she emptied her cup anyway. She needed just a moment to really gather her thoughts to explain what had come to her.

"Mum and dad were sure I would remember the date last week, so when I had that nightmare they automatically thought it was about Dana. But I didn't remember at all. I think they, poor things, put that idea in my head. So then I go and have a nightmare that was about Dana. But talking it all through with you guys makes me see I've been worrying over other stuff. In my dream last night there was a girl I couldn't make out. But she had long blonde hair. She reached for me and asked me for help. I think it was me asking myself for help. Some sort of weird self-therapy. There, that's what I think, crazy it might be, but you Corrinne know the mind doesn't act rationally when you're asleep."

Corrinne nodded in agreement and Clia squeezed Hally's hand. They both looked convinced. Hally glanced at Wes. He was smiling, also convinced. Hally felt relief deep inside her, it broke free on a sigh.

"So no more nightmares and no more worrying over stupid stuff. It's time for classes now, and then just two more days until we all have a great weekend."

Hally stated firmly. She tugged on Clia's hand as she stood up, ready to take on the day.

The day flew by for Hally. She enjoyed her lessons, took copious notes and contributed considerably in the discussions. It was almost a surprise when it was time to pack up and head for Wes'.

It was quite a walk across town to Wes' house, but one she thoroughly enjoyed. His home was on the outskirts whereas hers was in the middle. His was bordered by trees and backed onto fields and farmland, hers, surrounded by other houses. As she got closer she noticed a definite drop in the temperature. By the time she slipped through the gates to the back of the house, her nose was cold and her cheeks were flushed.

"Hi babe."

Wes greeted her with a hug and kiss as he opened the door. She wrapped her arms around him, luxuriating in his warmth.

"Brr, that's got really cold out."

"Yeah and it's always a bit chillier here on the edge of town."

Wes said as he rubbed her arms.

"Come on I'll make you a hot drink. Think it's time to pull your winter coat out."

Hally nodded as she shed her jacket.

"Suppose so."

She grumbled. Wes looked over his shoulder as he spooned coffee into two mugs.

"I had a winter conversation with Corrinne on the way home yesterday. Didn't think it would come this soon though."

Wes slipped his arm over her shoulder.

"Well I'll keep you warm. Anyway, winter can be just as much fun as summer."

He tickled her ribs forcing the sullen look into a giggle.

"I know, I got it all from Corrinne. It just means more time indoors though."

"More time for indoor activities."

Wes said waggling his brows. Hally burst out laughing.

"Cheeky. But true."

She replied. Standing on her tiptoes she planted a loud kiss on his lips. He turned her in his arms and the kiss became fuller. Only when the kettle clicked off did they separate.

Hally thought about the calm, pleasant evening she had spent at Wes' as he walked her home. Kate, Wes' mum, had come home with Ellie around three in the afternoon who immediately launched herself at her daddy. Wes lifted his toddler in the air twirling her, making her squeal. She grabbed his hair to hold on.

"Gen daddy gen."

She gabbled as Wes stood still.

"Say hello to Hally first."

He told her. Ellie gave Hally a beaming smile.

"Hewo Hawy."

Hally smiled back.

"Hello Ellie. Have you had a good day?"

The toddler twisted her father's hair in her fingers and frowned. Her tiny tongue appeared just between her lips, clamped between small perfect white teeth.

"Um, a wittle bit. I go to pwe-school now and my fwend Wowa cwied."

"Yes I know you do and oh dear why did she cry?"

Hally asked, used to the child's way of speaking. Ellie, letting go of Wes' hair waved her hands about gesticulating.

"She not wike her mummy weaving her. Deb took her to da carpet and pwayed with her. I did too and she not cwy anymore."

She gave Hally a very serious nod as she said the last few words.

"Well that was very nice of you Ellie. It's good when friends play with you and make you happy."
Ellie grinned.

"Gen daddy?"

Wes laughed and lifted her high up. He twirled and she squealed, her dark curls swirling about her face. Kate flicked the switch on the kettle and readied mugs.

"She loves pre-school and her speech is getting much better since she's been there. I was a bit worried, she used to babble so much, and it was quite hard to understand her at times but she's improved a lot."
Kate said to Hally in a hushed voice as Wes played with his daughter.

"I know Wes was too, but not so much now she's talking better."
Hally replied softly.

"But then it will be something else to worry about."
Kate said looking closely at Hally. For a moment Hally felt very uncomfortable. It was like Kate knew all of her secret niggles about Ellie, even though she had told no one. She felt a blush creep up her cheeks, the clicking off of the kettle her saviour.

Nothing further had been said, much to Hally's relief. Michael, Wes' dad came home and they all ate dinner. Hally and Wes played with Ellie, bathed her, read to her and put her to bed. It was comfortable and felt so right to Hally. So by the time Wes walked her home she was fully back in the land of everything perfect.

They lingered at the back door kissing and cuddling before Wes said a final goodnight, headed back down the path, turned and waved as he disappeared through the gate. Hally pushed open the door and slipped into the warm kitchen. It really had turned cold early for September.

"Hello angel."
Mum said coming into the kitchen. Hally shivered a little as she took her jacket off.

"Cold out."

She replied. Mum pulled Hally into her arms and gave her a warming hug.

"I was just saying the same thing to your dad. We've put the heating on so your room should be nice and cosy for you."

"Mmmm lovely. I hate getting into bed when it's cold."

May laughed. Hally always grumbled when the weather got cold but she lit up when it was frosty, crisp or snowy.

"You know the winter's not that bad."

She said rubbing Hally's shoulders. Hally let out a big sigh.

"You're the third person to tell me that."

She stepped out of the circle of her mother's arms.

"I'm off to bed. Night night mummy."

She kissed her mum and turned for the door.

"Dad's in the study."

May called to her departing daughter.

"Ok."

Hally called back. She stopped by the study to say goodnight to her father then plodded up the stairs. She really was tired and a warm snug room sounded very inviting.

Sometime during the evening mum had been in and closed the window. Hally, despite enjoying the warmth in the room, still felt it was a bit stuffy. She strolled to the window and opened it. Wide at first then feeling the chilled air on her face, pulled it back just enough to let in the fresh air.

With her elbows resting on the window sill she gazed out at the night. It was very still and dark. A few clouds drifted across the sky blotting out many of the stars, but it was calm. The big storm from the night before had completely blown out. For a while she simply let her mind wander. As usual it took her to places where Wes was ever present.

Still in her happy, comfortable, imaginary world, Hally turned from the window and prepared for bed. She slipped into pyjamas but tired as she was she didn't feel like sleep. Her room which recently had become a place to set her nerves jangling, was once again peaceful and secure. She was sure it was down to the fact that she had concluded her nightmares were actually about herself.

With just her lamp on Hally pulled one of her favourite novels from the shelf. She plumped her pillows, slipped under the duvet and settled down to read. A couple of pages in and her phone chirped. It was Wes' usual message that he was home safely. Hally happily texted back and turned back to her book.

Something was tugging her hand. She didn't want to be pulled from bed, from reading her book. She knew it was late and that she would probably be tired at college the next day, but she just simply loved this book and didn't want to be disturbed. The tugging persisted, annoying her. With a deep sigh she raised her eyes from the pages and looked over the top of the book to see what was bothering her. She frowned. A shimmery figure hovered by her bed. Long silver blonde hair fell in front of a face she couldn't make out except for its smile. A soft blurred hand covered her own, light and almost transparent, cool but not cold and strong enough to be felt.

Hally gripped her book in one hand as she was gently pulled forward. She felt no fear even as the face came closer. It was glowing, the blonde hair luminous but undefined. Opalescent lips moved, forming silent words that Hally tried to read.

"What? I don't understand."
Hally whispered. The figure backed away, relaxing its grip on her fingers. Hally reached forward.

"Don't go."

She pleaded, her voice no louder than a soft breeze. The figure floated further away.

"Soon."

Hally heard it say as it dissipated.

The thud of her book hitting the floor woke Hally suddenly. She was still sitting up in bed having dozed off whilst reading. Her first thought was where had the shimmering figure gone? Her eyes swept the room expecting to see it somewhere but she was alone. So it had been a dream she told herself. Yet it had seemed so real.

She scrunched up her face in concentration, determined to recall every moment of it. She could picture the figure, still not clearly but better than before. She remembered the tug on her hand and looked at it. She believed she could still feel the pressure of the silvery fingers on her skin. She knew it was trying to speak to her but the words had been silent except for one. She sat up quickly.

"Oh."

She said aloud. She remembered the one word she had heard as the incorporeal figure faded.

"Soon? What does that mean?"

She murmured.

"And if it's me what do I mean?"

Hally slumped back against her pillows feeling thoroughly frustrated. She was now very sure that the form in her dreams was indeed herself. But analysing what it all meant was getting on her nerves.

"Stupid. It probably doesn't mean anything at all. I bet Corrinne would tell me that or Mr Austin. Hally girl you're just making something out of nothing. Forget it and go back to sleep dipstick."

She told herself moodily. Closing the book and putting it on the side, she flipped off the lamp and pulled the duvet right up to her chin. She squeezed her eyes closed, determined to get back to sleep, dreams or no dreams.

****

Wow so much has happened. I really did connect with Hally. It was amazing. She heard me, she really did hear me. I asked her to help me but just as things were getting clearer she woke up. So now I know. I can reach her when she's asleep.

She's not scared anymore either. I like that. From what I heard though she thinks I'm her. Weird that, considering how horrible I was when I was alive. Nothing like Hally at all. She's sweet, kind, tries to look out for other people and help them. I mean she did me, once a long time ago. Oh I so wish I hadn't been such a bitch. If I'd only told her what was happening. I know being taken into care was awful and I really didn't want that to happen again, but I'm sure it would've been better than this.

I feel so stupid now. Why oh why did I fall for his lies? Because I was a needy little girl who thought he was in love with me. I mean, any girl can see how good looking he is. Any girl my age would fall for a guy older than her, Hally did. But her Wes is not anything like him. But who is he? Oh that is bad. I remember things about him but not who he is. How can I possibly tell Hally what happened to me if I don't know who he is? It is so crazy. I can feel his touch still, hear his voice but I cannot see his face. It's like, as everything else becomes clearer and I remember more that has happened, who he is fades further away. Hmmm I'm going to have to think of some way to get this across to Hally.

So backtrack. What was I on about? Oh yeah, Hally asleep. She came home and thankfully was happy and unafraid. I really did not like scaring her. Ha ha not funny Dana actually. You did so much of that intentionally when you were alive and I'm ashamed to say enjoyed it. Why did I? I think if someone had got into my head, you know like a doctor, they would have told me it was because it was a way of taking control. Stupid stupid Dana. You should have spoken to Mr Austin. He would have listened, would have helped. Now it's too late.

Hey! Stop feeling all sorry for yourself. It can't get you anywhere now. You're dead D.E.A.D dead. Look forward, try and get help now, not for yourself but I'm sure there are other girls who could end up like me, if he doesn't get stopped.

Backtrack again. Hally fell asleep reading and I saw, felt us begin to connect. I know I could sort of feel her hand. I had to concentrate hard to actually be able to grip. At first it was like holding water. It kept slipping through my fingers, trickling away. But with a lot of effort it began to solidify like ice. It didn't feel cold though just harder and I could pull her. I was so glad she wasn't frightened it helped me hold on.

She came with me, sat up. I could see her eyes and her expression. Ooh that's a word from school that I don't think I ever used but can somehow now. So she was staring at me. I don't think she could see me clearly though. Wonder if I can work on that too. She spoke to me, asked me what I wanted. I tried, I really did try and tell her. The words wouldn't come out though. Then I could feel myself going. I couldn't hold the concentration anymore. But I had to let her know that I would be back. I think she heard me say 'soon', I do hope so.

She's sleeping again now. I don't want to try again tonight it will wear her out. She's so good at her school work, uh I suppose college work, I don't want to make her so tired she can't concentrate. It's hard though, not like I can go to sleep. Maybe, I hadn't thought of that before, since before I was sort of slipping in and out of her room, but maybe, if I sit and close my eyes. Ah I know I can't sleep but I can close my eyes. That's sort of like resting. I mean it's quiet anyway and this way I can try and think of ways to really tell Hally what happened to me.

Chapter 12

Hally awoke to bright sunshine streaming through the slats in her blinds. She climbed out of bed with a smile. After the dream she had slept well, and if there had been any more dreams she didn't remember them. Showered and dressed she bounced down the stairs to the kitchen. Nathan was already tucking into his breakfast moaning when she scruffed his hair as she passed.

"You're cheerful today."

Mum said pushing bread into the toaster.

"Slept well and it's sunny."

Hally replied pointing at the window.

"Might be cold though."

Mum said teasingly. Hally shrugged.

"Ah but it is still sunny."

May laughed at her daughter's optimism. She was so pleased to see Hally out of the strange mood she had been in since the weekend. She handed her a mug of tea and watched as Hally took a sip. Hally smiled.

"What?"

She asked. May lifted her shoulders.

"Nothing. Enjoy your tea. Toast will be ready in a minute."

Hally, mug in hand ventured out of the back door to test the temperature whilst she waited for her breakfast. The sun was very bright but there was a definite autumn chill in the air. Hally didn't mind too much and took a deep breath. The cold air filled her lungs but like she had told her mum it was sunny.

She met the girls as usual, and as they strolled towards college told them about her latest dream. Corrinne especially agreed with Hally's analysis of the dream.

"I think you're right Hally. The dream girl is you and all the stuff in your head this week got in the way."

"But…what does the dream Hally mean then by soon?"

Clia asked not so convinced. Corrinne shrugged.

"Beats me."

Clia mock punched her arm and Hally giggled.

"What? Just because I'm studying psychology doesn't mean I know how to interpret dreams, yet anyway. It's only been a few weeks."

"And there's us thinking you had your doctorate already brainiac."

Clia chuffed out. Corrinne pouted.

"Stop taking the mick."

She said sulkily. Hally looked at them both a frown of confusion on her face.

"Have I missed something?"

A stab of old fear pricked at her heart. It was left over from her school days after she started going out with Wes. She had been terrified Corrinne and Clia would drift away from her, become two close friends instead of three. Clia linked her arm unaware of her inner trembling.

"Nah, last night Rhys said Corrinne was so brainy we should call her Doctor Corrie. I told her this morning and she got all embarrassed."

"No I didn't!"

Corrinne spurted out. But the flame in her cheeks told the other two a very different story. Hally linked her other arm through Corrinne's.

"Chill Doctor Corrie."

She said. Corrinne pursed her lips trying to look cross but she couldn't keep it up and burst out laughing. Still linked and laughing the three girls plodded on to college.

The day progressed normally. Hally met up with Wes and the girls at lunch, Rhys and Gregg joining them. The two boys were close to finishing their apprenticeships and Thursday was their day at college. Hally always enjoyed herself when all six of them were together. She was perfectly happy with her small group, didn't need any other close friends and prayed it would be like this always.

"Earth to Hally."

Wes nudged her.

"Oh sorry. I was miles away."

The others laughed, used to Hally's occasional mind wanderings.

"I was just saying the forecast is good for the weekend."

Wes said. Hally sat up straight.

"Excellent."

She replied.

The conversation turned to the plans for the weekend, so by the time lunch ended it was all arranged. They were getting the train to Exeter on Saturday morning, shopping all day, cinema in the evening, then the late train back. Between them they had decided to change the cinema from Sunday to Saturday evening leaving Sunday to just hang out.

Surreptitiously he listened to the conversation between the six. He found it very interesting. So they would all be in Exeter on Saturday. He felt a thrill of excitement deep inside as Hally tossed her long blonde hair over her shoulder, anger when her boyfriend draped his arm around her. He didn't like that. She should be his.

Not wanting to be noticed he didn't linger, thinking about their planned trip as he left the cafeteria. Hally was really too old for his liking, normally. But she was pretty, intelligent, and well he just fancied her. There were others, the younger ones to play with and of course Penny, just to keep her quiet because she wanted what Dana had had.

Although she was getting rather too demanding, so maybe it was time to sever that tie, carefully though. Penny wasn't like Dana. Getting rid of her wouldn't be easy. He would have to cajole her into breaking it off, let her do her immature 'You can't dump me because I'm dumping you first' stuff. But Hally, he imagined a much more grown up sort of relationship with her. That she wouldn't comply never even crossed his mind. She would be his. But what to do with her after? That was the question he had to figure out an answer to before he made his move.

At the door he turned, glancing a sneaky peek at Hally before entering the corridor. He had time, lots of it. There was no need to rush. She was already beyond his target age range, so yes plenty of time to watch and wait. He would watch this weekend. He would go to Exeter too. They wouldn't notice him. He could blend in when he wanted to, become almost invisible, he was very good at that.

He could even go to the cinema and sit near them. Yes, that would be fun. Watch the same film as Hally and find out what interested her. So by the time he had her she would see he was far better for her than the boyfriend, because he would know so much more about her. He should do some shopping too. The things he had weren't suitable for the sort of relationship he had in mind with Hally. No, he should buy things that are for grown-ups. He smiled as he pictured them in his mind. Now he had a plan he felt happy as he made his way across the campus.

Hally and the girls sat in her bedroom and went over the day, each telling the others about their course and studies. Hally was most keen to talk about the girl she knew fancied Wes. She had seen her during the afternoon, hastily walking down the corridor that Hally knew would take her to Wes' class. Hally had been peeved that her warning had not been heeded.

"I found out her name is Louise. Looks like I will have to have another chat."
Hally told Corrinne and Clia.

"Be careful Hals. Wes did say she meets someone from his group. Maybe that's where she was going."
Clia said. Hally frowned, she hadn't thought of that. But Clia could be right. She would look really stupid if she went diving in having a go if Louise was innocent.

"Hmm suppose so. I just didn't like the look she gave him the other night. And..." She paused for effect. "...after I spoke to her she went and tried flirting again. So I think she's still after him."
Hally told them indignantly.

"I'd be the same if she was after Gregg."
Said Corrinne sitting up straight.

"Hmm me too I suppose."
Clia said relenting.

"I just can't stand other girls going after someone else's fella. It's so so...bitchy."
Hally fumed.

"Hey that reminds me. Guess what Rhys told me."
Hally and Corrinne both raised their eyebrows waiting for Clia to divulge. Clia paused for dramatic effect a tactic the other two were used to.

"Well apparently Martin Cob has ditched Penny."
"Really?"

Hally sat forward interested. Clia nodded.

"Rhys heard a couple of lads talking. Supposedly, Penny turned up after college yesterday. She was furious because Martin has ignored her since you saw them in the Hotspot. Anyway she starts having a go, and Martin he just stands there and lets her rant. Then when she takes a breath he tells her to get lost, well actually his language was a bit more colourful but you get my meaning. Says there's someone else, says he's had enough of her. Penny went nuts, started yelling about how he can't dump her, that no one dumps her, and get this..." Clia giggled. "...Martin stands there with his hands in his pockets and goes, I just did, get over it. Then he walks away. Of course, at first Penny stood speechless, then she screams after him no you didn't because I'm dumping you. God I'd have loved to have seen that."

Hally leaned back against her beanbag and grinned. It seemed Penny was finally getting what had been a long time coming. She was so used to having her own way it felt good to know things weren't going so smoothly for her. A tiny frown appeared across her brows a thought entering her mind.

"Hals did you hear me?"

"Um, what? Sorry."

Hally said to Clia.

"I said, Rhys also said that no one has seen Martin with anyone else, that he just said that to get rid of Penny."

"Oh well serves her right."

Hally replied her earlier thought forgotten.

"I think that whole gang is disintegrating now that Dana's gone."

Corrinne said.

"Or most of them are just growing up."

Hally said. Corrinne and Clia nodded in agreement and for a moment the three sat in comfortable silence.

****

Corrinne and Clia are here with Hally. They all came back from college together. They're like sisters, so close and caring. I mean they really do care about each other. I think they've known each other since they were very little. I've known Penny for years, maybe not as long as these three, but long enough so it should mean something. But it doesn't. Penny never did see us as sisters. If she had, then surely it would be her I would be trying to get through to.

I remember once a long time ago. We hadn't been in secondary school very long. Mum was out as usual. I don't think she had come home the night before. Penny came 'round after school. We made junk for dinner. Then it seemed so cool to not have an adult tell us what to eat. Penny said then that she loved being my friend. What I now know is what she actually meant. That we could spend so much time without any adult supervision. I mean she was, still is I think spoilt. Gets everything she wants. New clothes, the best phone, latest tablet, everything.

What she also got with that lot is a mum and dad who kept an eye on her. Oh boy did she hate that. She used to go on and on about it. 'They won't let me do anything.' And 'You're so lucky Dana you can go anywhere, do anything you want.' And I thought it was so cool too sometimes. What teenager wouldn't? She used to lie to her parents too, bet she still does. She would tell them that my mum was always home, rarely went out. So her parents trusted her, believed her.

My mum didn't know about it and she really wouldn't have cared. Keeping me out of her hair was her main objective. Oh wow here I go again. Big words coming into my head. Anyway, back then I'd already started to get a reputation for being the cool, hard, very attractive girl. I, and I can't really say I know how, but I drew a crowd. Girls like Penny who thought it was great to come to my house and party, their parents in the dark about it. Then the boys joined in.

So when did I start bullying Hally? I remember it was in the first year of secondary school sometime near Christmas. Why what happened? Think Dana it might be important. She was little, really shy. I remember that. Corrinne and Clia were with her. I think uh...yeah that's it. It was cold and icy. She slipped on the path and all her stuff went flying. I had already got quite a gang by then and when I laughed at Hally so did they. It gave me a real buzz. No one had ever done anything before just because I did.

At primary school I was just lumped with all the other thick kids and those who had troubled backgrounds. There were one or two bigger ones who did some bullying, but the school was much smaller and a whole lot tougher on them. I didn't get involved, kept my head down and just waited out each day. I was tired all of the time, just couldn't wait for each day to be over, so I could go home. It wasn't a nice place to be but there I could sit and not think. There was food in the house. Tinned and packets mostly, but it was easy to chuck together so I didn't starve. I never had much fresh stuff but I simply did not care.

Mum was never there. You know I don't even know if she went to work. I think, yeah I remember she used to change jobs a lot. What I do know is she met loads of men. She was out most of the time. Days could go by and I wouldn't see her. Then she got found out one time and I got hauled into care. Why they gave me back to her I do not know but they did. For a little while she was there all of the time. I think because social services were keeping an eye on us. Eventually though they thought she had cleaned up her act and left us to it.

We moved house. Our town isn't that big but big enough so you can move to where you're not known. I started a new primary school, and because I absolutely hated being in foster care I learnt how to put on an act. I made myself stay clean. I kept the house tidy, so to the neighbours it just seemed like we were a normal family. Because of that we didn't move again. Mum even put on a front, made out she was the perfect single mother, working hard to look after her daughter. To this day I do not know why she wanted me back. Her life would have been a whole lot easier if she had left me in care, mine too I suppose. I might even still be alive.

Anyway I grew into a pretty girl with a great figure. I took a leaf out of mum's book and used my looks. I became the leader of the gang and the boys flocked. Of course I also got to know him. It was so cool. At first he would just talk to me and tell me how attractive I was. Then he started getting more flirty and that was all right with me. He was so gorgeous, still is I suppose. He made me feel like I was important, so much that I would do anything he asked me to do.

Because of him I got even more cocky. So that day when Hally fell over and I laughed and so did the others, something in me bubbled over. It was elation, wow big word again but that is what it was. It felt so good I wanted to test it again. Corrinne and Clia both helped Hally up, picked up her stuff too. But the path was really slippery and she went down again. That was all it took. I not only laughed but called her a clumsy boy chick. The others giggled. I didn't even really know what I meant, it just sounded funny. Then I really got going. Hally was tiny everywhere. I had great boobs, she was flat chested. So still laughing, I told her to lay back on the path and be a sledge for her friends since she was as flat as an ironing board.

It went from there. Over the years I did everything I could to take the mickey out of her. My life was going nowhere. She was doing well in school, naturally bright. She was getting taller and even though she still didn't have much boobage she was getting prettier. Her hair was the same colour as mine but it was cut better and shone. I was jealous but no way was I going to show it. So I did the only thing I could think of, bully her and my gang followed.

It was so easy from then on. Hally went bright red that first day, put her head down and stayed on the path until I decided to leave, my crowd following. Her friends tried to stick up for her but we were too many.

Any chance I got after that to call her names I took. I didn't think for one moment how much it was hurting her. I got a bit physical sometimes too. That's when her parents came into school complaining. I got hauled before the head for a bollocking and even had a few days exclusions. But I didn't care. There was no one at home, so to me it was a nice break from the boredom of school.

I found nothing in school that interested me. Lessons were full and I couldn't do most of the stuff anyway. At least that's what I thought. Now I know I could have if I'd listened and made an effort. But back then none of it mattered. I had him, he cared, loved me. I didn't even consider the future.

I should have though. When I got into trouble with the police after Hally's birthday. I should have seen my life was in chaos. Even when he wouldn't back me up, got mad at me actually for telling the police about the booze, I didn't realise where I was heading.

Well now I know exactly where, here and very dead. He's out there alive, probably forgotten all about me by now. Stop Dana, just stop wallowing. It's done. All you can do is keep trying to connect to Hally, tell her what happened. To do that you have to concentrate, listen to what they're saying. That way you might find out something that will help you.

So back to what Hally and the girls are talking about. Their day at college and the weekend. They're going to Exeter on Saturday all day. She won't be home until late. I wonder which film they're going to watch. Hey I don't even know what's out now. A lot can happen in a year. A year? I suppose it must be since Hally is in college but how far into college is she? From their conversation I get that Corrinne and Clia are too. But not Penny. Apparently she stayed on at school. Ha! I bet she didn't get very good grades in her exams so she has to take them again.

Maybe if I have a scout about Hally's room again I can find out exactly the date. I can't remember the day itself that he killed me, just that it was close to the end of the summer holidays. Yes, that's what I will do on Saturday. I have to fill the day somehow. In between I think I'll give Hally a rest. Not try and get through, it really wears her out. That's not fair. So yes I'll just listen to everything that goes on and give her a break. Then maybe when I try again it will work better.

****

Hally realised the conversation had completely led them away from the girl Louise who fancied Wes. She wondered if Clia had done it deliberately. She shrugged inwardly. If that was the case, then never mind. She was probably overreacting anyway. But she would keep an eye on the girl. If it looked like for one second Louise was trying to get her claws into Wes, then she would be on it.

Corrinne and Clia stayed for dinner then left for home. Rhys was seeing Clia that evening and she wanted to get changed and put on night time makeup, as she called it. Gregg was helping his dad refit the garage roof, Corrinne told them, so she was going around to his. Wes was working at the Hotspot tonight. Hally knew she could go and sit in the café and he would be happy to have her there. However, she decided to spend the evening with her family. Her days were so busy divided between college and Wes, she didn't get a lot of time with her parents and brother.

May was very pleased that Hally was staying in. She missed the days when her daughter had been younger, had a much lighter and easier life. She was happy that Hally was happy, had a lovely boyfriend and a full social life. Yet at times she wished she could have frozen time when her little girl was still little.

As a family they sat in the lounge and watched television. Because being together was quite rare, May allowed Nathan to stay up an extra half hour. She also brought in treats. He tried for more time when she finally told him it was bedtime but the huge yawn gave away his tiredness. Hally giggled and held out her hand.

"Come on squirt, let me take you up for a change."
Nathan grinned thinking he would be able to play her into letting him stay up longer but dad chimed in.

"Won't work Nathan. It's bedtime. You've had longer already."

Nathan pouted and drew his brows into a thick line. Hally gave him a tiny poke in the ribs. He tried to resist but a giggle escaped between his firmly pressed lips. Hally took his hand and gently tugged him towards the stairs.

"Come on. I'll read you one page from your Crewman comic whilst you settle down."

"I can read that by myself. I'm not little anymore."
Nathan replied indignantly.

"I know you can and of course you're not. But don't you think it will be fun listening for once. Especially when I can do the voices."
Nathan mulled it over for a moment. Then he was the one tugging Hally's hand.

As brother and big sister climbed the stairs, Nathan filled Hally in on the goings on of his comic book characters. Hally listened attentively, enjoying the moment. Her little brother was growing up but there were some things that reminded her he was still just a little boy.

They reached Nathan's room, her brother diving for the bed. Hally held onto his hand and pulled him back.

"Teeth."

She said. That one word brought Nathan's chin to his chest.

"Ohhh do I have to?"

He mumbled. Hally nodded and gave him a gentle shove towards the bathroom. Nathan went reluctantly and Hally followed, standing outside the door to make sure he actually did brush his teeth, and not just stand for a minute faking it. She smiled to herself when she heard him humming to himself around the toothbrush.

She left him to it and went back to his room. There she found his comic and thumbed through it, refreshing her memory of the characters so she would get the voices exactly right. Nathan bounded in and jumped onto the bed wriggling his way under the duvet. Hally settled herself next to him and rearranged the covers around him.

"Which bit do you want me to read?"

She asked. Nathan showed her and lay back against his pillows ready.

Hally thoroughly enjoyed herself reading to him. She brought the characters to life using her voice, and watched Nathan's expressions as he became absorbed in the story. She ended up reading more than one page, because Nathan's eyes were beginning to close and she thought he would fall asleep if she kept going. He did so she quietly closed the comic and laid it on his bedside table. Without disturbing him she gave him a light peck on the cheek.

"Sweet dreams little boy."

She whispered as she tiptoed out if his room.

May and Colin were snuggled up on the sofa watching the news when Hally returned to the lounge.

"All settled."

She told them.

"Goody good."

Her dad said.

"Anything interesting happening in the world?"

Hally asked as she curled up in a chair. Her dad shook his head.

"We were just waiting for you to come down. That drama you like started so we set it to record. We can watch it now together."

May said. Hally smiled at her parents and got comfy as Colin pressed the remote and the programme began.

★★★★

Ah that's so sweet. Hally and her little brother. I wish I could walk into his room with her and listen properly to her reading to him. But I can only stand here in the doorway and listen, because everything beyond is still foggy. But it's nice listening to her. I remember Hally in school. We were never in the same English class, she's far too good. But sometimes the sets would share their work. Now that I think about it probably to get us thickies to see how it should be done.

Anyway, no good harping on about all that now it's in the past. So the teacher would read out stuff written by the other kids, Hally's work sometimes. I mainly switched off, wasn't interested, except I do remember when I heard Hally's stories or poems I felt something. I tried so hard not to, to be cool and annoying. You know, interrupting and laughing, getting the other kids in the class on side as rebels. But deep inside her work affected me.

Crazy how these things keep coming back to me in dribs and drabs. I know my brain wouldn't bother remembering them if I was still alive. A shame that but hey ho, nothing I can do about it now.

I think I'm going to have to concentrate more on what is going on though. I keep missing things. Like Hally, Corrinne and Clia were talking about Penny but then I went and lost their discussion. It's quite scary really, like I'll just fade into nothingness if I let my mind wander. That cannot happen. I have to stay put. I have to try and make it known that I was murdered. It's going to be so damned hard though.

Penny what about Penny? Oh I am so frustrated. They were definitely talking about her. Wait, about her being dumped that's it. Oh Dana when did Penny even get a boyfriend? So long, so much time gone by. I don't even know what's been happening. Penny never had boyfriends, just bed buddies. Ah I remember her saying that. Maybe she changed, grew up and got serious. I don't know.

Hally's just come into her room. She looks happy, tired but happy. There are so many questions I would like the answers to but not tonight. I said I would leave her be for a while and I will stick to that. But soon I have to try and get those answers because then I hope, he will get caught.

Chapter 13

Hally awoke bright and early on Saturday morning. She practically leapt out of bed she felt so alive. Two whole nights of perfect, restful sleep. All her dreams had been happy, memorable, normal Wes type dreams. No nightmares or strange and weird ones about blonde girls.

****

It's morning. I'm getting very good at working out day from night now. Just a little concentration that's all it took. Focus Dana. If I keep telling myself that then I can keep track.

Hally is up. She's happy and bright. She's going out today. See, I'm getting good at remembering the things that are happening now. The past, the close past, not way back, is well, fuzzy except the last hours of my life. That's very clear, except him he's not clear. Some things are, like how it felt, his voice, but not his face and name, wonder why?

Anyway Dana don't brood. You are going to be alone all day. You have things to do. Oh it's so nice watching Hally get ready. Her clothes are nice, not designer stuff like some of the girls but still nice. She's putting on jeans and jumper so it must be colder outside today. Of course now I can't feel what that's like, weird I know. She doesn't wear a lot of makeup. I used to. Wow I remember that. I used to wear a lot of makeup.

Penny did too. Only she could buy hers, really expensive stuff. Me I'm ashamed to say, even though there's no one here to hear me, I used to steal a lot of it. Some of it mum left behind when she went off. Some of it I did buy when I managed to nick some money out of her purse, cheap lippy and so on. But when I got the chance I would go into one of the shops in town and slip the good

144

eyeshadows, mascara, foundation into my pocket. I was good at shoplifting, never got caught.

Later he would make me put on his choice of makeup. But only when he was with me. I wasn't allowed to wear any of that makeup out. He used to tell me it was for his pleasure only. He had a whole draw full of it. All different colours and all the top brands. At first I would slap it on thickly. I thought that's how it was supposed to look. But he would make me wipe it all off and start again. Then he showed me some videos on YouTube of girls doing their faces. He liked it when I learnt how to do it like them. I still used a lot but it looked better. He liked that.

It wasn't just the makeup that I used to pinch. Sometimes it was little items of clothing like undies. But he never knew that. He liked me to wear the stuff he bought. It was nearly always white and lacy. He got ever so angry if I was wearing black knickers and bra. I used to have to remember to change into plain pastel cotton pants with little flower prints before we met up. Then he was pleased and would give me the frillies. I don't know why the black ones were bad and then I didn't care. It was just so nice having someone show me some love and affection. Of course now I know different.

Then there was all the silky stuff too. When we were alone and I was all made up with the nice white undies on, he would go into his cupboard and pull out a box. He would make a big thing about giving it to me and I would have to smile and bat my lashes and tell him thank you, all giggly and girlish. Then he would lift the lid and I would have to pull back the layers of tissue to find the present. It was always a silky white or pale pink, I forget the word, shem something like that. Anyway it looked like a short nightie. I would have to raise my arms and let him slide it over my body. He would kiss me and hold me and love me and make me feel wanted. Huh very wanted wasn't I right up until the time he killed me.

Crikey I've gone right off track. Dana get a grip. Today you are supposed to be looking over Hally's room whilst she's out. Find out what the date is, what time of year it is and so how long I've been gone.

Hally's ready now. She's just looking at herself in the mirror. She's so bright and alive. Her skin still has a tan. That means it can't be too long after the summer. Hmm maybe it has only just happened, like days or only a couple of weeks. I mean I could have got it wrong when I saw her essay. Ah well she's leaving now. I'll give her a little wave even though she can't see me. She's stopped at the door. She's looking over her shoulder a little frown on her face. Maybe she's forgotten something. No she's leaving. Did she see me? Oh that would be very nice to not be so alone.

****

Hally bobbed down the stairs her phone in her hand ready to text Wes as soon as she reached the kitchen. Wes had stayed at home overnight so he could bathe and feed Ellie, and spend a little time with his daughter before his parents took over. They had a full weekend planned for the toddler so he took advantage of the time ahead.

Hally flicked on the kettle and dropped bread into the toaster as she tapped out a message for Wes.

Up and nearly ready. Love you xxxxx

His reply came quickly.

Be round in twenty. Love you too xxxx

Hally was waiting and eager to leave for their day out when Wes stepped through the back door. He pulled her into his arms for a hug and kiss, said hello to her parents and Nathan, then the two of them headed out hand in hand. May looked at her husband and smiled.

"Glad to see she's back to her old self."

She said. Colin nodded.

"Me too. How about we take Nathan to Funzone?"

Nathan heard his father and squealed with delight, jumping up and down on the spot.

"Yay yay."

He shrieked gleefully. May put her hand on his shoulder stilling him.

"Go and get ready then. I'm going to put some laundry on so be quick because I will be."

She told him, challenge in her voice.

Nathan fled from the kitchen and they heard him thump up the stairs to his room. Funzone was his second favourite activity, his first football. That had been cancelled today. The local playing fields come pitch were sodden from the storm earlier in the week. So practice had been cancelled to protect the grass in readiness for a match the next day. Funzone was a huge soft play centre for all ages and Nathan loved it. They knew it would probably be packed but they didn't mind.

In no time Nathan was back. May texted Hally just to let her know their plans even though she would be gone all day. Then they set off for a full day of fun themselves.

Hally received her mum's text as she and Wes strolled hand in hand towards the train station. They were meeting the others there. She had dressed for the weather today, jeans and light jumper. Autumn really was setting in. Cheeky, chilly fingers of cold tried to slip inside her jacket, but Hally had zipped it right up keeping them at bay.

"You're chirpy today."

Wes said swinging her hand lightly. Hally bounced on her toes acting more like Nathan than her sixteen years.

"I've slept well. I feel great and I'm looking forward to a brilliant day."

She told him stepping in front of him to plant a kiss on his lips. Wes laughed as they both nearly fell over.

Corrinne, Clia, Gregg and Rhys were waiting by the automatic ticket machine when Hally and Wes arrived at the station. Their timing was perfect. They only had to wait ten minutes for the next train. Piling on they found four seats facing each other with a table in the middle, and two seats on the other side of the aisle. The girls grabbed three of the four seats leaving the boys to decide where to sit. Gregg sat with the girls, Wes and Rhys taking the extra two but sitting sideways. The train began to fill up but soon they were chatting as it pulled away from the station.

****

If I make myself concentrate, I can actually walk across the room instead of drift from place to place. See, I've walked to the window. It looks a bit dull out there. The trees and bushes are swaying too, quite windy. Hally looked dressed for a colder day. I wish I could feel the air then I would know.

Now if I turn away from the window and take a step, there I'm at her desk. It's all in your mind Dana. Effort and thought. You can do it. The desk is very tidy. Hally has a bright pot, it looks hand painted with her pens and pencils in it. I reckon her little brother made it for her, it looks like something a little kid would make. She has a laptop too. A small one with a pink case. Ah text books, they're definitely not ordinary school ones.

So the essay? Move a little bit Dana. Yes, there it is and in the daylight I can see her name on it and the college. So it is the year after I was murdered. And the date on the essay, Hally has put Monday September the fourteenth, but I know today is Saturday. Aha she has a calendar hanging above the desk. So that means today is the nineteenth. Does that mean anything? I don't know but it is good to know the exact date. Sort of puts things into...um, I know there's a word for it but I cannot remember it. That's if I ever knew it. But what I mean is, things don't seem so flaky now I know what day and date it is.

So if it's the third week in September and I remember it was still the holidays when he killed me, but close to school starting back, then I've been dead for just over a year. Wow that's a frigging long time and where have I been during it? Why haven't I tried to get through to Hally before now? Too complicated and probably will never know.

Anyway now I know the date and I can work out day and night, I can keep track of the days. No more drifting through time and space and not knowing where I am. Just thought, maybe and it's a very big maybe, if I can concentrate even harder and focus more, perhaps I can find a way to move through the rest of the house. I could even try hard to move objects but not yet. Even though I cannot touch things I do sort of feel tired inside, especially after doing something new. It's very weird. I know I can't sleep but when I stop still for a while it kind of refreshes me.

Hally's mum just came into the room. She tidied a bit. Not like there was much to tidy though, Hally is very neat. She took some laundry out of Hally's little basket and then just stood for a while in the middle of the room. I heard her whisper a little to herself. She sighed and said 'My baby is growing up so fast.' My mum would be over the moon about that. Well wherever she is I don't expect she's even thinking about me and how old I am. In fact, I remember something from when I was little. It was my birthday. Hey that's it. Today is the nineteenth of September, that's why it means something, because tomorrow is my birthday.

Wow my birthday. I would have been sixteen. Sweet sixteen and many many times kissed. Actually if I was still alive this year I would be seventeen. But I never made it to sixteen. If I had though I wonder if I would have got myself a job? Would I have been planning a party? The Hotspot, that's where I would have had it. I love that place. It's always lively and friendly. Funny thing is there wouldn't have been any booze there. My crowd liked to drink, did it often in secret since most of us were too young. But at the Hotspot it wouldn't have mattered because we would have a few before we got there and lots more after. It's just the place is a fun place to be.

So what was it that triggered my birthday memory? Ah yes when I was little, my birthday then. I was six. I woke up in the morning all excited. I never got much for my birthday ever, the odd bit of clothing or a cheap toy. Only this year I had seen this doll in a shop window. It was gorgeous. So I asked mum if I could have her for my birthday. She told me she would see. She told me if I was really good. So I was. On my birthday morning I ran downstairs all happy and expectant. Only she wasn't there. The house was empty. Nothing unusual in that. I thought she would roll in around mid-morning like she always did. But the day went by and she didn't come. It was a Saturday so no school.

About six in the evening I heard the door go and voices. Hers and a man's. She strolled into the sitting room with a bloke on her arm. One I'd never seen before. I jumped up from watching tv, smiling, hoping to hear her say happy birthday. But instead she just told the bloke who I was. I said hello to him and then asked her for my birthday present. She frowned, then I could see she remembered. But, oh this hurts even now, she told me that I hadn't been good enough for a present, that I never could be. Then she turned her back on me and dragged the guy up the stairs.

That night really late I crept out of my room and out of the house. I had nowhere to go. I didn't even know what I was going to do. I walked until I got to the park. It was very dark and cold but I didn't care. I stood by the lake and stared down into the dark green water. Tears flooded down my cheeks and I felt so alone and miserable. I whispered to the sleeping ducks to help me. I begged for someone to find me and take me to a nice place. But of course no one did.

I cried until I was too tired to stand. Then I crumpled to the grass and fell asleep. The waking of the ducks woke me. I was freezing and frightened. As much as I wanted a nice person to come and look after me, mum had told me I would never be good. So I thought if anyone found me they would take me to the police and lock me away. I hated that thought so I made my way home. The door was still unlocked and mum was still in bed. She didn't even know I had gone out.

I never did get that doll or any other pretty present from her, and I never again asked for something special. When I went into foster care I should have seen that it was the better place to be. But by then I was too independent. I didn't like to be told what to do. There were no rules in my home. I thought that was cool but now I know it was lack of care from my mother.

Hally's mum loves her so much. Just those few little words that she whispered makes me see that. I'm glad. I wonder if Hally had a party for her sixteenth birthday? I bet she did. Nice presents too. Alive I would have been really jealous. Now, not at all. It's like all the hatred has gone from me. But I can't feel completely peaceful either. Angry yes, I still feel that. Towards my mum, him, because it's their fault that I'm here, dead but here. Yes, I have to blame mother too because if she had looked after me and loved me, I wouldn't have had to go to him for that love. I could have been strong and aware like Hally is. I could have had a future.

Ah Dana, perk up. It's no good imagining all the ifs and buts of your life. That's just a waste of time. I know you have plenty of that, time, you're dead. You have for evermore. So think and make good use of it.

Hally's room. What haven't you looked at yet? Well the things you don't have to touch since you can't. The desk, there's the painted pot, the laptop, the essay. She has a pile of notebooks, all with pretty covers and a shelf above the desk. The calendar is hanging from it. I wonder who chose it for her? Hmmm looks like pictures of a boyband. I don't know who though so maybe they're new. On the shelf are some photos. Ah that must be her grandparents then, her family. Ooh gorgeous hunky boyfriend Wes, the girls Corrinne and Clia. Looks like a photo album next to the framed photos. Shame I can't flip through that and look at more.

****

The city was busy but the bustle boosted Hally's good mood. The last week had been heavy and depressing, the nightmares casting a shadow over her life. Since they had stopped, she felt light and free and very determined to enjoy the day with her boyfriend and friends.

Wes, Gregg and Rhys followed their girlfriends into various shops. They knew the girls well enough to know what to say and what not to say, as Hally, Clia and Corrinne tried on clothes and shoes. In return the girls waited patiently whilst the boys checked out the latest video games and technology.

The day flew by. It seemed no time before they were collecting their pre-purchased tickets for the cinema. They queued for popcorn, Coca-Cola and other snacks then strolled to the screen showing their film, where they settled down to watch the latest disaster movie about an earthquake.

On the way back to the station the six chatted about the film. They laughed at the obvious bad spots and over dramatization, and praised the production for its special effects. Hally leaned into Wes as they strolled, tired but happy.

The station was quiet. Mid evening on a Saturday night being the time when families had already gone home and grown-ups weren't quite ready to go out. The temperature had dropped leaving a very definite wintery feel to the air. Hally shivered as she snuggled up close to Wes on a bench whilst they waited for their train.

"Brr it's cold tonight."

She said. Wes rubbed her arm up and down.

"Looks like autumn has either taken a break or has left permanently."

Corrinne stated as she dragged a thick scarf out of her big bag and wrapped it around Hally's neck. Hally giggled but pulled the soft folds close. She could always count on Corrinne.

"Thanks Corrie that's lovely and cosy."

"You're welcome."

Corrinne replied.

An announcement over the tannoy told them their train had been delayed and would be twenty minutes late. It was annoying but not a disaster.

"Coffee anyone?"

Wes asked. They all accepted his offer.

"I'll come with you. I have to nip to the ladies on the way."

Hally said letting Wes pull her up.

When they reached the small café, Wes went inside to order the drinks and Hally made her way towards the sign for the toilets. She followed the arrow for the ladies which took her around the other side of the brick built block. Without realising she found herself on a separate platform. This was completely deserted and so quiet it seemed like she had stepped into a different dimension. She shuddered and almost turned back, but shook off the prickle of fear running down her spine, telling herself to stop being silly.

Despite her conviction that she was perfectly safe, she hurried inside and locked the cubicle door, her ear cocked for the sound of someone following her in. No one did. She rushed through her hand washing and grabbed the door handle to exit then stopped. She was afraid and didn't really know why. For a few seconds she paused, certain there was someone on the other side of the door waiting for her.

Determinedly shaking off her fear Hally tugged on the door. Her heart skipped a beat as she expected an unknown being pushing it towards her, imagined herself trapped and unable to call for help. Taking a deep breath, she wrapped the strap of her handbag around her hand and closed it into a fist. She would fight she thought, use her bag as a weapon.

She dragged the door open quickly, relief flooding through her when she found she was alone. Barely breathing she fled back towards her own platform. The sounds and sight of people gave her comfort. Relaxing her shoulders and slowing her pace Hally glanced over her shoulder, her heart jumping into her throat. At the far end of the deserted platform stood a man. He was standing slightly sideways, almost facing the empty tracks. She couldn't see his face clearly, just a glint of his eyes as his head was covered by the hood of a thick grey hoody. All she could tell was that he was big. She turned away almost running to the café where she could see Wes inside. The man had done nothing wrong, probably hadn't even seen her, yet she still felt unnerved.

Wes smiled as she entered and then frowned.

"Hally?"

She tried a smile back and it worked, a little.

"I'm ok."

She chirped but Wes could see she was not, refraining from questioning her in the café. Taking the coffees in a cardboard holder they headed back to the others. Once there Wes handed out the drinks then raised his eyebrows.

"You looked scared out of your wits."

He said as he sat down pulling her into his arms. Hally went willingly, the fear completely gone, the memory of it not. She shrugged, feeling silly now. But the others had already turned to face her waiting for an explanation.

"Just my wild imagination."
She told him. He wasn't convinced and she knew it. The look on Corrinne and Clia's faces telling her they weren't either.

"Ok I got scared. The ladies' toilets are on the other side on another platform. It was empty and oh so quiet. I freaked, thought someone had followed me and there was no one to help me."
She went on to explain in detail, hesitating when it came to mentioning the man, but finally telling them everything and how she felt.

"Babe if I'd known you would be on your own I would have come with you and waited."
Wes said as she sipped her hot coffee. It warmed her and soothed her.

"Next time I'll make sure you do. At least until I know I'm not going to the loo on a deserted platform, or anywhere else like that."
Clia burst into giggles.

"Hey what's so funny?"
Hally asked. Clia looked at her grinning.

"What a sight that would be, Hally taking a pee on a deserted platform."
Hally took a mock swipe at her friend the others joining in with the laughter, her previous tension wiped away.

Their train finally arrived and they piled on. Wes sat next to Hally and they cuddled up, the other two couples doing the same. There was no need for conversation on the return journey between the six, it had been a full and enjoyable day. Once back in their home town they walked together until the roads divided. Corrinne, Clia, Gregg and Rhys heading one way, Hally and Wes the other towards her home, the incident on the Exeter platform barely a blip on her mind.

He stood silent and still in the shadows of the dark deserted platform. He was pleased with himself. He hadn't had to follow them all day thankfully, shopping was not one of his favourite activities, a necessity today, just not very enjoyable.

He had followed them onto the train that morning without any of them realising. It was quite easy really, becoming invisible, the wig and beard perfectly disguising him. He had chosen a seat close to them, knowing as teenagers they would chatter uninhibited and loud enough for him to get an idea of where they were going. That was one of the things he so liked about the younger ones, they planned everything and talked about it, so anyone nearby knew too.

Of course they had made a few changes throughout the day but that didn't hinder him. Altering which shops they were visiting wasn't important. What was though was knowing what film they were going to watch and the show time. He snickered to himself remembering, he had been very clever. He had sat just a few rows from them in the cinema, barely watching the movie, unnoticed. He had watched her though, Hally. He liked the way her hair flipped about when she moved, imagined how it would feel sliding through his fingers. He hadn't liked the boyfriend snuggling up, oh no not at all. But he would change that soon. She would be snuggling up to him before long.

Now he watched as Hally came around the building onto the silent platform. He could take her then and there and no one would even bat an eyelid. He snickered again, there wasn't anyone else on the platform to observe his actions. But he would wait. Jump in too soon and there would be questions. He had to time it right.

He watched as Hally came out of the ladies and fled to the other platform. He could see her eyes, feel her fear and that made him happy. The girls, all of them, should fear him. She had seen him, but not seen him. He had removed the beard but kept his head and face completely covered. He was wearing plain jeans and boots, nothing that would draw attention. He blended in, looked ordinary so no one would be able to describe him.

He didn't need to get on their train. It didn't matter what time he got back. He might even stay late in Exeter, make an evening of it, that would be fun. After all, following her about today had been recreational. He hadn't planned to do anything to her, he just wanted to watch her. He was in no rush and taking his time was all part of the thrill, would make it so much better when she was finally his.

The night was still as Hally and Wes walked arm in arm to Hally's house. It was the time of evening on a Saturday when people started out for the town. On the way they met several teenagers they knew. A few stopped them to chat and ask them if they wanted to go into town with them, others grinned and just said hi.

On another Saturday night Hally would have said yes to joining them. Tonight she didn't have the energy. It was a pleasant tiredness induced by the long day. She knew once they were home she would perk up again and Wes was staying over, a sure way to raise her zeal.

Hally's parents were snuggled up on the sofa when they walked into the lounge. Mum was about to get up but Hally put up her hand to stop her.

"Stay there. I bet you two are whacked after a day at Funzone."

May sank back against her husband and smiled.

"Not half as much as Nathan. We went out for pizza after and when we got home he didn't complain once about getting into his pyjamas. He sat on the sofa for a while playing with Crewman and Gripper then went to bed without a peep. We didn't even get the usual 'May I have?' about the Crewman games."

Hally smiled. Nathan loved his action toys, all from a series of stories in comics, on tv and DVDs. These had extended into video games but May and Colin had so far avoided letting their youngest child get into those. They preferred him to use his own imagination, using the action figures to create his own tales. They knew though it wouldn't be much longer before they would be socially forced into the gaming world. Nathan had a PlayStation but the games were all simple and educational.

"Wes is a dab hand at video games. I'm sure he wouldn't mind introducing Nathan. That way he can learn how not to get too fixated."

Hally told her parents, Wes nodding in agreement by her side. Mum sighed.

"That would be a big help. He has been nagging us a bit lately about getting a new Xbox or PlayStation. I'm just worried that he will want to stay in all of the time rather than play out."

"Mum you know he'll try it. You also know he won't fight you too much when you tell him no. You and dad have never spoilt him. You could have, he's so cute, but you haven't. It's not like you're going to just hand a pile of games to him and tell him to get on with it. I bet you won't even let him have them in his room. So he gets to do the same as other kids his age and you get to monitor his usage. There, all happy."

"When did you get so wise kid?"

Colin asked his daughter. Hally grinned shrugging her shoulders.

"I learnt from the best."

She replied. Her dad grinned, a tiny patch of pink staining his cheeks in embarrassment.

"I suppose so. He is nine and most of his friends already have a library of games. I just have to accept my little boy is growing up."

May said almost to herself. Hally kneeled on the floor and gave her a hug.

"Happens to us all mummy. Now we're off upstairs, it's been a long day."

Hally kissed her parents goodnight then she and Wes made their way up to her bedroom. As they passed Nathan's room Hally peeked in. Her little brother was sound asleep. He was sprawled diagonally across his bed on his back. The duvet was half on him and half off, Crewman by his side. Hally quietly slipped into the bedroom and gently lifted the cover over him. He didn't stir. Backing out of the room she whispered to Wes.

"He must be tired. Usually he mumbles something when any of us covers him up. Tonight not a chirp."

****

Wow the light's going from outside. The day has flown by and I didn't even notice. I'll have to work on that like the other things. I want to be able to keep track, not drift. I can hear voices outside the room. It's Hally and Wes, they're home. Wonder what sort of day they've had? The door's opening. She looks tired. Happy but tired. I'm glad. She deserves that. I might have to keep my eyes closed though since Wes is obviously staying over. Hopefully I can shut out sound too.

****

Once in her own room Hally plonked down on the edge of her bed. She dropped her bag on the floor not bothering to remove her phone. She didn't need it. Wes was with her and she didn't need the alarm.

"Phew don't know about Nathan crashing I think I will too."
Wes sat next to her and put his arm around her shoulder drawing her close.

"Me too. It's been a strange week."

"I don't think I'm too tired for a little kiss and cuddle though."
Hally told him threading her fingers through his hair. Wes pulled them both backwards and obliged.

Wes drew her up against him and wrapped them both in the duvet. Hally felt herself unwind as Wes massaged her neck releasing the tension in her muscles. She closed her eyes and let his comfort wash over her. Soon she was asleep.

Hally awoke suddenly. She lay in her bed, Wes by her side cuddling her. As tired as she was she couldn't get back to sleep. She could hear Wes' steady breathing, feel his chest against her back rising and falling rhythmically, but it didn't lull her. As carefully as she could she lifted his hand away from her tummy and slid to the edge of the bed. Without waking him she slipped from under the duvet and tiptoed to the window.

Standing looking out, Hally let her mind wander. She went over the day smiling to herself. It had been a really good much needed day out. Mr Austin had told her to put all her worries aside and enjoy the weekend. So far that's what she had done.

"You ok?"

Hally jumped, startled at Wes' whisper. Turning, she saw him throw back the cover and pad across the darkened room to her side. He touched her cheek with the back of his hand lovingly.

"You made me jump."

She said keeping her voice low.

"I'm sorry babe. But are you ok?"

Hally leaned into his outstretched arms pulling them tight about her waist. She tilted her head up and looked into his worried eyes. A little light from outside showed the frown of concern on his face.

"I'm fine. I just woke up, couldn't sleep and didn't want to disturb you but I did anyway."

"Anything on your mind?"

He asked giving her a gentle squeeze. Hally stifled a giggle.

"Plenty. I've just been thinking about the brilliant day we've all had. My brain just won't shut down even though I am very tired."

"So no nightmares or scary thoughts then?"

Hally shook her head.

"I've barely been to sleep yet so hopefully not. I don't think that fright I got at the station will affect me either. It was just me being silly. I mean that bloke in the grey hoody was only standing on the platform. He wasn't anywhere near me, wasn't even looking at me." She tapped her head with a finger. "Just my imagination going wild and freaking me out."

Wes tightened his grip around her and nuzzled her neck. Hally let herself relax into his arms. He was warm and made her feel safe. They stood like that for a while, Wes swaying her slightly from side to side. Only when she began to feel cold did she turn and lead him back to bed.

****

Oh my God. Did I just hear right? Was it? No it can't be. Hally and Wes talking about their day, well the bit I heard anyway. I did manage to shut out sound when they went to bed, closed my eyes too. Then suddenly Hally's voice came through very clear.

Someone frightened her at the station. Not just any old stranger either. It was him. She saw a man on the platform, he spooked her. I didn't hear all of it though but enough to know she got freaked out. What was very clear though was what the man was wearing. A grey hoody.

I mean loads of men, girls too, have grey hoodies. But even though I cannot see his face in my mind I can see that hoody. He used to wear it with the hood right up so his face was covered. It was thick and made of a heavy fabric. I can even remember the smell of it.

He would laugh and tell me that the big hood kept him looking like a teenager. Of course I thought it was funny, that he was funny. But then what did I know? I believed everything he told me. I let him control me, encourage me to be bad, especially at school. He thought that was very cool.

So was it him on the platform? Oh Hally I hope to God it wasn't because if it was then it means he's after her. I heard her say he didn't look at her, wasn't anywhere near her. But he's very good at sort of blending in. That's how he can get away with so much because nobody really notices he's there, when he wants it that way. Then when he does want to be seen and heard, he's charming and oh, I can't get the right word, he's just big, not right but what I mean is people react to his presence.

Of course when I was alive I thought that was brilliant. It meant we could get up to quite a lot without getting caught. He did all sorts of sneaky stuff alone too and no one knew. Now I think there was a lot I didn't know.

So what can I do? Well listen and be aware to begin with. Keep an ear out for any mention of him. I mean Hally won't realise who he is, but if she sees a hoody man again and talks about it here, then maybe I can work out if it really is him. And if it is? Oh Dana, you have to try and find a way to communicate with her. He can't do to her what he's done to me. I will not let him. I just don't know how right now but I will work it out.

Chapter 14

Hally awoke from a deep, restful and dreamless sleep. Wes was still flat out next to her his arm laying heavily across her tummy. Carefully and without waking him, she slipped out of bed and padded across the room to the door. The house seemed quiet and she wondered what time it was. As she passed Nathan's room, she saw his door was open and his bed empty. So her little brother was up. Her parents' door stood ajar too, their room also empty. She frowned and mulled over where her family might be.

Detouring from her intended destination, the bathroom, Hally trotted down the stairs. The big old grandfather clock, that granddad had moved from his house to theirs, ticked loudly. Hally glanced up at it on the way to the kitchen and was surprised to see it was just after ten. They had slept in.

The kitchen was empty and tidy. Three mugs and cereal bowls rested upside down on the stainless steel drainer, a sure sign her parents had breakfasted with her brother and were now out somewhere. Hally twirled slowly, looking for the note she was certain her mum had left her. She smiled to herself. It was propped up against the kettle. Hally opened the single sheet of paper as she flicked the switch on the kettle and saw her mum's neat handwriting.

Angel Hally.

We let you two sleep in. Have taken Nathan to football. Be back before twelve. There's bacon in the fridge.

Hally grinned. Nathan played for the Colingford's under tens football team. He loved his football and loved his parents going with him to watch. The kettle clicked off and Hally made two cups of tea. Just as she was adding milk to Wes', he appeared in the doorway. His hair was standing in spikes and he looked a little bleary eyed.

"Morn…ing beautiful."

He said on a big yawn. Hally giggled and handed him a mug.

"Mum and dad have gone with Nathan to football." She waggled her brows. "And they've left bacon in the fridge."

Wes took the cup in one hand and Hally in the other. He gave her a big kiss and pulled her into a hug being careful not to spill his tea.

"Mmmm just what's needed on a chilly Sunday morning."

"Is it?"

Wes frowned.

"What?"

"Chilly."

Hally said. Wes grinned.

"Don't know, haven't been out. But the sky looks it."

Hally shook her head a little and unlocked the back door. She pulled it open and peeked out closing it again quickly.

"Brr it is. So best get this bacon a cookin'. But after a shower."

She said flipping her hair over her shoulder as she trotted out of the kitchen. She was quick, and in no time was back tugging on the fridge door and taking out a packet of smoked bacon.

Minutes later the bacon was sending out a mouth-watering aroma as it sizzled in the pan. Hally and Wes chatted whilst waiting, sipping tea and buttering English muffins.

"What do you want to do today?"
Hally asked. Wes grabbed her around the waist and kissed her full on the mouth. Hally giggled.

"After breakfast."
She mumbled against his lips. Wes leaned back and winked. Hally slapped him lightly on the shoulder and wriggled free, just in time to save the bacon from burning.

As they munched on their bacon muffins they discussed what they would do with the day. Both were up to date with their college work so were completely free.

"Want to go and watch Nathan?"
Wes asked around a mouthful of muffin. Hally smiled.

"Mmhm he'd love that, me too. I don't go and watch him enough."
With that decision made they finished their breakfast, cleared away and got ready.

It was quite cold when they left the house and Hally was glad she had decided to put on a thick jacket and gloves.

"Wow it is cold out today. I was hoping for an Indian summer but looks like autumn skipped straight into winter."
Hally complained. Wes swung her hand.

"Nah it'll warm up again you see. Don't be so quick to discard the season. Look at the trees, their leaves are gorgeous and only just dropping. We've got a while to go before winter sets in properly."

Hally looked up and sighed. Wes was right about the leaves and she so hoped about the weather too.

They heard shouts and cheers minutes before they reached the recreation centre. As they passed the chain link fence on the way to the entrance, they saw two football games going on. One was the older boys, the other, Nathan's game. Hally's parents were standing on the side-lines watching intensely.

Hally and Wes joined her parents. Nathan spotted his sister and gave her a wave, at the same time deftly kicking the ball straight into the goal. His team mates jumped on him and bounced about throwing air punches. The spectators cheered and Hally's dad raised his arms above his head waving them about.

"That's my boy!"
He yelled happily. Hally grinned and felt the elation.

"They're three up. Nathan scored two."
Mum told her and Wes, excitement and pride very evident in her voice. Wes clapped Colin on the shoulder.

"He's a nifty little player."
He said, Colin nodding in agreement.

The sun pushed through the clouds as the match progressed. By the time the whistle went calling full time, Hally had unzipped her jacket and removed her gloves. She could feel the excitement from the small crowd watching, felt it build inside herself, a broad grin spreading across her face as Nathan's team squealed and jumped about in jubilation. They had won, four goals to one, Nathan scoring the final goal and achieving a hat trick. Hally giggled as her little brother waved his arms over his head, nearly toppling off the shoulders of his team mates, as they carried him around the pitch. Colin was barely containing his own joy and pride, May wiping a tear from the corner of her eye.

The family joined in with other team member families, chatting and rehashing the game, whilst they waited for their offspring. The men especially discussed tactics comparing their children to their own experiences. Hally listened to her own dad relaying a couple of past moments when he had won a game for his team.

"He's chuffed to bits isn't he?"

Wes whispered in her ear. Hally nodded.

"I'm not really sporty. Even PE at school. I didn't enjoy it that much. Swimming, now that I love but only for fun. I'm just not that competitive."

"Oh I don't know." Wes nudged her. "You get pretty feisty when we play the Angels game."

Hally turned her face into his shoulder and snickered. He was right she did like to win. The challenges and puzzles excited her more so when she was ahead of Wes in the game.

"Can't help it. You bring out the devil in me."

She mumbled into his jacket. She felt him huff out a chuckle.

The young players began to appear from the small building next to the pitch. It housed showers and changing facilities, separate from the main recreation centre, thereby ensuring the centre remained clean. Especially today since the pitch was still very muddy. Nathan bounded out and ran up to his family.

"Did you see!"

He screeched as he ran into his mother's open arms.

"Did you see?"

He repeated, his cheeks flushed with excitement, his hair wet from his shower.

"We did, we did."

May said as she hugged her baby boy to her chest. Colin came up behind and tickled Nathan.

"A hat trick son how cool is that?"

Nathan beamed at his dad as he wriggled free from his mother's grasp, taking his father's outstretched hand and jumping up and down. He swivelled around to face his sister his excitement infectious. Hally took his other hand and found herself bouncing on the spot too.

"You were amazing Natty."

She squealed, her cheeks flushed with pride.

"Coach says if I keep this up I could be captain next year."

He gabbled out.

"Do you want to go to Gesslers?"

Dad asked, aiming his question at Nathan but talking to the whole family. Nathan squealed out a yes jumping even higher.

Gesslers was busy but that was always expected. It was a large family run restaurant with three sections. One intimate with booths, a formal dining area and then a large open plan space that could accommodate bigger groups. It was very popular for either family meals or parties. Hally loved it.

Over lunch Nathan gave them virtually a minute by minute account of the match as if none of them had seen it. They all indulged him.

"How come Granddad didn't come and watch?"

Hally asked her mum.

"He's joined a seniors group. Several of them have lost their husband or wife and he was getting so lonely. They've gone to Plymouth for the day on a bus trip. He says it's not really his thing, but I think he's enjoying the company. The group meets up at the community centre a couple of times a week in the afternoon. They have tea and cakes and so on. I think it's good for him."

Hally felt a prickle of emotion deep in her heart. She missed Gran every day, so Granddad must find it very hard. She hoped he would be able to get past the pain a bit and have some happiness without the love of his life. Her mother covered her hand and squeezed. She missed her mother deeply and also didn't want so see her father unhappy.

"He's getting through it. It's still so fresh, January, but feels like a lifetime."
Mum said to Hally quietly. Hally nodded, it had been hard for all of them and time was the only way they could get through it.

They took their time over their meal, and when they finished and headed out for home, found the sun had won the battle against the clouds and breeze. The sky was clear and blue, the air warm. Hally didn't bother putting her jacket on as she strolled hand in hand with Wes next to her parents and brother. Nathan had calmed down and walked in between their mum and dad. She smiled remembering.

When she was a little girl, before Nathan was born, she had done the same. Mum had one hand dad the other. Sometimes she would simply lift her feet from the ground, complete trust in her parents to hold on. They would gasp in surprise but never let go. Other times they would count one, two, three and swing her between them high. She would squeal and giggle, her tummy flipping inside as her parents lifted her from the pavement, feeling joy only a child can feel.

At home Nathan dived upstairs to get changed and mum flipped the switch on the kettle. Her cheeks were bright and her eyes gleamed. Hally could tell she was happy and that made her happy. A tiny nudge of thought poked at her brain, Dana. How could her mother, her only parent up and leave her like she did? Hally felt the sadness wash over her at how lonely Dana must have been for so long.

"You ok?"
Wes whispered. Hally looked up startled and nodded.

"I'm fine. It's been a brilliant day, weekend actually."
She purposely pushed thoughts of Dana to the back of her mind as she took the mug of coffee her mum handed her.

She wouldn't let sadness intrude on this wonderful time with her family.

Hally stood at her bedroom window looking down onto the garden. It was quiet. Wes had gone home and texted her night night. Nathan was tucked up sound asleep, worn out from the day. Her parents were in bed too. She felt tired but in a good way and wasn't ready to settle down for sleep. At that moment if she tried she was sure she would simply lay awake.

In the darkness of the night the leaves and branches of the trees looked black, silhouetted against a backdrop of dark sky dotted with glittering stars. It was a poetic view. Hally smiled to herself. If she was still in school she would have written about what she was seeing for English. Her college course didn't require such composition.

A second later she was nestled on a beanbag, a pink patterned notebook in her hand. Just because she didn't have to write down her thoughts didn't mean she shouldn't. She opened the notebook, it was one she had bought on a whim and so far hadn't used. On the first page she wrote her name. Underneath and without pausing for thought she wrote.

For Wes. My thoughts are my heart and my heart is yours.

She then turned the page and began to write the poem inspired by the night.

The darkness has brought peace to the night.
The colour has faded from the day.
But bright is my heart. A rainbow.
Your love keeps it aglow.
Your touch holds its form.
Your kiss the gold at each end.
So never the darkness comes in.

Hally finished her poem and closed the book. She rested her hand on the hard cover for a moment. She would fill the little notebook with words of love for her one true love. Her grandfather was lonely without his, she would make sure that Wes would always have her words to hold close if something were to ever happen to her.

She gave herself a little mental shake. She was sixteen, had a long lifetime ahead of her with Wes. Her earlier thoughts of Dana crept back in. Dana hadn't had a long life. Nor had she had anyone to care about her, to write words of love for her. A tear seeped beneath her lashes, and a small sob escaped her lips for the sadness she knew had beaten the girl to take her own life.

"I'm so sorry Dana. I should have tried harder."
She whispered to the night.

Hally wiped away the moisture and carefully placed her little book in the drawer of her desk. She turned to her bed, determined not to dwell on what had happened to Dana.

****

Hally is writing something. I remember she's very good at that. She was looking out of the window, a little smile on her face, peaceful. Then she took a cute notebook from her desk and sat on her beanbag. For a minute she sort of mulled over what she was going to write, then I watched her pen fly over the page.

She's stopped. Closed the book. Just sitting there holding it gently, lovingly, like something precious. I wonder what she wrote? It would be something pretty I know. Because that's what she used to do in school. I could never write anything pretty.

Sometimes we got told we had to write a poem or a story. Of course tough little me would go for rude or dirty just to raise a laugh. My poems always started with, there was a someone from somewhere, da dee da and so on. I got into quite a bit of trouble for those. Stories? Um, well yeah, never could get to grips with them, no imagination. Or so I thought. Bet I could write a real corker now. Back then my life was just so sh... Dana don't, rubbish. My life was rubbish. School work was the last thing on my mind.

Being dead I think of how it could have been. How I could have been. My mind, it's free. Weird, I can think, can see beyond the misery of each day I was alive. Now if I could I would write and it would be good and special and pretty. Teachers would want to read it, others too. They would want to share it with the rest of the school. But it can never be, not now.

Wait Hally's talking. Well whispering really to herself. Maybe she's saying what she wrote out loud. No, my name, she's saying something about me. She's, oh no, she's crying, apologising for not helping me. Hally I wish you could hear me. I'm right next to you so close, you don't have to apologise you did nothing wrong.

Hally's climbed into bed and snuggling down. There was something before, ah yes him. At least I think it was him, the man in the hoody. I do believe it might have been him and I must try and connect with Hally now, not wait like I thought I would. I have to warn her to be careful. But to do that I have to let her know I was murdered. She has to see that none of this is her fault. She tried to help me, now I have to try and help her.

Tonight, it will be tonight. I don't want to scare her though. I think I can bond with her without frightening her. It will take a lot of effort but I have to make it work. This is so important, probably the most important thing I have ever done.

Before, I thought it was just about me. You know making Hally see I was killed, that I did not take my own life. But what I heard, the man in the hoody could be him. He could be watching her, maybe going after her. I don't know. After all, it seems I didn't really know him at all. I thought I did but God how wrong was I.

****

Hally turned over under her duvet. She was so cosy, warm and snug. She was dreaming of Wes just as she did most nights. It was a lovely dream and one which she wanted to stay in. But that didn't happen. Her dream of Wes changed, replaced with the one of the girl with long blonde hair, herself. She tried to shake it off, push it away and return to the soft kisses of her boyfriend.

It didn't want to be budged. The image of the girl in front of her stayed firm. She was holding out her hand, beckoning with her fingers. In her sleep Hally tried to ignore the girl. She turned her head away hoping the other her would go away and let Wes back in. She didn't want a chat with her dream self. She was over all of that. All she wanted was her boyfriend. But when she looked over her shoulder, just a tiny glance, the girl was still there.

Hally was cross. The dream girl would not go away. She would just have to make her, force her away, concentrate on bringing the Wes dream back. In the dream she spoke.

"Go away."
Hally said to the blonde girl. But she only smiled. Hally frowned.

"You are interrupting my dream. I don't want you here right now."

The dream girl wavered, faded slightly. Hally felt triumphant. It was working and soon Wes would be back. She opened her mouth to speak again but something disturbed her. She turned, looking for its source but there was nothing.

Looking back, the dream girl was just a faint outline drifting away. Hally grinned, she was going, leaving. Now her boyfriend could return. Waiting for Wes she didn't at first feel the tug on her body. Then it was all she felt. Still in sleep she smiled. She thought it might be Wes, thought he had come to her room and was gently waking her. She didn't want to wonder how he had got into the house. That didn't matter. The tug strengthened, dragging her from sleep.

Hally came awake slowly. Her eyes were still closed but she knew she was awake. Her dream self was gone so was the tugging. She could feel her bed beneath her, the duvet covering her, the pillows under her head. When she opened her eyes she would see Wes she was sure.

Feeling a little too warm she threw back the cover and sat up opening her eyes. The room was dark, empty. Disappointed that Wes was not there, that believing he would be had been part of her dreams, she reached for her mobile and pressed a button, the screen lighting up. It was two twenty-two. Hally frowned thinking it was an odd time to wake. Knowing something had disturbed her, not knowing what, was all rather weird and annoying.

Then the memory of the tug she had felt crept into her thoughts. She shuddered a little, nervous but not knowing why. She cast a glance around her room, all was silent. She was alone as expected, awake and not happy about it. It would take her ages to get back to sleep now and she had to be up in a few hours for college.

Hally pushed the duvet off and slid her legs over the side of her bed. She rested her feet on the floor and scrunched her toes into the carpet. She rubbed her palms over her face and ran her fingers through her tangled hair.

"Ouch."

She whispered as her fingers snagged the ends of her long hair.

Feeling really cross now Hally stood up. She knew sleep was out of the question, she was too wide awake. She padded to the window and pulled the blind up. Perhaps something in the garden had been the source of the disturbance. She unlatched the window and opened it wide leaning out to look. The air was very cold and made her gasp. Quickly she drew back and grabbed the duvet wrapping it around her body. Warmth seeped into her.

Snug, she again leaned out of the window. The garden was still, the road beyond quiet. There was nothing she could see that could have awoken her. Sighing she closed the window and sat on a beanbag. She hated being woken in the middle of the night and having no idea what had disrupted her sleep.

With the window closed she began to feel too warm. She stood up and shook the duvet back over her bed replacing it with her dressing gown. It was much lighter, but still covered her, keeping out the autumn chill. She took a deep breath, held it and let it out on a huff.

Clicking the lamp on, Hally took the little notebook from her desk deciding she might as well write some more poetry, since sleep was distant. She plonked down onto a beanbag and with the end of her pen resting against her lip, thought. Ideas began to flood in and soon the pen was flying over the page.

Hally was so absorbed in her writing she had no idea how much time was passing. She had written half a dozen individual poems when a speck of light caught the edge of her eye. She paused, pen poised on the next word, turning her head. A glimmering shimmery light hovered then disappeared before her mind had time to register its presence.

Hally frowned, leaning forward to lay the book and pen on the desk. She blinked, rubbed her eyes and shook her head. She lifted her phone and saw she had been writing for over an hour. She yawned, tired and a little droopy.

"Best go back to bed girl you're seeing things."
She mumbled to herself.

She slipped her arms from her dressing gown and reached up to the peg on her door. As she turned towards her bed she caught a glimpse of the shimmering light again. She stopped and waited. It didn't dissipate. Hally felt a tiny knot of fear in her chest. She held her breath, frozen to the spot. The light wobbled, its edges sharper than its centre but it didn't come closer, wavering next to her desk.

Hally finally let out her breath slowly and quietly. She took a tentative step towards her bed. The glowing shape stayed where it was. Hally took another step, keeping her eyes firmly fixed on it. Slowly as though trying not to frighten a timid animal, she eased her way to her bed and lowered herself to the mattress. Her initial fear had passed. She felt no threat from the apparition, more curiosity now.

Hally stared at the shimmering form. It glowed silvery like moonlight, almost transparent like vapour. The more she looked the more the shape became defined. The edges separated from the whole, stretched to become arms and legs. The middle parted as a glowing head emerged. A figure, faceless and featureless floated just above the floor near her desk, coming no closer.

Hally pulled her duvet over her lap, gripping the fabric between clenched fingers. She couldn't take her eyes off the spectre. Even though she wasn't afraid she was filled with suspense, waiting and wondering what it was, what it wanted. Memory flicked a switch on in her brain. She had seen this before but had dismissed it, blamed the thunder storm. Now she knew it was real not her imagination. But she had no idea what to do.

The apparition hovered. Hally watched and waited. Questions flooded her mind. Should she speak? Approach it? She did nothing. Then as though in slow motion the figure lifted an arm. Fingers glimmering and frayed at the edges reached towards her. Hally held out her own hand, solid and warm. The form glided towards her, they connected. Hally's hand was enclosed in a warm glowing mist. She expected it to feel damp like clouds but it was dry and soft, feathery.

Hally moved her own fingers and the ghostly fingers wrapped around hers. They were not solid but she could feel them. She fisted her hand except her forefinger, watched the figure do the same, their fingertips touching. Hally held out her other hand so did the silvery form. Hally took it standing up. She felt a slight tug as though the being was pulling her up. It was so strange to be physically connected, to actually feel something that was so like air.

As she stood, Hally realised that the tugging sensation was the same as that which had pulled her from sleep. So this was the disturbance. The shimmering apparition was still holding her hands. It floated, barely moving, its silvery glow casting a spot of light on the carpet just below it.

Hally took a deep breath and let it out. She expected the form to shift, blown away by her breath. But it maintained its shape. Inside, Hally felt she should be afraid but there was something familiar about the spectre. Just as she thought this the shape began to change, become even more defined. Eyes, nose and mouth appeared in the face, the lips smiling sweetly at her. The head altered becoming less round as cheeks and chin protruded.

Hally was mesmerised, awed by what she saw happening before her. She watched as hair grew long and wavy down the back of the figure and fringed across the forehead. She could see lashes appearing on the eyes and brows over the eyelids, all shades of silver glittering like tiny stars.

The figure finally fully formed into that of a young woman. Hally gasped. It was the girl in her dream. She shook her head a fraction, confused and afraid. Was she still asleep? She was so sure she had woken up yet now she wondered. Was she losing her mind? She began to shake, that thought far more terrifying than if the spectre were actually real.

Hally stepped back from the figure pulling her hands free. The girl before her hovered with her hands still outstretched. The smile faltered and a frown appeared but she didn't move towards her. Hally pressed her fingers to her cheeks unsure of what to do, how to test herself.

"Are you real or am I dreaming?"

She whispered. The girl tilted her head forwards.

"Please. Tell me. Am I going crazy?"

The girl gently shook her head from side to side. The silvery hair, which had been blonde in Hally's dream, floated like wisps of smoke as she moved. Hally felt a tiny measure of relief. Perhaps this was real. Surely if she were asleep the girl would look as she did in her dream. Yet here in front of her she was different.

"Then please, who are you?"

Hally begged. The girl turned her head looking around the room as if searching. She looked back at Hally, her lips pressed hard together a deep frown across her brow.

"Can you speak?"

Hally asked. The girl again shook her head and lifted her shoulders. Her expression showed frustration. Hally puffed out a breath wondering how they could communicate.

"Are you me?"

Hally asked feeling a bit stupid. The girl grinned, shook her head. Hally felt relieved. She tapped her nails against her lips mulling over what to ask next that would answer her questions.

The girl drifted a little, moved towards Hally's desk. Hally reached out afraid she was going away. However, the girl stopped and pointed to the desk. Hally frowned having no idea what she was supposed to do. But she was now sure that this wasn't a dream and she wasn't going mad.

Hally joined the girl at the desk and shrugged. The apparition pointed to a notepad. Hally frowned. Could the figure hold a pen and paper?

"Can you write?"

She asked. The girl shook her head and Hally felt mounting frustration. The girl again indicated the notepad so Hally picked it up taking a pen from her pot too. The girl's mist-like fingers wrapped themselves around hers and Hally intuitively knew that she was guiding her. Hally placed the nib of the pen to the paper and felt her hand being guided. A letter, scrawling and rough formed a D. Hally gasped.

"Dana? You're Dana?"

The girl floated backwards and nodded. Hally shocked, dropped the pen and notepad back onto the desk and felt her legs wobble underneath her. All of the breath had gone from her lungs and she gripped the edge of the desk, fearing she wouldn't be able to remain standing. The Dana spectre reached for her, concern across the glimmering face. Hally watched the ghostly hand come towards her, felt it rest on her shoulder and finally took a deep breath.

Hally, her lungs once again full, tentatively stepped away from her desk. She didn't fall and felt relieved. Dana hovered close by worry in her silvery eyes. Hally faced the spectre, shaking and feeling very cold.

"Really, are you really Dana?"

Hally whispered. Without coming any closer Dana nodded. As she did so the face became so clear Hally recognised the girl she hadn't seen in over a year.

"Are you going to hurt me?"

Hally asked her voice trembling. Dana held out her hands palms out and shook her head from side to side quickly. Her eyes had grown large in her shimmering face, full of concern. Hally slowly sank down onto a beanbag realisation clicking into her brain.

"You came to me in my dream. Asked me to help you."

Dana nodded. Hally rubbed her hands across her face. She was weary and confused. The initial terror and shock had gone leaving wonder and turmoil. Dana needed her help but with what?

"Help you how?"

She said her voice shaky. She suddenly felt exhausted, barely able to hold her head up and her eyes open. Dana reached out, her soft fingers stroking the top of Hally's head. Hally looked up into eyes full of anxiety and knew it was for her. Dana clasped her hands together as if in prayer, tilted her head and laid it on her folded hands. Then she pointed to Hally and to her bed.

"You want me to go to sleep?"

Dana smiled and nodded, pointed at Hally and mimicked a yawn.

"Will you come back?"

Hally asked dragging herself to her feet and plodding to her bed. Dana nodded and followed her. Hally slid into bed and pulled the duvet up to her chin. Dana hovered next to her, her hand resting on Hally's head. Hally felt peace wash over her as she closed her eyes. Briefly she flicked them open and Dana was still there. When she closed them again sleep overtook her.

****

Wow, that went far better than I thought it would. At first I was sure Hally would really freak out. For a moment she did get scared and I wondered if she would call out for her mum and dad. But she got it under control and she believed it is me.

What was really exciting though was how I managed to guide her hand on the notepad. I didn't know I could do that. I hadn't even thought about it until it actually happened. It was like something else was in control. But I know it was me. I think maybe that things were disconnected, woo big word, haven't done that in a while. Anyway, disconnected, yes like broken wires. That happened to my hairdryer once. It used to switch off in the middle of drying my hair. Then if I wiggled the lead it would come back on. I remember he said it was a broken wire and wiggling it made the ends touch and work again.

So me, my body and brain, no that's not right because my body and brain are dead. Well whatever it is, let's say my spirit or soul. Yes, that sounds better. My soul disconnected from my thoughts. Can thoughts survive after the body is killed? Hmm so many questions and no one to answer them. Ha ha unless an angel happens to drop by and give me a lesson or some pointers on being dead.

Drifting Dana. So somewhere along the way my thoughts started to join together with my soul. That's the only way I can describe it I think. Because what I was thinking, saying to myself was all over the place at first. Then as the world around me started getting clearer so did my mind. I could see and hear and think all at once.

Now that one little moment, that one tiny touch and I made something happen, something physical. Wow another grown up word, I'm liking this. Anyway Dana, keep it together this is important. So if, and this is a huge if, I concentrate I might be able to leave this room. If I can do that I can try and communicate with Hally at other times, maybe even speak to her. Well that's my plan. At last I have one, somewhere for all of this to go with the ending HIM caught and locked away.

Chapter 15

Hally waited where the roads met for Corrinne and Clia. She was early but she had needed to get out of the house. If she had stayed longer, mum would have noticed something was definitely wrong. Because it was for certain.

What had started out as a dream had become a reality. Well that's how it had seemed at the time. Now in the cold light of day she was no longer sure what had happened during the night. She knew something had, because when she awoke she went straight to her desk and found the notepad with the D on it. That's when the trembling had started, so much the book shook in her hands.

She had fled from the room to the shower. The water had calmed and soothed her a little. So that once back in her room she lifted the pad and with a steady hand examined it. The single letter, shaky around the edges, was definitely formed in her own hand. She remembered doing it. She also remembered the glowing apparition, the Dana ghost that had guided her. That's when the shaking began again.

She had put the notepad in her drawer shutting it away, blotting it out. Then with determination she dried her hair and told herself over and over that she wasn't crazy. But a niggle in the back of her mind kept telling her different. Something epic had happened during the night, and she wanted to believe it was Dana trying to tell her something. That at least would mean she wasn't losing her mind. But common sense kept telling her it wasn't possible. Dana was dead. Had been for over a year. Why would she be trying to connect with her now? More so why her?

Before she left her room Hally took the book she had begun writing poems in, turning to the very last page. She thought for a moment and then wrote her deepest thoughts.

She closed the book on a sigh feeling a little better, thinking that at least if her mind trekked off to some far off never never land, Wes would know she needed him to bring her back. She left the book on top of her desk instead of putting it away, so it would be found with ease and went downstairs.

Standing on the street, the cold autumn morning trying to penetrate her jacket, Hally pondered. She would tell the girls, no doubt about that. Corrinne might even be able to give her some idea of what was going on. They came into view and a peace settled over her, her jangling nerves quietening. This was real, she didn't feel nuts, she felt just like herself and very happy to see her friends.

The three girls greeted one another as usual. But Corrinne instantly spotted that Hally was out of sorts.

"Give."

She said simply and Hally felt tears immediately threaten. She swiped at them, determined not to give in to her emotions. She looked about and was glad the pavement was empty of other people. Corrinne moved closer placing her hand over Hally's. Clia stepped to her other side and completed the circle. Hally, keeping her voice low said.

"First please promise me you won't think I'm ready for the funny farm."

Clia grinned, opened her mouth and was about to retort with one of her normal witty responses. However, the look on Hally's face was so serious she closed it and simply nodded, Corrinne doing the same.

"Of course Hals."

Corrinne said in a soft voice.

Hally quickly explained everything, from the dream and after. When she was finished she was relieved to see her friends believed her. She had been so afraid they would be sceptical, question her own belief in the events.

"Hally this explains so much."

Clia said. Hally smiled.

"You really think so?"

Clia nodded and linked her arm through Hally's.

"Look girls, I wouldn't normally suggest this but how about we bunk off college today? My house will be empty. We can go there and chill out, talk about all of this and make a plan."

Hally nodded in agreement before Clia even finished speaking, but Corrinne frowned uncertainly.

"I um…don't know. We shouldn't really." She paused taking in Hally's worried eyes. "Oh go on then. I'm in."

Corrinne relented.

"I have to text Wes. He'll wonder where I am if I don't turn up. And I think we should let out parents know. I mean, just in case of an emergency."

Hally said her sensibility kicking in. None of the girls had ever skived school, it wasn't in their natures and being in college hadn't changed them.

"Ok miss goody good girl."

Clia agreed with a giggle.

"We're just no good at being bad."

She added as they turned back towards her house.

Once inside Clia's home, Hally called her mum, the other two doing the same.

"Can you please call college for me and tell them I'm not well. I know that's not true and I will explain later what's going on." She paused as her mum questioned her. "I am ok mum honestly. No, everything's fine between me and Wes. I just need a bit of time with Corrinne and Clia. I'll be home either normal time or before. I love you mummy."

Corrinne and Clia had similar conversations with their mums, all three hanging up within seconds of each other. Hally quickly texted Wes and waited for his expected reply.

Do you need me to come over? xxxx
Hally texted back reassuring him too that she was fine.

Well if you're sure. Bob's asked me to work tonight, but only 'til eight. Is that ok? I haven't said yes yet, so if you don't want me to I won't. Love you so much xxxx.

Tell him yes, I don't mind, really I don't. But will you come over after please? Wes I love you very much xxxx
His reply came quickly.

Straight after, I promise. Hally I love you very much too. xxxx

With mugs of coffee and chocolate biscuits the three girls curled up in Clia's lounge. It was warm and cosy. The sky outside had darkened threatening rain. Hally just knew it would be cold rain and shivered.

"You ok?"
Clia asked. Hally nodded sipping her drink.

"It's going to rain and it's getting colder out."
Clia laughed and nudged Hally with her elbow. Coffee rippled from side to side in Hally's mug and just missed slopping over the edge. Hally giggled, the other two joining in. It felt so normal to her, the three of them snuggled drinking hot drinks and being silly.

The moment passed and Hally knew it was time to discuss the night before. She took a deep breath and began.

"So I'm not going bananas. That means Dana really has come back and is trying to get through to me. Right?" She said to Corrinne and Clia, a beseeching expression on her face when she finished telling them.

"Well I know you're nuts Mackeller but you're so not flipping out." Clia stated matter-of-factly. Corrinne cracked up and Hally couldn't help but join in.

"Woo I feel so much better." Hally laughed.

"Ok we've established Dana's ghost has come to you. She doesn't want to scare you it seems or haunt you. So what do you think she does want or need?" Corrinne said, more seriously. Hally shrugged in frustration.

"I have no idea. Like you said, I don't think she wants to harm me. She was different but the same. That makes no sense. What I mean is she looked exactly like she did back in school. But her face it was...um...calm, peaceful and friendly, not at all like it used to be when she delighted in bullying me. And, oh oh crikey, I've only just remembered, before, when I thought my dream person was me asking myself for help, it was really Dana."

Both Corrinne and Clia gasped. Pieces were finally beginning to fall into place, make sense. All of the confusion over the past week was replaced with realisation. Dana had actually come back. Her ghost was and had been trying to connect with Hally, and she didn't want to harm her in anyway. She just needed help. Hally decided then and there that no matter what people thought about her sanity, she was going to do all she could to help the dead girl, where she hadn't been able to when Dana was alive.

Hally relaxed back against the cushions on the sofa. Until then she hadn't realised how tense she had been, had been since the first dream had woken her. She lifted her mug and swallowed cool coffee.

"Yuck it's gone cold."

She grumbled. Clia unfolded her legs from beneath her and held out her hand for Hally's cup.

"Give it here. I'll go and make some fresh."

Corrinne passed her mug too and Clia trotted off to the kitchen. Corrinne sighed and ran her fingers through her hair.

"So, any idea what Dana needs help with?"

She asked. Hally shook her head.

"Not the foggiest."

Clia came back into the room. She had two mugs balanced in one hand, holding them precariously by the handles, and the third in her other hand. She speeded up as she approached.

"Ouch ouch. Hot hot."

She squealed. Hally jumped up and took the two mugs, Clia sighing dramatically.

"Any conclusions?"

She asked plonking into an armchair and drawing her feet under her. Corrinne shook her head.

"Nah just trying to guess exactly what Dana means by help."

Clia leaned back and shrugged.

"God that girl. She couldn't leave you alone when she was alive and now even dead she's causing you grief."

Hally smiled at her friend. She knew Clia wasn't as harsh as she sounded. Dana's bullying had affected her friends too. So many times when Hally had been in tears or hurt, they had been there for her, stood by her side. They could have left her, joined the cool kids, Dana's gang, but they never once betrayed her. So Clia's words, Hally knew, were her way of defending her just as she had done back in school.

"I know Clia. In some ways I wonder if she has come back just to get at me some more. But then when I think about how she looked, how she acted, I really do think there's something important that she needs my help with. Hopefully I'll find out soon."

For a while the girls sat quietly sipping their fresh drinks contemplating the situation. Hally especially wondered what it was Dana needed, and more so how she Hally would accomplish that.

"Ok so I suppose I'd better hope she comes to me later, tonight maybe."

Hally said startling her two friends. For the second time that day coffee very nearly made it outside the mugs.

"Don't do that Mackeller."

Corrinne grumbled holding her cup out in front of her in case the drink did drip over the side. Hally giggled. This was normal, this was safe. Because no matter how much she told herself Dana wasn't going to harm her, the back of her mind screamed a warning, beware.

Hally arrived home before her little brother came in from school. She had decided that her mother deserved some sort of explanation, just not the true one. She could tell her mum anything usually, but this, Hally decided it was just too far-fetched. Voicing it to the girls had been hard, but being teenagers themselves she knew they would accept it, enjoy the mystery. Her mum would try and understand, would perhaps believe her but she wasn't ready to test it.

May was in the study when Hally walked in. As soon as she saw her daughter she turned away from the computer and took her hand. She led her to the kitchen and gently pushed her into a chair at the table.

"So?"

She didn't have to say anymore. Hally swallowed. She had prepared a little statement in readiness.

"Well I had a bit of a rough night and when I met up with the girls I was just so tired. Clia said she'd been up a bit too and Corrinne is finding some of her lessons a bit harder than she thought. So Clia suggested we bunk off and have a chill out day."

May frowned and opened her mouth to speak but Hally held up a hand.

"Don't say it. I know it's not the way to approach college. But mummy, I've never done it before and won't again. We, all of us just needed a bit of relaxation and time to get our heads together. And it worked."

She said the last bit on a big smile and a chirpiness in her voice. She didn't feel too guilty in the lie, especially as Corrinne had actually complained a tiny bit about one of her lessons, not as much as Hally had made out, but enough to give some credence to the fib she had told.

May pressed her lips together and drew her brows close. She studied her daughter's wide open eyes and knew she couldn't reprimand her. She didn't entirely believe Hally's explanation, but she also knew her daughter well enough to know she wouldn't do anything that would cause trouble. Whatever was going on she felt confident Hally and her two friends would get through it without it being detrimental to their studies.

"Ok for now I accept what you say. But if you're finding college too much then tell dad and me now. Like we said before, if you need to take time out, college can wait. We don't want you getting so down and tired that it affects your health."

She said flicking the switch on the kettle. Feeling even more guilty Hally replied.

"I'm fine mum honestly. Today was exactly what we all needed."

Her mum nodded and held up the coffee and tea canisters.

"Ooh tea please. I'm totally coffeed out."

After tea and innocent chat, mum headed out to meet Nathan from school. Hally suddenly felt nervous being left alone, but shoved her fear to the back of her mind. She sat with the television on, not watching, glancing at the lounge door to the hallway. Biting her lip, she stood up twice taking a step towards the door. Twice she chickened out and sat back down.

The news came on and Hally finally plucked up the courage to get up and go upstairs to her room. On the one hand she hoped Dana would appear, on the other she wished she wouldn't.

The door to her room was ajar. Hally placed her palm flat on the wood and took a deep breath pushing it wide open. She let out the breath she was holding as she found the room empty and exactly as it should be. Mum had been in sometime during the day and changed her bedding. The blinds were up and the window slightly open. The day had brightened, sunshine gleaming through the glass, spilling warmth and light across the walls and furniture.

Hally took a step inside and paused. Nothing happened. She gave herself a mental shake and resolutely walked over to her desk. Her little book of poems, as she now referred to it, was where she had left it that morning. For a moment she wondered if her mum had looked inside it. She shrugged. If she had she never mentioned it but she really didn't think she had.

When she was younger like a lot of teen girls she had kept a diary and mum had never peeked at that. She felt her cheeks warm as she remembered some of the things she had written. As puberty kicked in she had written language she would never have dreamed of using verbally. It hadn't taken her long to come out of that stage, and feeling so embarrassed she had destroyed the diary. Six months' worth of ranting and venting emotion was shredded in her parents' mini shredder. She hadn't ever regretted doing it.

Hally lifted her book of poems and opened it to the back page. She read what she had hastily scrawled that very morning. It sounded frantic in her mind but she wouldn't scrub it out. As crazy as she had felt composing it, she still felt it was important. A just in case poem. For a moment she drew her finger across the words then flipped the pages to the beginning. She plonked onto a beanbag, the sun warm on her face, and began writing more poems for Wes.

****

I think something is not right. With Hally that is. It's early, well for Hally to be home it's early, I think. I mean I can't be certain that she shouldn't be home this time of the day. But since she's at college now I sort of feel that's where she should be. But no, here she is nestled on her beanbag writing in her little book.

But hey what do I know? After all, it wasn't so long ago that everything was cloudy and foggy when I couldn't tell night from day. So although now I can see clearly, and the clock tells me it's early in the afternoon, I can't be sure that Hally shouldn't be home.

Hmm even to my mind that all sounded a bit garbled. So backtrack. If I'm right Hally should be in college this time of the day. But here she is comfy on her beanbag writing in that little book of hers. She doesn't look sick or anything but I sort of get the feeling that something is amiss. I like that word. Say it again Dana, amiss. It sounds classy, ha ha me classy? Well maybe being dead does that, makes you less um, common I don't know. Because let's face it, popular you were, pretty most definitely but classy not flipping likely.

I think, if I tried, I could appear, let her see me. But it doesn't feel right just now. Before, I could only watch her unseen. Now with concentration I know I can be seen, by Hally anyway. But I don't think it's fair to her to keep popping up all of the time. I have to let her have her normal life sometimes.

****

Hally was so absorbed in her work she didn't realise there were sounds on the landing until Nathan's voice rang out.

"Ha...lly I'm ho...ome!"

Followed by a thud on her door. Hally grinned and pulled herself up. She dropped the book and pen on her desk and dived for the door. She yanked it open.

"Boo!"

Her little brother yelled, his face centimetres from the door. Hally jumped and made a grab for him. He was too quick, ducking away from her grasp.

"You little demon. I'm gonna catch you and tickle you 'till you're wiggling like a fish."

Hally squealed chasing after him.

She caught up with him at his bedroom door. Nathan wriggled but couldn't escape. Hally poked him in the sides but only a little bit. Her brother was very ticklish and just the tiniest dig would send him into fits of giggles.

"Get off me. Hally no...!"

Nathan hollered as he twisted and sprang free from her grasp. Hally followed in hot pursuit, laughing as they both bounded down the stairs.

"I'm coming titch. Fingers a ready for tickling."

Hally screeched after him.

****

Ok maybe I've got it completely wrong and Hally's perfectly fine. Maybe my sense of time is still off, or I just have no idea when Hally should and shouldn't be in college. Because she's just jumped up full of beans when her little brother called out he's home. And when she opened the door she happily went chasing after him. Surely if something was upsetting her, or she was unwell, she wouldn't have done that. So I suppose I have to try even harder to get a sense of the when and where.

Oh oh my God. I don't believe it. I'm at Hally's bedroom door and I can see the landing. This is amazing. Before I could hear the sounds outside her room, but couldn't see even when the door was open. It was like looking into thick fog. Now I can see the hall and the other doors and the top of the stairs. Beyond is still just mist. Hally and Nathan have disappeared but I'm not scared anymore. I thought that if I concentrate I could go further than Hally's room, and now I do believe that can and will happen.

A strange thing though. Why is it that when I look out of Hally's bedroom window I can see the garden clearly? Yet outside her door I can only just now see the landing but no further. Hmm I'm going to try a little experiment if I can. It will mean someone opening the window. I'll have to be vigilant, here I go again remembering big words I didn't even know I had learnt, yes vigilant. I will wait and as soon as Hally or someone opens the window wide enough for me to put my head out, I will see what happens. If I'm right in my thinking I won't see anything except the mist. I reckon I can see the garden through the glass, but I bet it will disappear if I try to go out or put any part of me out.

Well now that I have that plan what next? Effort is what's next. Everything that happens from now on needs one hundred percent effort. Hah that's what the teachers used to say. Mr Haines especially. He would bellow, 'Dana you have to give it one hundred percent all of the time!'. Of course I would snigger and make rude signs behind his back. But he was right. He'd be proud of my determination now. Pity he will never know about it.

Oh, I've just noticed Hally's little book is on the desk and it's open. Ah now I can have a look at what she was writing. Hmm it looks like a poem. She's headed it Wesley her boyfriend. The words, her words, are so beautiful and full of love. I feel like crying. My chest is tight and I'm shaky, I'm, what is the word? oh yes, emotional.

****

May watched Hally over dinner but kept quiet. Colin suspected something but decided to wait until he and his wife had time alone to ask. He got his chance when Wes arrived after his shift at the café, and he and Hally disappeared to her room.

"Ok give."

Colin said gently to May. She took a deep breath and relayed the earlier events. Colin frowned as he pulled his wife into a cuddle.

"Hmm she's been on and off since last weekend. Let's see how things go from tomorrow. If it looks like she's struggling, we'll both sit down with her and have a chat."

May nodded in agreement, snuggling into the comfort of her husband's strong arms.

Hally on the other hand was feeling just fine. She and Wes were happily sitting in her room talking about their day. Where she had been completely open with Corrinne and Clia about Dana, she only told Wes as much as she'd said to her mum. It wasn't that she didn't trust him to believe her, she knew he would, she just didn't want to voice it aloud just in case. The girls, well they had known her all their lives and would accept anything she told them, the same as she would for them. She felt a tinge of guilt for keeping it from him, but rather that than have him think she was off her rocker.

Wes leaned back against the beanbag he was settled in and folded his hands behind his head.

"Guess who came into the Hotspot tonight?"

"Uh…Wesley, half the teenagers in town."
Hally replied a hint of sarcasm in her voice. Wes pounced.

"Ooh sarcy sarcy Miss Hally."
He ribbed her as he pulled her onto his lap. Hally giggled giving him a poke in the chest.

"Go on then who?"
She asked. Wes planted little kisses on her face mumbling in between.

"Not telling you now."
Hally let him get away with that for a few minutes. She was enjoying his kisses and attention, turning her head this way and that for more.

"Who?"
She said again as his lips met hers. Wes grinned and gave her a full kiss which she lapped up. Then satisfaction gleaming in his eyes he pulled back.

"The ditsy girl who waits outside my class."
Hally felt her face heat up, two red spots appearing on her cheeks.

"What did she want?"
She said enunciating each word, her tone just short of anger. Wes grinned again and wrapped his arms around her.

"Me."
Hally's mouth dropped open in a perfect O.

"What, she actually said that?"
Hally exclaimed once the shock passed. Wes nodded.

"She came right up to the counter and said, 'Hi Wes. I really fancy you. Will you go out with me?'"
Hally was fuming.

"The cheeky cow. I told her straight to keep her eyes off you, that you're my boyfriend. How dare she!"
Wes rubbed his hands up and down her arms.

"Babe hey it's ok. That's exactly what I told her."
Wes soothed. Hally relaxed into him.

"Tell me what you said, word for word."

Wes stroked her hair and kissed the top of her head.

"Well at first I laughed. I mean, it was so bizarre. Then she looked at me all seriously and I knew she actually meant it. So I said um, don't think so. I have a long term girlfriend and I love her very much. You've seen me with her so why would you ask?"

Hally felt cheered.

"What did she say then?"

"She said it didn't matter, she wouldn't mind. I got a bit angry then. So I told her to get lost, I didn't cheat and would never want to cheat on you. Then she said you wouldn't have to find out. That's when I asked Bob to get rid of her. He chucked her out, told her to stop bothering a member of his staff. She wasn't too pleased."

Hally grinned. She liked Bob, Wes' boss. He had always treated Wes more like a son than an employee, giving him hours that fit with both his studies and Ellie.

"Good old Bob. But looks like I'll be having more words with her again. I obviously didn't make myself clear enough the last time."

"That's fine by me babe. She's weird and I honestly did think she was hanging around the class for someone else."

Hally smiled and covered his cheeks with her palms. She leaned in and gave him a long deep kiss. He held her tight and she knew he loved her and her alone. She had nothing to be worried about. But that wouldn't stop her giving the girl a piece of her mind, making it crystal clear that Wes was her boyfriend and would always be.

Snuggled up on Wes' lap her eyes closed, Hally let her thoughts drift to what she was going to say to the girl at college next day. Maybe because she had missed classes today the girl had taken it to mean she could poach her boyfriend. Hally would rectify any such thoughts. Various conversations materialised in Hally's mind, all concluding with the girl running away with her tail between her legs, and Hally left feeling elated.

Hally could still feel Wes' loving warm hands wrapped around her. She could feel his chest rising and falling as he breathed deeply, could hear the beat of his heart through his T-shirt. It was relaxing, calming. She opened her eyes slightly. They had left the blinds open and just the lamp lit the room. Shadows from waving branches outside flickered across the walls. Everything was normal.

Hally blinked. As she did a tiny puff of silvery light shimmered and disappeared near her desk. She opened her eyes wide. At first there was nothing. Then the light appeared again and began to grow. Hally didn't move, didn't speak. Slowly the glow formed into the ghost Dana. She hovered close to Hally's desk. She looked over at the two of them and waved, a smile across her ghostly lips. Hally moved her head a fraction looking up at Wes. His head was leaning on hers, his eyes closed.

"Wes."

Hally whispered.

"Hmm."

He replied his eyes still closed. Hally nudged him. He looked down at her.

"What's up?"

He murmured. Hally glanced towards her desk. Dana was still there floating just off the ground. Wes stretched.

"Whoa I'm knackered. I think I dozed off for a bit. Do you mind if I head off home?"

"No course not. That's what I nudged you for."

Hally whispered, glad he had provided the excuse because it was obvious he couldn't see the apparition in front of them.

Hally stood up and tugged Wes' hand. He arose yawning and stretching. Flicking off the lamp Hally led him to the door, looking over her shoulder before passing through. Dana, glowing and shimmering even more brightly in the now darkened room, stayed where she was smiling. Hally only hoped she would still be there when she got back from saying night night to Wes.

Even though she was in a hurry to get back to her room, Hally couldn't rush Wes out of the door. Not only would he wonder why, she didn't want to. His goodnight kisses were sweet and lingering. His cuddles and soft touch were perfect. He was perfect and nothing, not even a ghost was going to interrupt their usual departing routine.

Eventually Wes did pull away and said a final goodnight. Hally watched him stroll down the back garden path as usual, waved when he got to the gate and waited until it closed behind him. She desperately wanted to bolt for her bedroom but her parents would think something was wrong. So hoping Dana would still be there she sedately padded to the sitting room and said goodnight to her parents. She walked normally up the stairs but once on the landing dived for her bedroom.

Dana was exactly where she had left her. Hally shut the bedroom door and stood with her back against it, unsure whether she should be terrified, mystified or just crazy.

"Are you really here?"
She whispered. Dana nodded, a serene smile upon her lips. Hally let out a deep breath she hadn't realised she had taken. This was all so weird. Many times in the past, her, Corrinne and Clia had discussed ghosts and spirits. As young teenagers they had over dramatized the after-life, spooked it up on Halloween for effect, but ultimately hadn't really believed ghosts existed. Now Hally knew they did.

Dana's shimmering form watched Hally's expression. She didn't come any closer and Hally suspected she was concerned about scaring her. Hally felt nervous and wary but not afraid. She took a tentative step towards the apparition. Dana simply smiled, her long silvery hair sparkling like tiny crystals. Other braver steps and Hally could reach out and touch the ghost. Again Dana remained in the same place. Hally stretched out her arm reaching forward with her fingers. Dana slowly lifted her own ghostly arm and once again the two connected.

Hally hadn't known what to expect. The night before when the ghost had touched her it felt like a soft warm mist. Now Dana's fingers had substance. As Hally held the fingers and watched in awe, Dana slowly changed from transparent to diaphanous.

"Can you speak?"

Hally whispered so low it was barely a sound. If her parents heard her talking, they would assume she was on the phone to Wes or one of the girls. But she didn't want to risk one of them coming in to check. Dana seemed to take a breath. Her gossamer chest swelled slightly and she opened her mouth but nothing came out.

Dana's silvery brows drew together in what Hally guessed was frustration as she clamped her ghostly lips closed. Hally still held onto her hand, nodded and smiled in encouragement.

"Try again."

She murmured. Dana ran her tongue over her lips as though moistening them. Hally waited in anticipation. Again she nodded in encouragement and tweaked the delicate fingers.

"H... aa...ll...y."

Dana said, the sound of Hally's name a mere breath of wind. Hally grinned.

"You did it."

She said, her voice softly muted. Dana's form altered. It became completely transparent and for a moment Hally feared she would disappear altogether. Then it shifted, the edges becoming clear like a sketch. Hally blew out a breath of relief. It seemed it was quite an effort for Dana to make a sound, that her energy had to be focused. Hally hoped it wouldn't all be too much for her.

"Dana what do you want, can you tell me?"

Dana hung by the desk and glowed. Patiently Hally watched and waited as Dana seemed to settle, her form once again appearing less transparent. Her chest rose as on a breath and she opened her mouth again.

"Hally."

This time the word was clear. Dana grinned, her ghostly eyes shining with excitement. Hally grinned back.

"I'm here Dana."

She said. Dana nodded knowingly and spoke again.

"You...tried...before."

With every word uttered her form wobbled and faded, as though every ounce of her energy was expelled each time she spoke.

"Take your time Dana. I won't leave you."

Hally told her. Dana frowned and gave a quick shake of her head. The movement lit up the room, as tiny droplets of light scattered through the air, then re-formed as though pulled together by a magnetic force. The sight made Hally gasp in wonder.

Dana glistening and ethereal, bobbed just above the floor and Hally waited on bated breath.

"Please."

Dana uttered. Once again she dimmed, flickering like a candle in a breeze. Then her glow returned, pulsating outwards from where her heart should be.

"Help...me."

Hally knew this was the moment when she would finally discover exactly what Dana had come to her for. She didn't move, barely breathed, afraid Dana would blow away on her breath. Their hands still joined, Hally paused giving Dana time.

"I...was...murdered."

Dana spluttered and vanished.

With Dana's glow gone, Hally was plunged into darkness. She gasped in shock both from Dana's parting words and the suddenness of the lack of light. Her hand was still suspended in air, but no longer had anything to hold onto. For a minute she was rooted to the spot, unable to assimilate what Dana had just told her.

****

Oh my God. Finally, I spoke to her. I so thought she was going to be completely freaked out. But she wasn't. Yes, she sort of looked a bit nervous, but if it had been the other way 'round, I swear I would have peed my pants. Not Hally though. She seemed more curious than scared and concerned for me. Because it was damned hard I admit. Before when I was just there watching, it was easy. But talking, that took a lot of energy. I could feel myself disappearing when I first tried. It felt like um, like I'm made of air. So when I spoke all the air came out of me. Like when you let down a balloon. Then I had to sort of um, suck it all back in again, like taking a deep breath.

I could feel it filling me, stretching me and then I could talk again. But it was so exhausting. Now I'm drained, deflated and I don't think Hally can see me now. God I hope I can go back again. Hmm I can see the room, it's clear. So I haven't disappeared completely. There's no fogginess and ah there's Hally.

Oh figs, she looks um, like she's in shock. Crikey, I didn't mean to do that to her. Wait, ah she's moving, she's at the window. Maybe she just needs a bit of air. I mean I finally got to tell her the most important thing but it did come out a bit quickly. I had planned to sort of get 'round to it. But the strain of talking. It was so much like fainting. I so wanted to explain in detail. To tell her everything. But just one or two words took the energy right out of me. So in the end I had to just say it.

****

A noise small and indistinct jolted Hally from her frozen state. Just a little buzz from beside her bed, but enough to jar her into motion. She spun around, her eyes wide as she realised the noise was her phone. She grabbed it from her bag, Wes' usual message lighting up the screen. Hugging the phone to her chest she began to tremble, her heart pounding so loudly she could hear it. The room seemed empty of air. Quickly she fled to the window and yanked it open. Leaning out she took gulps of clear fresh air. Although it was chilly, Hally didn't mind, it was what she needed.

Feeling slightly calmer, Hally read Wes' message, his words soothing her. She tapped a goodnight reply, sent the message and held the phone until its light went out, plunging her once again into darkness. Thoughts swirled through her mind, questioning the reality of what she had just experienced.

For some time Hally stayed exactly there, her head out of the window breathing the cold night, filling her lungs, replenishing her senses. Here at the window, the breeze tugging her long hair, she could think about Dana's words. Had she really heard her correctly. Hally shivered, some from the cold but mostly from what she believed Dana had told her. She had been murdered, hadn't committed suicide at all.

Finally taking a very deep breath, Hally pulled her head back inside but left the window open. Her room still seemed stuffy, suffocating. She shivered. Glancing around she wondered if Dana would return and tell her more, but she was alone. She padded to her bed and began to undress. Once in her pyjamas and dressing gown she felt warmer and less exposed. She took her book of poems from her desk, and with a pen resting against her lip, slipped under her duvet. The warmth of the cover relaxed her, now she could think clearly. She turned to the back of the book and thought for a moment. Then she wrote another poem for Wes.

Holding onto the little book like a talisman, Hally leaned into her pillows and let her thoughts trail back to her contact with the Dana ghost. It really had happened, that she was sure of. She had another moment of terror, her mind telling her it couldn't be real, but she shoved that right out of the way. Dana had come back. Dana was a ghost. Dana had sought Hally to help her because Dana had been murdered.

Hally had too many questions and no answers. The main ones, why had it taken over a year? Who had killed Dana? And why her, Hally? Dana had bullied her for years. She had hurt her in many ways. The only conclusion to the last question she came to was that she had offered Dana help where it seemed no one else had.

Hally closed her eyes. It was getting late and she was tired. The questions churned around in her mind but no answers came. As sleep took her, the one thing she focused on was that she would help the girl, who when alive had gone out of her way to cause her grief.

★★★★

Poor poor Hally. She looks worn out too. Did I do that? Maybe when we touched I absorbed, ooh I like that word, her um, life force. Maybe a little of her spirit joined with mine and gave me the strength to speak. But will that harm her? I can't do that. So now I will let her sleep, leave her to recover.

Tomorrow I will let her do with what I told her in whatever way she chooses. If she believed me I think she will help. If she didn't, well I will have to try again. Not necessarily so she finds out who killed me, but to protect her. Because the more I think about it, the more I'm sure the man in the hoody at the station was him. And I'm also sure that she is in danger from him. Maybe this is my actual purpose. To stop him from hurting her, doing to her what he did to me. If only I could remember exactly who he is, describe him even. It's so darned frustrating.

Chapter 16

Everything about Hally's room was completely normal when she awoke. She still had her notebook with her, but the pen had fallen to the floor. The book had slipped from her fingers in sleep and was wedged under her pillow. She tugged it free and opened it to find she hadn't written anything in it in her sleep, as her dreams had suggested.

As she stretched, her thoughts suddenly collided and memories of the night before flooded in. At once she felt breathless. She pulled herself out of bed and made herself calm down. Nothing had happened to her in her sleep. In fact, she had slept deeply and peacefully. Her dreams had been happy ones. That's why she had wondered about the notebook. In one of her dreams she had written page after page of love notes and poems to Wes.

Dragging her fingers through her hair Hally turned slowly, taking in every inch of her room. It looked just as it should. Nothing was out of place and there was definitely no ghost hovering by her desk. Still, Hally knew it had all been real. That wasn't what was bothering her, making her hold her hand to her heart and check her breathing. No, her fear was what Dana had told her and what on earth she was going to do about it. What she could do about it.

Dressed and breakfasted, Hally successfully kept up a show of normality to her mum as she headed out of the door to college. She was anxious to meet the girls and tell them what had happened, get their advice. When she spotted them coming towards her it was more than just the usual joy of seeing her friends. It was relief that she had someone to talk to and tell about Dana's revelation.

"Hiya."

Clia beamed.

"Hey Hals."

Said Corrinne who then frowned after her initial greeting.

"Hally what's wrong?"

Clia looked from Corrinne to Hally, suddenly realising Corrinne was right. Hally didn't look her usual perky self.

"Did you tell Wes?"

Clia asked jumping to the wrong conclusion. Hally shook her head and put up her hands palms outward.

"Hey you two. One at a time. Wait…"

Hally said as both her friends opened their mouths to speak. Quickly they clamped them shut and let her continue.

"No I didn't tell Wes, didn't want to have to try and explain. Telling you two was hard enough. Wes would think I'm bonkers."

She linked her arms through her friends' and began walking in the direction of college talking along the way.

"She was there last night in my room."

Hally heard the girls gasp but ignored it.

"And…get this. Dana did not kill herself. She was murdered."

Hally felt herself pulled backwards as both Corrinne and Clia stopped still on the pavement. A man behind them tutted and sidestepped around them. They took no notice, their eyes rooted on Hally.

"What did you say?"

Corrinne asked her voice trembling slightly.

"Yeah Hally, did I actually hear you right, Dana was…murdered?"

Clia said the last word in a hushed tone. Hally took a deep breath.

"Yes you heard right. Look, keep on walking and I'll tell you what happened. I don't want to be late for college and that's something else I have to tell you."

The three kept up a steady pace as they crossed town to the Colingford College. All the way there Hally talked, telling them every detail of her time spent with Dana. The girls made occasional sounds and murmurs but refrained from asking any questions until she finished.

"So she didn't tell you who did it or why?"

Clia asked just as the gates came into view. Hally shook her head and then nudged Clia to be quiet as Wes came towards them.

"Morning break ok?"

She whispered as she greeted her boyfriend.

"Hi babe. I know I worked last night, but Bob's asked me to go in tonight, just to close up as Raj has to be somewhere. Do you mind?"

Hally wrapped her arms around his waist and looked up at him.

"Babe that's fine. Look, why don't you stay home before work and spend some time with Ellie?"

She looked at the girls.

"Are either of you seeing Gregg or Rhys tonight?"

Corrinne and Clia both shook their heads.

"Want to come to mine then?"

Eagerly they nodded confirmation.

"There, you get to see your little girl, bathe her and play and all that. And us three can have a girlie night. No doubt Corrinne will bug us into doing some college work first, but then we can chill out and talk about you guys."

Hally told Wes. Corrinne gave her an *I'm not like that* look, making her giggle and Wes gave her a kiss.

"Ok then if you're sure?"

Hally kissed him back murmuring reassurance. Then they all strolled onto the campus.

The grounds were busy as students milled about until classes began. The day was bright with warm autumn sunshine, so nobody wanted to be inside until they had to be.

"Oh by the way, what was it you wanted to tell us about not being late?"

Clia asked as they found a bench to sit on. Wes threw his arm over Hally's shoulder and gave her a knowing look.

"Oh just that I have to have words with a certain crazy lady, who thinks it's perfectly ok to hit on my boyfriend just because I'm not there for one day."

"Oh ouch."

Clia replied.

"And you don't mind her having a go?"

Corrinne asked Wes. He grinned and shook his head.

"Looking forward to it. The girl wouldn't take my no for an answer. She kept rabbiting on about how ok it was if I wanted to cheat on Hally. I say let Hally have a go. I'm betting the nutter will back off then."

"Aha look who's just come through the gates."

Hally said standing.

"Be just one minute."

She stated, holding up her forefinger. Then she swung her hair over her shoulder and marched towards the girl.

"I want a word with you."

Hally said firmly as she closed the gap between her and the girl. The girl looked up startled.

"Uh um, who are you?"

She stammered, trying for ignorance. It didn't work with Hally. She knew the girl knew who she was and wasn't letting her get away with it. Quickly she changed tactics.

"What's your name?"

She asked, pretending she didn't know already. Taken off guard the girl blurted her name out.

"Louise."

Hally smiled a non-too friendly smile.

"Well then Louise. I know you know who I am and I suspect why I'm here talking to you."

Hally began. Louise immediately started shaking her head quickly from side to side in denial. Hally didn't pause.

"Well to be absolutely clear, so there is no misunderstanding in future, I am Wes' girlfriend. His very long-term permanent girlfriend. He loves me and only me. He doesn't want to cheat on me with you or anyone else." Louise began to blush. "Ah I've hit the nail on the head. So you do understand, excellent. Now stay away from him or I will hurt you."

With that said, Hally turned her back on Louise and stomped across the campus to the waiting girls and Wes. She had a grin on her face which Louise could not see. Despite her threat to hurt the girl, she knew she never would. It wasn't in her nature. But she was very good at drama and could pull off an act first class.

"That looked intense."

Wes said when she reached him. Hally wrapped her arms around his neck and pulled his head down for a long lingering kiss.

"Ok, tart's gone."

Clia stated. But Hally kept the kiss going a bit longer. It hadn't all been for show.

"Come on Oscar nominee it's time to go to classes."

Corrinne said tugging on Hally's arm.

The girls decided at morning break to leave the discussion of Dana until they met up in the evening. Hally was relieved as she was nervous discussing it in public. Wes came into the cafeteria just after them and said he had to go to the library, leaving the girls by themselves.

"So did either of you really not have plans with the boyfriends tonight?"

Corrinne looked a little sheepish.

"You did didn't you. What did you tell him?"

Hally exclaimed. Clia gave Corrinne a little poke in her ribs making her squirm.

"Go on spill Bryant."

Corrinne twiddled her dark hair around her finger.

"I just said we were having a boy free night."

She mumbled. Hally leaned forward and gently took Corrinne's hand away from her hair.

"Oh Corrie. You are my sweet, lovely friend and I really appreciate you giving up your boyfriend time. But you're naughty. Gregg adores you and you him. You should be seeing him."

Corrinne grinned.

"It's all right. I'll make it up to him and he knows it."

Hally and Clia giggled.

"So what did Miss Flirt With Wes have to say?"

Clia asked. Hally grinned.

"She didn't say a word. Not like I gave her the chance to anyway. I made it very clear that she was tramping on my turf and I wasn't putting up with it."

Clia snickered.

"Tramping being the operative word."

"And I said I'd hurt her if she didn't lay off."

Both her friends burst out laughing. They knew Hally would never lay a finger on the girl.

"Well um, since you won't actually do that, let's hope she gets the picture."

Corrinne whispered. Hally sat up straight.

"She will. I was very convincing."

Clia glanced up at the large clock on the wall over the counter.

"Time to get going. Meet at lunch ok?"

Hally and Corrinne agreed and the three strolled out of the cafeteria to their respective classes.

The rest of the morning flew by and before Hally knew it she was making her way to lunch. As the day had remained warm and dry many students had taken to the grounds. Hally intended to do the same. She just wanted to get a sandwich from the cafeteria first. On her way to the counter she spotted Corrinne.

"Hi seen Clia?"

Corrinne looked over her shoulder and pointed. Clia was weaving her way through the tables towards them.

"Hiya. Got mine already."

She said holding up a plastic tub.

"Me too."

Said Corrinne.

"Goody good. You two go and find a nice sunny spot and I'll be out in a mo'."

Hally told them.

Hally paid for her sandwich, stuffing it and her purse back into her bag.

"Hello Hally."

She looked up, startled at the man in front of her.

"Uh hi Martin. How are you?"

Martin Cob held his arm out indicating a vacant table.

"Could I have a word with you please?"

His voice was soft and quiet, surprising Hally. She couldn't remember actually ever having a conversation with him, but she did remember his voice being loud and harsh. She shrugged and nodded leading the way to the table.

Martin waited until she was seated before sitting himself. He leaned his arms on the table, his palms held together as if in prayer. His face looked old and sad, much older than his actual years. He didn't appear like the Martin she knew and despised during her school years, and Hally wondered if his time in prison had caused this change. He didn't seem to be in a hurry to speak whereas Hally wanted to get outside with her friends. She cleared her throat.

"Uh what did you want Martin?"

"Can you tell me about Dana?"

The shock of his request must have shown on her face.

"I'm sorry. I didn't mean to upset you. You tried to help her once, so I heard. I just wondered if there was anything…"

He said sincerely, leaving his sentence unfinished.

Hally gave herself a mental shake. For a moment she had an awful suspicion that he knew about Dana's ghost. Then reality kicked in and she realised that was ridiculous. So she took a deep breath and spoke.

"Tell you what Martin?"

He leaned back in his seat and sighed. His eyes were full of despair and for a moment Hally thought he would cry. Then he brushed over them with his fingertips and took a deep breath, letting it out on a shudder.

"Anything. Anything you know that can help me understand why she did it. I know it was my fault, I pushed her too far, but to kill herself? Then to top it all I couldn't go to her funeral, say goodbye properly."

Hally pondered his words. He really did seem to think it was his actions that had caused Dana's death. She stared down at her hands for a while, trying to work out a way to help him without having to give anything away. A thought crossed her mind giving her a spike of fear. Maybe it was his fault. For all she knew Martin was the one who had murdered Dana. But she couldn't tell him she knew Dana had been murdered, that could be dangerous for her.

She didn't want to believe the man in front of her could be that sort of person. Even though he had done so many other bad things, murder was something else altogether. And he seemed genuinely miserable and confused about Dana's death. She wanted to think well of him, believe he had changed and relieve his anguish. But she couldn't take the chance.

"Um, I um...don't think it was just what happened at my party. She had stuff going on at home too."
She paused, unsure of how much he knew about Dana's life. He nodded, his eyes down, giving her confirmation that he did know about Dana's mother.

"You know, maybe she didn't actually kill herself."
Martin looked up, a deep frown across his brows and Hally feared she had said too much, that he had guessed she knew.

"What do you mean?"
He asked, his voice sounding more like the old Martin. Hally shuddered, glad she was in the college cafeteria surrounded by people.

"Uh just that perhaps it was accidental. You know, she hoped someone would find her and stop her, that she didn't mean to actually, you know, go through with it." She paused. "And I heard she had drunk a lot too."

Martin exhaled, his shoulders slumping as he unfolded his hands and let them lay lax on the table. The little burst of what Hally thought had been anger had gone, replaced with a bleakness in his eyes.

"I'm sorry Hally."
She frowned.

"What for?"

"Everything. For getting mad just now. For giving Dana the stuff to get your parents into trouble at your party last year. For like I said everything. Being the dickhead I was, causing hurt and upset all around. I have changed. I'm not that person now. I can't undo all the bad I've done but I can never do any of that stuff again. But none of that brings Dana back."
Despite her nervousness, Hally covered one of his very big hands with her own little one. He didn't move.

"You loved her."

She stated. Martin nodded, his eyes welling up. A tear escaped and trickled down his cheek. He made no move to wipe it away. Hally had no idea what to do, how to comfort him.

"There you are Hally. We've been waiting for you. You all right?"

Hally let out a sigh of relief as Clia came up behind her and spoke, Corrinne by her side. Martin dragged his hand away and turned his face so the girls couldn't see his misery.

Hally jumped up from her seat. She was anxious to get away from Martin. She couldn't help him, didn't know if she even wanted to.

"Hi um, yes I'm fine. Come on let's go and eat our lunch. I'm sorry Martin, I have to go. I hope things get better for you soon."

She said, stepping away from the table as fast as she could, Corrinne and Clia close at her heels.

Once outside she slowed down and took a deep breath.

"Phew. Thank you, both of you. I didn't know how to get away."

"What was going on Hals?"

Clia asked. Hally darted for an empty bench and plonked down. She grabbed her sandwich from her bag and yanked off the wrapper, taking a large bite. She chewed, swallowed then told the girls everything.

"Well Rhys did say Martin had made an effort to change his life."

Hally nodded and continued eating her lunch.

"I know. It's just at the moment I sort of feel sorry for him but don't, do you get me? I mean, why come and ask me about Dana right now when all this you know..." She lowered her voice to a whisper. "...spooky stuff is going on."

"Maybe just coincidence."

Clia said practically. Hally clamped her bottom lip between her teeth.

"Hmm I hope so. All I can say is I was very glad we were in a crowded room. I mean, I don't think he really had anything to do with Dana's murder, but well, who knows? I'm not taking any chances just in case. I'm definitely steering clear of Martin Cob in future."

Corrinne and Clia both nodded in agreement, both frowning in consternation as they all continued with their lunch. Hally sighed, then grinned as she spotted her favourite man Wes coming towards them, a big comforting smile on his face.

Well well well he thought as he strolled out of the college gates and along the pavement. He was very chirpy today. Not only had he been close to Hally, close enough to touch all of that glorious blonde hair, but the conversation had been very interesting. Informative and interesting.

He frowned, just a tiny bit as he reached his destination. So it appeared Hally was a little suspicious about Dana's death. That only amused him. After all she couldn't know, that was impossible. Only he knew. Yes, she was very intelligent, much more so than his usual choice of girls, but still, not even being smart could have given her any clues. She wasn't psychic. He held back a grin at that thought.

No, Hally was no doubt just being over dramatic. He knew she was good at that. The little display this morning with the girl over the boyfriend proved that. He had enjoyed it immensely. Maybe the boyfriend would find solace in the other girl once he had Hally.

Now he had to work on his plan of how to accomplish that. Annoyingly she was always with her friends, family or the boyfriend. Most people spent some time alone, so statistically there had to be a moment when Hally would too. That's all it would take, a moment. He could be so stealthy when he chose. No one would see, no one would know. It would be quick and furtive. She would most likely fight and wasn't that an exciting thought. But still no one would see.

As he got his things ready, he created a mental map of all the places he knew Hally went to. One way or another one of them would provide him with an opportunity. He let out a breath of anticipation. Very soon she would be his to do with what he liked.

Chapter 17

Home was cosy and comfortable, Hally thought as she sat at the dining table with her family. The early evening had cooled but it was still dry. A perfect autumn night. She tucked into her dinner, grinning at Nathan's attempt to avoid eating his broccoli.

"Won't work."

Mum said, even though no one would have guessed she was even watching her son. Hally giggled as Nathan let out a very big, very dramatic sigh.

"But I don't liiiike broc'li!"

He wailed. Mum ignored the tone.

"Yes you do. You just pretend you don't."

Mum said. Nathan picked up his fork and stabbed a spear of the vegetable. He held it up like a lolly-pop.

"Hally's not eating hers."

He tried. Hally huffed, stuck her fork into a large spear on her plate and put the whole thing in her mouth.

"Yes she is."

Mum said her tone light but firm. Nathan dropped his shoulders in resignation and nibbled around the edge of the broccoli.

"Good boy."

Mum said continuing with her own meal. Hally had to bite back a laugh. It was a routine Nathan practised with any meal that contained broccoli, parsnip or swede. Mum always won.

After dinner Hally helped her mum clear away. As they did they chatted over their day, Hally not imparting anything to do with Dana. Once finished Hally trotted off to her room to do some college work before the girls arrived. She stepped through her bedroom door, hoping Dana would be there. But the room was empty.

Deep in concentration Hally didn't notice the time go by, until her door opened and in strolled Corrinne and Clia. She dumped her folder on her desk and smiled. The girls greeted her back. Corrinne dropped her big bag on the floor by a beanbag and Hally laughed as it went clunk. She raised her brows. Corrinne shrugged.

"Funny time of the year, funny weather."

Said Corrinne. Hally didn't have to ask. She knew her friend so well. The bag was sure to contain a whole fresh outfit, umbrella and boots as well as anything else Corrinne might need.

Once the three were settled, and passed information back and forth about their boyfriends and families, a little silence ensued. They were all waiting in anticipation for one of them to bring up the subject they were eager to discuss, Dana. Finally, Clia broke the silence.

"Have you seen her today?"

Hally shook her head. Corrinne slowly looked around the whole room.

"Wonder if she's with us now listening?"

Hally shrugged. She had no idea if Dana could appear at will. No idea if she could remain invisible and watch and listen. It unnerved her a little. How many times had Dana been present when she and Wes had been loving?

She gave herself a little mental shake. What of it? It wasn't like Dana could go and spill all her secrets to anyone.

"So did she tell you who did it?"
Clia asked as if carrying on the conversation from the morning. Again Hally shook her head.

"I don't think she had enough energy to say more at the time. Just what she did tell me was a strain. I could tell. She sort of went completely see through after speaking then came back after a little while."

"Oh. Then it's going to be ever so hard for her to tell you everything."
Corrinne said sympathetically. Hally nodded.

"Oh I really hope she comes when you two are here even if you can't see her."

"Now that would be very cool."
Clia stated excitedly, rolling off her beanbag onto the floor.

"I wonder if there's anything we can do to you know, invoke her?"
Corrinne said hushed and serious.

"What you mean like a...a séance?"
Hally replied nervously. Then they both jumped as they heard a moaning sound from Clia. She was sitting on the floor crossed legged, her hands held up in front of her, her eyes closed.

"Dana, Dana are you here? Come to us, come to us. It is time."
She muttered in a deep monotone voice. Hally grabbed Corrinne's hand afraid for their friend. Then Clia opened one eye and winked at them. Hally and Corrinne fell off their beanbags in fits of giggles.

"You idiot."
Hally hissed still laughing.

Clia unfolded her legs and kneeled up. She had a wide smirk across her face.

"Oh you should have seen your faces."

"How do you know? You had your eyes shut."

Corrinne blurted out. She was still feeling the effects of Clia's little act, and though she was smiling her expression indicated she was peeved.

"They weren't completely closed. Come on I got you. Admit it Bryant."
Clia said making a grab for Corrinne. Corrinne ducked out of the way and Clia went flying. Hally burst out laughing at her friends' antics.

"Hey you two. Keep banging about like that and mum will wonder what we're up to."
She said it lightly. They all knew May wouldn't really intrude. She had seen the girls through many years of play.

Corrinne grabbed a handful of Clia's hair playfully and gave it a gentle tug. Clia whipped around and began wiggling her fingers near Corrinne's tummy.

"No no…that's cheating."
Corrinne squeaked keeping her voice as low as possible.

"Let go of the locks and I won't tickle torture you."
Clia replied.

"Uh girls."
Hally said attempting to interrupt their shenanigans. Neither girl responded.

"Corrinne, Clia."
Hally voiced more loudly. This time they heard her, turning towards her.

Hally had her arm outstretched, her forefinger pointing towards her desk.

"She's here."
She whispered. Corrinne and Clia scrambled up from the floor and hurriedly seated themselves on beanbags.

"Where Hals? I can't see her."
Clia said an urgent inflection in her voice.

"Neither can I."
Murmured Corrinne. Hally flicked her hand slightly.

"By the desk. Just like last night."
"What's she doing?"

Corrinne and Clia said together. Hally tilted her head to one side and smiled.

"She's watching us and she's smiling."

"Talk to her Hally."

Hally stood up and slowly walked towards Dana. She wasn't glowing as brightly, and Hally suspected it was because the main ceiling light was on in the room.

"Turn off the light."

Hally whispered back over her shoulder. Clia got to it first. As the room darkened, Dana's inner glow pulsated, growing and expanding. Hally sighed. She could see her clearly now.

"Can you see Corrinne and Clia?"

Hally asked her. Dana nodded. Hally thought she was refraining from speech as it expelled so much of her energy.

"Can you hear everything, not just me?"

Again Dana nodded. Hally reached out her hand as did Dana, Hally enclosing the ghostly fingers within her own.

"Hally."

She whispered.

"She said my name."

Hally told the girls. They both sat completely still.

"Ask her who killed her."

Clia said, a little bluntly Hally thought.

Dana turned her head, her shimmering hair, swirling like mist. She looked right at Clia and Hally realised she only had to relay Dana's words to her friends.

"I...don't..."

Dana began, her words no louder than a breath of wind. Hally watched her dim as she struggled to speak. She squeezed her fingers closed, covering the ghostly ones that were Dana's. As she did she noticed Dana becoming clearer again. An idea formed in her head, quickly materialising.

Hally brought her other hand around and cupped Dana's hand in both of hers. Dana glowed even more brightly.

"Say something Dana. Try."

"Hally."

Just one word but it was clear and had volume. Hally grinned. Corrinne and Clia looked at her questioningly.

"What's happening Hally?"

Clia asked. Hally indicated with her head for them to come to her side.

"I have an idea. Don't know if it will work. Clia take my hands in one of yours, you too Corrinne. Then stretch your other arm right out towards each other."

Hally watched them do as she asked and Dana did too.

"That's it. Make a circle. Hold hands. Dana's in the middle."

As Corrinne and Clia's hands joined, Hally's smile widened. Her idea seemed to be working for Dana was now glowing like a lighthouse beacon.

"What are we doing Hally?"

Corrinne asked. Hally gave a little nod to where Dana floated within the circle the girls had made.

"She's really bright now. I think our energy, our life is giving her strength. I think she might be able to talk more now. Can you Dana?"

Dana smiled her beautiful ethereal smile at Hally. Her chest rose as though taking a breath and her mouth opened.

"Hally. It's better. I can talk."

Hally passed on her words to the girls.

"There's so much to tell you. But the one thing you want to know I can't tell you. I can't remember. He, I remember the sound of his voice, his touch, but not who he is or what he looks like. What I do know is, he is dangerous. I so want him punished for what he did to me but I don't want you to get hurt by finding him. It's enough that you know I was murdered. Don't go looking for him please, it's too dangerous."

She paused giving Hally a beseeching look. Hally frowned.

"What? What's she saying Hally?"

Clia whispered. Hally told her two friends what Dana had just told her.

"But I don't think I can do what she's asked. I mean it's not right that the man who did this should walk free."

"I agree Hally, but how can we find out who he is if Dana can't remember him to tell us?"

Corrinne added. Hally sighed in frustration.

"I need a wee."

Said Corrinne making Hally smile. She looked at Dana.

"We're going to have to break the circle, just for a little while."

Dana nodded and slipped her silvery fingers from Hally's, drifting away a tiny bit.

Corrinne darted out of the room throwing back over her shoulder.

"One minute."

Clia and Hally plonked down on the beanbags, Hally running her fingers through her hair.

"Is she still with us?"

Clia asked. Hally nodded. Dana, glowing like silver mist hung near the desk. Hally could see she was watching and listening to them. She had a tiny frown across her brows, and Hally suspected it was because she Hally had decided not to heed her warning.

"It's all right Dana."

Hally said and Clia frowned. Hally puffed out a breath. It wasn't easy being the only one who could see and talk to the ghost.

"I think she's worried because I said we can't just ignore what's happened."

Dana nodded in agreement. Just then Corrinne came back into the bedroom.

"That's better. Now we can carry on."
She announced sauntering over to the desk and holding her arms out.

The girls re-formed their circle and once again Dana's glow increased.

"I have questions too."
She told Hally who repeated her words for Corrinne and Clia.

"Ok ask me."
Hally replied.

"Why did everyone think I took my own life?"
Hally repeated Dana's question and heard Corrinne suck in a breath. This was going to be difficult, not just for her to tell, but for Dana to hear. Still the girl had the right to know. So Hally braced herself and told Dana what she knew about how she was found. She could see her words had an impact. Dana's face changed. Gone was the smile replaced with misery. Her eyes sparkled and Hally saw what appeared to be droplets of shimmering moisture sliding down her ghostly cheeks.

"Oh please don't cry Dana."
Hally whispered. Both Corrinne and Clia showed concern on their faces as they stared at the spot where they knew Dana hovered.

"I couldn't cry before. I didn't know I could. Inside I had the feeling but there were never any tears. It feels very strange now because my eyes don't feel wet."
Dana whispered back.

"But it's all right Hally. I understand now. He made it look like that. No one can change what's happened. It was terrifying though, choking, not being able to breathe."
As Hally passed her words on it hit her.

"Oh my God. I just realised. That dream I had, the really bad one, it felt like I couldn't breathe. And Dana was in it. So, oh this is quite scary, I think maybe I was feeling what happened to her."

Hally gasped to her friends. Both of them looked horrified. Clia tore her hand away from Hally's and covered her mouth, her eyes big and round.

"Clia it's ok, honestly. She didn't mean to harm me I'm sure. Please make the circle again."
Hally begged.

As Clia tentatively covered her hand again, Hally watched Dana. She was moving her head, looking from one to another, concern very evident on her glimmering face.

"I'm so sorry Hally. I didn't know that would happen. I had only just realised I was dead. It was a shock and somehow I passed my terror of it happening onto you."
Dana said.

"It really is ok Dana."
Hally replied.

"I don't even know how I came back, or why it was you I came to, especially as it was so long ago. All I can think of is that you were kind to me once."

"Dana slow down. We're here. Take your time and explain everything."
Hally coaxed.

She watched Dana gather her thoughts, take another of her ghostly breaths, and listened as she told her everything from the beginning. In between, Hally relayed it all to the girls. Sometimes there was a lull in Dana's words, where Hally was able to finally join the dots, where things made sense. Corrinne and Clia often making comments too. So by the time Dana had brought the three up to the point they were at, everything was clear.

"I need a break."
Hally said.

Dana understood and broke the contact. She didn't disappear, just drifted and dimmed a little. Hally dropped to a beanbag, the girls following. She leaned her head forward and covered her face with her hands. She felt impotent. If Dana couldn't give them any information to identify her murderer, how were they going to find him? They couldn't go to the police. What would they say? *Oh by the way, this girl, she's a ghost and she came back and told us she didn't kill herself, someone else did.* That would go down really well. They would probably be thrown out for wasting police time or locked up as insane.

"So what can we do Hals?"

Corrinne gently asked Hally. Hally shook her head.

"Hally, remember that bloke who freaked you out at the station.?"

Said Clia. Hally nodded, sat up and uncovered her face.

"I know Clia. Dana thinks it was him whoever he is. She thinks that he's after me. She doesn't know why but that maybe that's the reason she's come back now. Not just so she can have justice but to stop him hurting me. It's all very confusing and vague. I mean, I didn't see him properly, just a man on the platform. For all I know the poor guy is totally innocent. Oh I just don't know what to do."

Hally let out a huge breath. Her two friends sat opposite her neither knowing what to do or say.

After several minutes of sitting silently, each girl contemplating their next move, Hally straightened her back and took a deep breath.

"I've got an idea."

Corrinne and Clia both perked up and Hally watched Dana lift her head in interest.

"I'm going to see Mr Austin tomorrow. I finish college early. I'll go to the school and see if he's free."

"And?"

Clia asked making a circular motion with her hand.

"I'm not sure yet. I'll think of something. It's the only suggestion I've got."

"Well you can't go blurting out you've been chatting to Dana's ghost."

Clia said.

"Hmmm, now that's exactly what I was going to do."
Hally replied sarcastically.
"I only meant…"
Clia began hurt in her eyes.
"Clia I'm so sorry. I'm frustrated, tired and to be honest a bit scared. If Dana's right and some weirdo is stalking me, then maybe saying something to Mr Austin, in some way might help. You know, get it out into the open. He might be able to advise me on what to do. I won't go in guns blazing that a ghosty told me. I'll make something up."

Clia looked appeased and even Dana seemed to agree with Hally from her expression. She was also nodding her shimmering head again, hard enough for tiny crystals of light to appear in the air around her.

"That's settled then. Dana agrees that's the best way forward. So that's what I'll do."

They hadn't realised how late it had got until Hally looked at the clock. Corrinne and Clia both decided they should get off home, and Hally went downstairs with them to say goodnight. She waved at the door, yawned and for a moment shuddered, not because it was cold but because she wondered if the mystery man was out there. If he was real was he watching her? Closing the door, she gave herself a mental shake. She was safe. She never went out alone in the dark, and daytime she was always around people. She wouldn't worry about herself. Her main concern was to find a way to discover the identity of Dana's murderer, and get him locked up for life.

With that thought in mind, Hally went into the lounge and said goodnight to her parents. Feeling exhausted she plodded upstairs to her room. Dana was bobbing up and down lightly by the window. She turned to Hally.

"Sleeeep."

She whispered, her form dimming with that one simple word. Hally nodded and readied herself for bed. Her phone chirped and she smiled.

Goodnight my gorgeous. Sleep well. See you in the morning. Love you lots and lots. Xxxxxx

Hally tapped out a reply and hit send. She climbed into bed and snuggled down. Dana hung in the air by the window watching her. She lifted her hands and pressed them together as if in prayer. Then she tilted her head and laid her cheek on her hands. Hally understood as she closed her eyes, Dana wanted her to rest.

★★★★

That was just so amazing. The girls, they made a circle with me in the middle. They gave me um, life. I know that's completely crazy and impossible but that's what it felt like.

I know I can still only speak to Hally. But Corrinne and Clia know I'm here. They believe Hally, believe I'm real. Even though they can't see and hear me I can see and hear them. I can answer their questions, well I say the words to Hally and she tells them what I've said. But it's still really cool. Now I don't feel so lonely. This existence, ooh big word again, is, oh here comes another, bearable. Being dead is not so bad now I'm not alone.

It's weird though. Sometimes I sort of feel tired then I go somewhere. I don't know where. It's a bit like going to sleep. Then I come back. To Hally's room that is, like waking up. Maybe that's exactly what it is. Do ghosts sleep? No one here to answer that question. No heavenly gates with pretty white angels to say, come on in this is paradise. But hey, there isn't a fiery pit with horned demons either.

I wonder if there are other ghosts about somewhere. Will I get to meet them? I think there must be. I can't be the only one. Perhaps after I've finished whatever I have to do they'll appear. Or maybe I will go elsewhere and we'll all get together and have a big never ending party. Ha that would be a laugh.

So back to what I have to do. I guess one or both of two things. Find out who killed me and stop him from hurting Hally. The more I think about it the more I'm certain that's why I've come back.

What I'm afraid of though, and really don't like, is Hally trying to find him. I wish she wouldn't. It's putting her in danger I'm sure. But then Wes is nearly always with her, or the girls. She's not stupid like I was. She doesn't go out alone at night. Night is the time he likes best. Oh I remember that too. Yes, night, because it was more romantic, he used to say. So Hally will be safe. She's always careful. I think if she only digs about in the day she'll be fine.

Maybe something will trigger more memories of him, who he is. Then she won't have to go looking. I will be able to tell her. She could then find a way to report him. Make it believable to the police so they can lock him up and throw away the key. I'll be very happy then, maybe for the first time in my life, ha I should say death.

Chapter 18

The morning brought drizzle, dark clouds and a strong breeze. Hally moaned as she munched toast and sipped tea.

"Sunshine didn't last."

She grumbled. Mum smiled.

"English weather angel."

Hally nodded and finished her breakfast. Reluctantly she collected her things and with her umbrella up left for college.

Corrinne and Clia came into view at the juncture of their roads as Hally reached it. She was relieved to see her friends. The night before now seemed surreal, and the normality of the girls' smiles and greetings set her feet solidly back on terra firma.

"How are you?"

Corrinne asked.

"I'm fine. I slept really well, all through. No dreams, well not nasty ones anyway. Plenty of ones with Wes in them."

She waggled her brows making the girls laugh.

"And Dana?"

Clia questioned.

"She was there when I went to sleep. Not this morning though. Maybe she has to rest too."

She shrugged.

"She'll be back."

She stated with certainty.

"Still going to see Mr Austin?"

Asked Clia. Hally nodded. Clia raised her brows but didn't comment.

"It really is the only thing I can think of."

Hally said on a note of desperation.

"Do you want us to come with you?"

Corrinne offered. Hally shook her head. As much as she would love having them come along, they both had a full day at college.

"No I'll be fine. The last time going into the school was a bit unnerving, but this time I'm prepared, and I don't think Penny will start again. You two mustn't bunk off college again, you'll get into trouble."

Hally could see Clia wanted to argue but refused to allow her or Corrinne to take time away from their studies. So the subject was closed as they made their way to the campus.

Wes was waiting at the gates. Hally folded her umbrella and leapt into his arms, winding her hands around his neck, kissing him.

"Good morning to you too."

Wes said once Hally let him come up for breath. She clung to him. More than anything she wanted to tell him all about Dana. But a niggle still held her back. Although she was secure in her relationship with Wes, some of her old emotional doubts about herself and her own worthiness added a fragility to it. It made her worry that Wes would find it hard to believe her, think she was bonkers and break up with her.

"Babe are you ok?"

Wes asked, concern evident in his voice. Hally slid down from his hold planting her feet on the ground. She looked up at him and forced a big smile across her lips.

"Of course. Just missed you last night."

It worked. Wes leaned his head down to hers and nuzzled her hair.

"Hmm, best absent myself more often if that's the greeting I get after."

He murmured. Hally aimed a mock punch to his bicep.

"Not a chance Mr Robinson."

Wes wrapped his arm around her shoulder and held her close. It was still raining so none of them wanted to linger. Quickly they trotted through the main doors and wound their way through the throng of students to the cafeteria.

The morning flew by for Hally. Before she knew it lunch time had arrived. She threaded through the stream of students lining the corridors towards Wes' classroom. From a short distance away she saw a girl leaning on the wall next to the classroom door. It was Louise. Fuming, Hally sped up. Louise spotted her coming and straightened.

"I'm waiting…"

She got no further. Hally held up a finger and pointed.

"I thought you got my message."

Hally said enunciating each word. Just then the door opened and Wes' class spilled out. Wes saw both Hally and Louise and stopped, a frown creasing his brow.

"Hally are you ok?"

He asked quickly putting his arm about her waist. Hally looked at Louise.

"*She* doesn't seem to have taken any notice of what *she's* been told."

Louise stepped forward and held a hand out to Wes.

"You have to tell her Wes."

Hally looked up into his eyes. Wes looked down at her, perplexed.

"I don't know what she's talking about Hally, I swear."
He stated.

For a tiny moment Hally doubted him. For a moment she was back in the hospital, Wes sitting by Ellie's side as she fought off a serious virus. That was when he had finally come clean and told her Ellie was his daughter not his sister. Seconds ticked by and Hally remembered all of the trauma that followed. Then her heart began to settle back to its normal rhythm as she also remembered the tears they had both shed when Wes explained.

She remembered how he had clung to her, whilst telling how he didn't know the baby's mother had gone ahead with the pregnancy until after the baby was born. Then, how Ellie's mum had dumped her on Wes and gone to Australia. How at sixteen his parents had supported him and helped him raise his baby girl. How they had moved from Oxford to start a new life. How he had never lied to her or let her down since.

"That we've been seeing each other since term began."
Louise piped up intruding on Hally's thoughts. Wes gasped.

"Hally no. She's lying!"
Hally stared into the eyes of the girl in front of her, saw the smirk across her face and wanted to swipe it away with a hard slap. She knew that would likely get her expelled from college. So with great difficulty she resisted. She did raise her hand though and was delighted when Louise flinched.

"I'm not going to hit you bitch. You're lying or delusional, we all know it. If Wes was going to cheat on me, he would go for someone with far more brains than you have."
She glanced up at Wes then back to Louise.

"And he will report you to the governors since you can't refrain from stalking him."

She saw Wes nod in agreement and Louise blanch. Hally smiled. It seemed her words had finally had an impact.

"Hally's right Louise, I will report it if you don't stay away from me and stop waiting outside my classes. I've told you before and I'm telling you again, for the last time I hope, I love Hally. We are together and always will be. You do not factor into that anywhere, go away and stop trying to cause trouble. You will not break us up."
Wes said firmly. Louise stubbornly stayed where she was, so Wes took Hally's hand, turned his back on the girl and led Hally down the corridor, not once looking back.

"Let's hope that got through to her this time."
Wes murmured as he stopped, pulled Hally into his arms and kissed her. Hally nodded.

"But I'm still going to report it just in case. That way it's on record."

Arm in arm they continued down the hall to the cafeteria. Inside they spotted Corrinne waving frantically. The place was again crowded, rain lashing heavily against the windows.

"Managed to get a table."
She said as they reached her. Someone tapped Hally's shoulder and she spun around to see Clia grinning at her. They had all brought lunch from home as they knew the wet weather would mean a queue at the counter, so they settled down to eat.

Two bites into her sandwich and Hally was eagerly telling Corrinne and Clia about hers and Wes' run in with Louise. They agreed that Wes should go ahead and report the girl, Clia telling Hally she should have given her a slap anyway. Hally giggled, explaining that as much as she would have loved to, college was too important to risk it.

At the end of lunch Wes walked Hally to her next class. He was finished for the day.

"Are you coming to mine when you finish?"

Hally didn't want to lie to him. But she couldn't explain why she needed to see Mr Austin either.

"I've got some work to do first. Then I will."
She said, feeling a little better that she hadn't out and out lied. After all, what she had to do was work of sorts. Wes nodded, kissed her and left her at the door to her classroom.

"Ok babe. See you later. Come over when you're done. Love you."
He called out walking backwards, waving as he did. Hally waved back, secure in his love as she entered her classroom.

It was still pouring down as Hally left the campus and hurriedly crossed town to her old school. She had her umbrella up and held close to her head, barely able to see where she was going. Water bounced back up from the pavement soaking the bottom of her jeans.

Finally wishing she had gone straight to Wes' instead, she entered the gates of the school and sloshed across the tarmac to the reception. At the door she shook her umbrella and shoved the door open with her shoulder. Inside it was warm and dry. Mrs Durant sat behind the counter tapping on a keyboard. She looked up, surprise in her eyes when she saw Hally.

"Hello. Have you got another appointment?"
She asked with a frown as though she had missed knowing about it but not quite sure how. Hally shook her head.

"Sorry no. I came on the off chance that Mr Austin might be able to see me."
Mrs Durant looked at her screen.

"Well he's free from teaching." She held up a finger. "One moment. I'll call him."
She picked up a cordless phone, pushed a button and waited. Then she spoke. Hally heard Mrs Durant ask if she could send Hally over. She nodded and ended the call.

"He's free. He said to go right on over."
She said handing Hally a visitor's badge.

Hally thanked the woman and opened the door. The rain gushed in wetting the entrance welcome mat. Quickly Hally opened her umbrella and ran across the courtyard towards the English department.

Mr Austin was at his desk waiting for her. He greeted her with a comforting smile and held out his arm towards the chair in front of him.

"Sit down Hally. This is a surprise. A pleasant one though. More nightmares?"
Hally looked about her for somewhere to put her dripping umbrella.

"Oh don't worry about that. What's a little water on the carpet?"
He said with a grin. Hally relaxed. She hadn't even realised she'd been tense. Dropping the umbrella to the floor she shrugged out of her jacket and sat down.

"No, no nightmares. But I do want to talk to you about Dana again."
Mr Austin leaned his elbows on the desk his hands clasped together.

"Ok. Go ahead. I'll help if I can."

Now she was here, Hally didn't have a clue what she was going to say. She sat and thought for a moment whilst Mr Austin sat patiently watching and waiting.

"Remember Hally. Whatever you say to me is confidential."
Hally realised he had sensed her trepidation. She swallowed, trying to formulate a way to begin. Finally, she took a deep breath.

"I can't get over the feeling that I should have, could have, done something to help her."
Mr Austin sighed and picked up a pen. He tapped it lightly on the pad in front of him.

"That's understandable Hally. I feel that I should have seen it coming, done something too. We can all look back retrospectively, believe we should have known, but in truth Dana didn't want any of us to know."

Hally twiddled with her fingers. Then in a voice barely above a whisper she said.

"I think, um, Dana didn't kill herself. I um…think she was murdered."

Mr Austin dropped the pen with a clatter.

"Hally there was never any suspicion that it was anything other than suicide. Why would you think that?"

Hally chewed her lip, pondering how to make him understand.

"She um, said…"

She stopped, suddenly realising what she was saying, knowing exactly how it would sound to a trained psychologist. Mr Austin frowned.

"She said? Hally are you telling me you believe you have spoken to Dana?"

Hally lowered her eyes and quickly shook her head. She had to think, get herself out of this. If Mr Austin thought she was talking to dead girls he would make a formal report, her parents would have to be told. Taking a deep breath, she launched into what she hoped would be a plausible explanation.

"No a…a dream. I had a dream."

She stammered.

"A dream?"

Mr Austin looked sceptical. Hally nodded.

"Um, yes a dream. I had a dream. Dana was in it. She said, she um…didn't kill herself. Someone else did."

Mr Austin's expression changed to one of sympathy.

"Oh Hally. This is not your fault. It never was. Your subconscious is trying to replace your feelings of guilt by finding an alternative scenario."

Hally bit down on her lip. This was not going the way she wanted it to.

"Ok."

She said more to herself than to Mr Austin.

"Dana did not commit suicide. I know she didn't but I can't tell you how I know." She dropped her eyes and whispered under her breath. "And you wouldn't believe me anyway."

"Try me."

He said. Hally shook her head.

"No, the point is I know she didn't, but I don't know what to do about it. Can you help me?"

Mr Austin clasped his hands together again and bumped his knuckles off his lip. He was deep in thought, his eyes not really focusing on Hally. She waited impatiently. Finally, after what seemed minutes but was only seconds, he lowered his hands and leaned forward.

"Hally I'm going to pop out for just a short while. Please wait for me here. I won't be long."

He stood up and pushed his chair under the desk. He gave her a brief nod of assurance, walked around her and out of the door, closing it behind him. Hally turned in her chair following his path, suddenly very nervous. She almost expected to hear the click of a key turning, locking her in, but she shoved the thought away.

It took her less than a second to decide she had made a terrible mistake coming here. Visions of Mr Austin returning with a posse to cart her off to some psychiatric unit spurred her into action. She bent down, grabbed her umbrella and jacket, threw her bag over her shoulder and dived for the door. She yanked it open, saw with relief that the corridor was empty and fled down it, shoving her arms into her jacket, to the exit at the end.

Outside the rain was falling in sheets. Hally raised her umbrella and ran across the courtyard, barely breathing until she exited the school through the gates. She kept her head down, crossed the road and walked as fast as she could.

The rain was loud against her umbrella, thundering in her ears. Her mind was in turmoil as she plodded along the wet pavement. Her goal was home but she feared what awaited her. Would Mr Austin call her parents when he discovered she had fled from his office? What would he tell them? What was she going to tell them? All of these questions churned through her mind, blinding her to her surroundings. So she barely noticed the car that drew up alongside her, or the person getting out coming towards her.

He bubbled with excitement as he watched Hally flee from the school. Finally, she was alone. He wondered what she was doing there, what had got her into the state she was obviously in, but whatever it was gave him the advantage. Chance was such a fine thing. Here he was, on his way home, and here she was at the exact same time.

At long last, he could do what he had longed to for some time. He had to be a bit careful though, after all it was daytime, the middle of the afternoon. But the rain was so heavy most people were indoors. Here close to the school the pavements were empty. All except for Hally, and she was walking so fast, with her head tucked under her umbrella, she wouldn't notice anything.

He drove slowly. Carefully keeping her in sight, hanging back and waiting until she was away from the school, just in case. Besides, it was a joy to watch her. Not only because she was pretty, and the swing of her hips as she walked excited him, but because he could tell she was distressed. That gave him a real buzz. When she had sped from the school he had seen the anxiety in her eyes. He loved that. He could use that.

Now as she trekked through the pouring rain he gradually began to close the distance. It had to be soon. He knew there was a lane a little way up that she would turn into. He couldn't follow her in the car up there. He sucked in a breath, held it, and let it out slowly as he drew alongside her, easing the car into the curb.

With the engine left running, he stepped out and pulled the passenger door wide open. He had to be quick now. He hoped she would come willingly but he was ready if she didn't.

"Hally?"

He put on his best, gentlest voice of concern, containing the glee he felt when she stopped and looked at him. He could see recognition in her eyes, and thankfully no fear.

"You shouldn't be out in this weather. Let me give you a lift."

He smirked inside. The fatherly tone was just right. But she was backing away. He couldn't let her go. The street was empty. This was his chance. He had hoped not to have to use the drug, but it looked like she wasn't going to get in the car without a little help. He brought his hand out of his pocket, and laughed as her eyes widened in fear at what she saw held between his fingers.

Hally opened her eyes. She was confused. Beneath her she felt something soft, warm and dry. At first she thought she was at home, on her own bed, but as her focus cleared she knew she wasn't.

Fear gripped her heart and she nearly stopped breathing. Her memory returned in a flood. She had been walking home, had very nearly changed her mind and gone to Wes'. But she needed to see her parents first, explain what Mr Austin was going to tell them. She hadn't been looking where she was going. Hadn't even seen or heard the car until it stopped by the side of her. Then when the driver came and spoke to her she just didn't think, not straight away.

She knew him. Had known him for a very long time. Still, all of the warnings she had learnt from her parents about getting into cars stimulated her senses. Suddenly she had been aware of how very alone she was. How deserted the pavement was, the torrents of rain minimising visibility.

She remembered he had spoken to her, wanted to give her a lift. For a moment she had been tempted. Then, as she lifted her umbrella and really looked at him, saw the grey hoody that covered his head, recognised the eyes that had briefly glanced her way on the platform, she knew exactly who he was. She had backed away, was going to run, but he was fast. She'd had no time to scream as she felt the sting on her neck.

Slowly Hally sat up. She felt groggy. She had never been drunk but guessed it might feel something like this. She looked about her. The room she was in was decorated all in pink and white pretty printed patterned wallpaper, a little girl's room. She frowned. Maybe she had got it all wrong. She shook her head, her mind clearing as the seconds passed, and began to tremble. She hadn't got it wrong. She didn't know where she was but she knew who had taken her, Dana's murderer.

Hally felt panic well up deep inside her. She swallowed it back, tried to breathe normally and calm herself. She focused on what Dana had remembered about him, the things he liked to do. She hated thinking that he would do the same to her, but if it kept her alive, she wouldn't fight unless she saw a way out. Then she would with every breath in her body.

The door opened and he walked in. He carried a chic, satin black garment which he laid next to her.

"Hmm good, you're awake. Now I'm going to undress you and put this on. Don't fight me. It will be worse if you do."

Hally kept her eyes closed tight as he stripped her. She expected to feel his hands upon her but only felt the silkiness of the chemise as he dressed her. She heard him laugh.

"Not yet my lovely."

He whispered close to her ear making her flinch. She opened her eyes, hating her fear and hating him.

"Why?"

She asked and saw him frown. He chewed his lip then spoke.

"To be perfectly honest I don't know. You're too old for my usual liking. I tend to keep to girls in their early teens. But I've been watching you lately and well I just fancy you. That's all there is to it. Of course unlike the other girls who will never tell anyone what we do together, you would. So when I'm done I'll do to you what I did to Dana, and of course no one will be any the wiser."

He stood up and pushed his hands into his pockets. For a moment he stared at her then let out a little sigh and left the room.

Hally swallowed back the terror that gripped her. He was wrong. Corrinne and Clia knew what he'd done to Dana but could they convince anyone else? She moaned, tears spilling from her eyes. Wes, her family, her friends, how soon would they know she was missing? Unlike Dana she had people who loved her, cared, would search, call the police. Could they find her? Yes, she told herself, and she would stay alive until they did.

Chapter 19

Wes put down the notepad he had been writing college notes in and frowned. It was raining heavily, the sky darkened by thick cloud, and he hadn't heard from Hally. He knew something had been bothering her lately and was worried it was to do with him, their relationship. The girl Louise hadn't helped matters either. But none of that explained why she hadn't come around like she said she would.

He picked up his phone, checked it was on and not on silent and frowned again. No messages or calls, that worried him. He contemplated calling her, but quickly changed his mind and decided to go around instead. He loved her so much, needed to know they were all right.

May answered his knock with a little surprised look on her face that was quickly replaced with concern.

"Where's Hally? Is everything ok?"

She asked as he stepped into the kitchen.

"She's not here?"

Wes questioned, concern pricking his heart. Hally always made sure her mum knew where she was. May's eyes flickered fear as she glanced at the clock. It was just after six.

"Colin!"

She called out to her husband. Hally's dad appeared in the kitchen doorway. At once he saw the stress on his wife's face, the fact that Wes was alone and felt his own face pale, knowing this was about his daughter.

"We...we don't know where Hally is."

May stammered, tears already seeping from her eyes. Colin wrapped his arms around her and trying to contain his own panic replied.

"Have you called Corrinne and Clia?"

Colin felt May shake her head in his shoulder and saw Wes do the same. He swallowed.

"Ok, we'll try that first. Maybe she just forgot to tell us."

He said injecting a note of hope into his tone.

"I'll try Clia you call Corrinne Colin."

Wes said pulling his phone from his pocket.

After very short conversations it was established Hally wasn't with either of her two friends. They however were on their way around. Wes got the impression they knew something he and Hally's parents didn't know.

"We have to phone the police."

May blurted out, taking fistfuls of her husband's shirt and gripping it tightly. Colin nodded in agreement. He glanced towards the lounge where Nathan was watching television.

"Ok I'll do it. You call your dad and let him know too. Ask him to come over and take Nathan back to his. He doesn't need to know just yet, not until we know more."

May shook her head.

"I'll call dad to come over but I want Nathan here. He'll know something is wrong, like when mum was ill, anyway. I don't want him getting wound up because he's being kept in the dark."

Colin nodded in agreement knowing his wife was right. Nathan had to be told.

Whilst Colin and May made their calls Wes felt he needed to do something. He couldn't just stand and wait. He left the kitchen and ran upstairs to Hally's room. As he stepped through the door he felt an overwhelming desire to cry. But he checked himself. Now was not the time to crumble. He wrapped his arms around himself and rubbed his shoulders. He felt helpless. Choking back the tears, he swept his burning eyes around. There had to be something here in her room that would tell him where she was.

For a while he simply stood in the middle of the room and stared. Everything in front of him was Hally. He could smell her, almost feel her. The wind howled and the rain slammed against the window, startling him from his reverie. He gave himself a mental shake and stepped over to her desk. He saw her little pink patterned notebook and picked it up, stroking the cover lovingly.

"Oh Hally. Where are you my darling? Please someone help me find her."
He whispered to himself.

He flipped it open and saw the inscription on the first page and smiled. She had written poems for him. He started to read them, feeling close to her as he absorbed her words.

Each one made Wes feel like she was pulling him to her. He thought if only they could tell him where she was, what had happened to her. Reaching the last poem Wes began to close the book. A flicker of ink made him stop. He flipped the pages to the back of the book and saw her poems hadn't ended at all. There were two, deep and slightly disturbing. He read them both, twice, a frown creasing his forehead.

Wesley.
I'm so scared.
I think I'm losing my mind.

So I've left this,
For you to find.
To know that right now,
I love you so much.
I know your scent.
I know your touch.
If I get lost,
Please search for me.
Please bring me back,
To reality.

The second one made him catch his breath and hold it.

When I sleep.
In my dreams
I see.
A silver girl,
I thought was me.
She smiles the same.
She calls my name.
And when I wake.
She doesn't wane.
There she hovers.
Close by me.
The girl, the ghost.
Only I can see.

Wes stood frozen to the spot except for the hand that held the book. That shook, making the pages flutter like a butterfly trying to escape. He let out his breath slowly and read the words in front of him once again. They terrified him. His heart pounded, loud enough he could hear it, hard enough to break through his chest. Was his beautiful, intelligent girlfriend losing her mind? Was she having some kind of breakdown? He shook his head in denial. It couldn't be so. That thought motivated him into action. Corrinne and Clia would be here soon. They would know what was going on. In the meantime, he would talk to Colin and May and show them the book. It might help.

Wes turned from the desk, the book held open with a finger. A flicker of light bounced near the corner of the desk near the edge of his vision. He blinked. It faded and came back growing into a tiny ball of silver. For a moment he was too shocked for his mind to register it. Then as it shimmered and floated, his mind began to wonder what it was. He watched in curiosity as it grew and began to take form. His eyes widened in surprise when he saw the image of a girl with long silvery blonde hair gradually take shape.

****

No no no not Hally. She's missing, gone. He has her I know he does. Wes is here in her room and I heard him say she was missing. I shouldn't have let her try and find him. Now he has her.

I have to do something. I have to remember. Then I have to try and tell Wes. I did it with Hally, I don't know how but I did. Dana concentrate everything you have. Make him see you, hear you.

This is so hard, too hard. It's not working. Wait, he's reading Hally's poems and there are tears in his eyes. Maybe somehow I can connect with him whilst he's thinking so deeply about her.

Oh no, I think he's going to leave. I can't let him go. I have to help. I'm the only one who can. Push Dana. Push hard. He's stopped. He's looking. I think he can see me. I think I'm getting clearer. I feel something inside of me getting stronger, bigger. Yes, he's looking right at me and his eyes are so big and round I think, no I know he can definitely see me. Now all I have to do is make him understand me.

****

Wes stood mesmerised, not believing what he saw in front of him. The girl was becoming more solid as he watched in awe. She looked at him, her long silver blonde hair falling about her like a sheath.

Before the initial shock wore off, Wes thought she was Hally. A jolt of fear stabbed his heart, his mind not wanting to register that his darling girlfriend could actually be dead. Then he realised exactly who she was and breathed again. The floating apparition was Dana. She hovered before him, her eyes piercing his. Her expression was full of worry and concern. Without even thinking about it Wes spoke.

"Dana?"

She nodded quickly, impatiently as if to tell him to get on with it.

"Do you know where Hally is?"

Dana's chest rose as she shook her head. Wes let out a long breath of frustration.

"Has someone taken her?"

Before he finished speaking Dana was nodding.

"Who?"

He asked.

Dana seemed to swell up, glowing brightly. Her silvery brows creased in a deep frown and her lips pressed together firmly. Wes concluded that she was struggling to find a way to communicate. He waited, hoping she could do exactly that.

****

Focus. Look at Wes' eyes. He's miserable. He can see me and he's asking questions that I know I have the answers to. I have to hurry too. I don't know how long Hally has got.

Remember Dana, remember it all. Watch Wes' face and use it to help Hally. Think back to when *he* was with me. How he touched me and the words he used to speak. Remember his voice. Remember how he felt when I touched him. His hair, it was thick and curly at the neck, short on top. His lips. Sometimes they could be soft and gentle other times hard and forceful. His voice, mostly his voice. When he wanted to be he could be kind but when he got angry he was very scary.

More, there's more. Keep concentrating because he is becoming clearer. He's tall, much taller than me. He's big and muscly. The grey hoody, focus on that because that's what I remember the most, its feel and smell.

Oh my God. I can see him. All of him. His face, his arms, his whole body. It's like he's standing in front of me. Wait, there's Hally. She's on the bed in the pretty pink and white room. She's frightened but alive. He has her tied to the bed posts. She's wearing something black and silky. Yes, I know, I remember. I know who he is and I know where Hally is.

****

Wes sucked in a deep breath as the apparition gazed at him intently. She seemed to be concentrating hard. He wanted to help her but he had no idea how. He wasn't even sure he believed what he was seeing. Had he conjured up the image in front of him because of everything Hally had gone through this past week and a half?

Unsure of his own sanity, Wes closed his eyes. When he opened them again Dana was still hanging in front of him. So she was real then, he thought. He had actually spoken to what he suspected was a ghost. He opened his mouth to ask another question but she dimmed. He paused in panic afraid she would disappear before he found out where Hally was. Because he was certain Dana knew.

In front of him Dana shimmered. The edges of her ghostly form became frayed and mist like. He waited on bated breath as she faded, becoming transparent. He reached out a hand, the one that held the notebook, as if to yank her back. Her silver eyes turned towards the book and she smiled elatedly.

One ghostly hand reached for his fingers and the book. Wes felt a soft warm mist engulf his hand and guide it back to the desk. He let Dana lead him. He felt a tug and the notebook leapt from his fingers and landed on the desk. The pages fluttered to a blank one and stilled, pressed open by Dana's almost invisible ghostly hand. Her misty fingers wrapped around a pen. It bobbled on the desk, then rose wobbling in the air. It steadied, its tip pointing down. Slowly, wavering, it connected to the page in the book. A tiny ink smudge appeared. The pen re-positioned and letters began to form into two scrawling words. Wes waited anxiously, barely breathing, then let out a gasp of shock.

Tony Wheeler

Wes looked up into the sad ghostly eyes of the girl who had been murdered by her maths teacher.

"Are you sure?"
He asked. She nodded slowly and deliberately. A shudder of terror penetrated his shock. He spun around and bolted through the door. He thundered down the stairs, nearly tripping, hanging onto the bannister for support. He sped through the kitchen door just as Corrinne and Clia came through the back door. Both girls were panting heavily.

Colin was on the phone, his hand gently stroking Nathan's hair who sat at the table looking miserable. May was pacing up and down the kitchen. Wes heard her muttering. "Not my baby. Please not my baby." And wished the same thing. Clia, eyes wide with fear grabbed Wes' arm. Corrinne was wan and visibly shaking.

"Wes what happened?"
He beckoned to them both and they followed him into the hall. There he quickly explained, hesitating when he had to bring up Dana.

"You saw her?"

Corrinne stammered. He nodded, surprised but relieved that they knew about the ghost.

"I have to speak to Colin. I know he's on the phone to the police but I know who took Hally. I don't have time to go into detail. We have to get to her."

The urgency in his voice spurred both girls into action. They each took a hand and dragged him back to the kitchen.

Colin had finished on the phone and was tapping it against his palm. Nathan was looking very afraid, as he clung to his father.

"I know who has her!"

Wes burst out. May flew to him, grabbing his biceps tightly. Colin sprang up lifting Nathan with him, coming to his wife's side.

"Who Wes, who has my little girl?"

May implored.

"Mr Greenleigh."

May frowned, the name wasn't familiar to her. Wes covered her hands with his. He glanced towards Nathan. The child looked terrified, but Wes had to tell them.

"He's a maths teacher at our old school. He teaches the kids who need extra help." He paused. "And he does some work at our college too."

Wes could see the questions intermingled with fear in May's eyes. Colin was frowning and Wes knew he wanted to ask how he knew this. But Wes didn't know how to begin and time was flipping by rapidly. They had to get to Hally.

"Call the police. Tell them!"

Wes yelled startling them all. Colin took a deep breath, passed Nathan into Corrinne's outstretched arms and lifted the phone.

"I can try. They told me because Hally's sixteen they have to wait before declaring her missing."

There was despair in his eyes as he tapped the redial on the phone. May was frantic. Tears were pouring down her face as she gripped Wes even more tightly.

"A…a teacher?"

She shook her head as if in doing so would make it not real. Wes wrapped his arms around her and nodded. She leaned her head into his chest briefly, then flung it back her eyes wild.

"Mr Austin Wes.!"

Wes frowned and opened his mouth, about to correct her. May gripped his jacket in an iron hold and shook it.

"I have his home number. Last year…oh never mind that."

She tore herself away from his hold and fled from the room. A minute later she was back with her own mobile, scrolling through her contacts. She looked up, satisfaction on her face.

"Here."

She showed Wes the screen then whipped it away and pressed it. Colin was still talking on his phone but he watched his wife carefully.

"Hello, Mr Austin."

They all heard her say. Wes let out a breath of relief, realising why May was calling. Maybe Mr Austin would know where Tony Greenleigh lived. He waited as he listened to May's end of the conversation. She was rapidly explaining the situation to Mr Austin but paused when it came to telling him how they knew about Greenleigh. She glanced at Wes and he knew she was wondering just that. But now was not the time to go into it. It was much too far-fetched for them to believe anyway. Instead he held out his hand, an idea quickly forming. May handed the phone over.

"Mr Austin it's Wes. Hally wrote some things in a notebook. I don't have time to tell you everything but one note made it clear, it is Tony Greenleigh who has taken her. Please if you know where he lives, tell me, it is urgent."

Wes waited, breathing heavily, his knuckles white where he was holding the phone so tightly. After what seemed like forever his grip relaxed and he sighed. A small smile appeared on his lips.

"Thank you. Yes, I'm sure they would appreciate that. I'll text you the address."
The conversation ended and both May and Colin looked at him beseechingly. The phone blipped in his hand and he opened the message.

"He's texted me Greenleigh's address. He's coming here to support you, apparently Hally went to see him this afternoon, so could you text him yours. I'm going to Greenleigh's to get my girlfriend back. Oh, what did the police say?"
Wes said.

"They're sending someone over. And I'm coming with you."
Colin exclaimed. May nodded to her husband.

"We'll stay and look after her, them."
Clia said, Corrinne nodding in agreement. At the same time the back door opened and in came Hally's granddad, panting and worried. He held his arms out to May and she fled to her father, sobbing as he enfolded her in his embrace. Nathan, wriggling free of Corrinne, dashed to his mother and granddad. Granddad's large hands pulled him into the circle, holding him secure. Colin kissed his wife and son and followed Wes to the front door.

"So where are we going?"
Colin asked as he lifted his keys from the table in the hall. Wes relayed the address he had memorised from May's phone.

"Right. So then are you going to tell me really how you found out?"
Colin said as they both jumped in the car. Wes snapped his seatbelt on and bit down on his lip.

"Let's get her first. You need to concentrate on driving."

Colin nodded in resignation and pulled the car away from the pavement.

The address Mr Austin had given them was on the outskirts of the town. Coincidentally it was close to Wes' own home and of a similar design. Colin drove up slowly and parked outside the closed gates to the driveway, extinguishing his headlights. From their position the house looked dark and deserted and Wes wondered at the truth of his source.

"You sure this is it?"

Colin whispered even though there was no one about to hear him but Wes. Wes took a deep breath and gave an almost imperceptible shrug.

"God I hope so."

He whispered back.

Both men got out of the car and all but tiptoed up to the gates. Both were relieved when they found them unlocked. Taking purposeful breaths, they walked up the path to the front door. It was old, wooden with rusting hinges and a dirty glass pane at the top. It looked like it hadn't been opened in years, and once again Wes feared they had got it wrong.

"Looks deserted."

Colin said in a hushed voice.

Wes, his heart pounding, lifted a hand and knocked hard on the door. They waited for what seemed like forever. Wes was about to knock again when a dim light came on beyond. Wes clenched his fists and saw Colin brace himself, anger on his face. They heard a bolt slide, a squeal from hinges that hadn't been used in a very long time and the creaking of swollen wood. The door opened just a crack. Dark eyes peered at them through the slit.

"Yes. Can I help you?"

Wes and Colin felt deflated. The voice was that of an old woman. However, neither man was about to give up.

"Does Tony Greenleigh live here?"

Wes asked. The woman smiled and nodded.

"My son."

Wes let out a breath of relief which was quickly replaced with fear. Surely the teacher wouldn't bring Hally here to his mother's house. But he had to be certain.

"Can we please come in and talk to him?"

Wes asked and Colin looked at him hopefully. The old woman smiled again and stepped back. She tugged at the door until it opened wide enough for them to enter. They stepped over the threshold into a dimly lit old fashioned hallway. It was then both Wes and Colin noticed the way the old lady was looking at them. She was blind.

"Mother!"

A man's voice called out sounding like it was some distance away. Wes and Colin heard dulled footsteps overhead and braced themselves as they became louder and nearer.

****

Oh God oh God. I've done it. I've finally remembered and I managed to tell Wes too. I hope they get to him and find Hally. But maybe I can help with that too because he's sneaky. He will pretend he knows nothing about her.

I saw the room. My room. Well he used to tell me it was anyway. The pink and white room in his house. It was very pretty. The wallpaper is old fashioned but it's still pretty, prettier than my room at home.

But what's important is that I saw it and Hally is there. I'm sure Wes and Hally's family will find a way to get the address, maybe the police will help. So what can I do to help? Aha concentration is the way to go. I did it with the book and pen. Wow I actually did hold the pen and write his name. Tony Greenleigh. My maths teacher.

All those times he told me to work hard and concentrate, well now I will do just that. I have to get to him and stop him before he hurts Hally. He hurt me and not just by killing me, but my heart. I loved him so much and thought he loved me. But he just used me.

Now I remember it all. Why sixteen and my birthday was so important. He was going to leave me and I was so upset. He told me I was too old for him. Sixteen too old? He's thirty-five and I'm too old. What a laugh. Well not really. So I got all teary and begged him not to go. He pushed me down onto my bed and told me to shush. He said everything would be all right. He said I should make a go of things with Martin. Huh, Martin's going to gaol and nearly got me sent there too. I told him that.

He held me whilst I cried, stroked my hair and then did all the other stuff I loved him for. After, he gave me chocolates and lots of wine. It made me very sleepy. My body felt heavy and sluggish, oh all the right words are coming now. Anyway I couldn't move and I felt his hands on my neck. At first they were soft and gentle. Then he pushed his thumbs into my throat and began to squeeze. I couldn't move. I couldn't breathe. I saw his eyes close to my face. He was grinning and then the blackness came.

Now it's all so completely clear I feel energised. Now I have to try something that I hope will work to help Hally. There's the door to Hally's room. Yes, I can go through it and nothing is fogging. The stairs are clear. I'm at the bottom. I can hear Corrinne and Clia with Hally's mum. They're talking but that's not important. I'm in the kitchen where they are. They can't see me but that's ok. I'm stepping out of the backdoor. The garden, I can see it all. I can feel the air about me.

I am lifting up, moving. The air feels free and fresh. It's whooshing by or maybe that's me moving really fast. Ah there it is, down below, his house. I'm rushing towards it. The door is open and I can see Wes and Hally's dad inside. Yes! I'm here now next to them and I can hear him coming. This is it, I know, we are going to save Hally.

****

Wes and Colin stood in the hallway next to the blind old lady and waited. The footsteps came nearer. A pair of slippered feet appeared at the top of the stairs then trouser covered legs. Casually the man came down the stairs a curious frown across his brow.

"Mother what's all this?"

He asked in a soft voice as he reached them. Wes felt his anger bubble up and burst out. He launched himself at Tony Greenleigh grabbing a thick handful of his grey hoody.

"Where's Hally?"

He growled. Tony stared at him unconcernedly. This spurred Colin into action and he seized a fistful of the man's hair.

"My daughter. Where's my daughter!"

"Mother go to your room please."

Greenleigh said firmly and the old lady padded away from them.

"Let go of me please. I really have no idea what you're talking about."

Wes knew the man was lying. He tugged him forward and raised his fist. Greenleigh didn't flinch. Colin yanked his hair but nothing seemed to deter him. He simply stood with a smarmy smile across his face.

"I'm going to tear this house apart until I find her."

Wes snarled as he got right into Greenleigh's face. Greenleigh shrugged then he froze. His eyes which had been firmly fixed on Wes' darted to somewhere over Wes' shoulder and opened wide. Wes saw fear and glanced over his own shoulder, frowning when he saw nothing.

"No no it can't be."

Greenleigh mumbled and twisted from Wes' grasp. Quick as a flash he bounded up the stairs. Wes and Colin followed at his heels.

****

There he is. God how I hate him now when I loved him so much once. He looks so smug coming down the stairs. So arrogant as he pretends he doesn't know what they're talking about. Well I'll wipe that smile off his face soon enough.

Ah, he's seen me. Oh look he's frightened. Good, just a little closer and yes he's running. He's sure to go to the room. I know there are other rooms in this house but he only likes the pink and white one and that's where Hally is. Yes, run you evil coward, run but you won't escape, not from me.

Wes and Hally's dad are following so he won't be able to harm Hally now. Haha he's going to try and shut the door on them. Well they're strong and angry so I don't think he'll be able to. But even if he does he can't shut me out. It's so easy now going from place to place.

****

Greenleigh fled along a dark hallway towards a door at the end. He shoved it open and turned to slam it shut, but Wes got to him first blocking his movements. Colin caught up and between the two of them pushed their way in. Greenleigh backed up until his back was against the far wall. His eyes were still wide in terror.

Hally lay bound to an old bed, tied with silk scarves. Her eyes were wide open flashing fear but relief. Another silky scarf stretched across her mouth preventing her from making a sound. Wes dived for her, yanking it from her face and tugging at the others, freeing her hands. He then pulled her up and into is arms.

Colin stared at Greenleigh, daring him to move, but the man seemed rooted to the spot. Wes was comforting Hally, who now sobbed into his shoulder, as he reigned little kisses across her head. Colin stepped forward and Wes relinquished his hold on Hally to him. Hally fell into her father's arms shuddering and shaking.

"Go away."

The three of them heard, the voice whiny and weak. With tears flooding down her cheeks Hally looked up at Greenleigh. He was now cowering in the corner. He held his arms out as though warding something off.

"You're not here. You're not real. Go away. No don't come nearer."

Greenleigh stammered waving his arms around his head.

Wes and Colin looked perplexed but Hally knew. She knew Dana was in the room. She knew Dana had managed to leave her bedroom and come here and Tony Greenleigh could see her and hear her.

"He's lost it."

Colin murmured but Hally shook her head. She was beginning to feel a lot calmer now she was safe.

"No dad. He hasn't. He murdered Dana though."

Colin gave her a look of sheer surprise and went to open his mouth to ask how she could possibly know that. He was interrupted by a scream.

"Dana don't. I'm sorry. Leave me alone. I will. All of it, all of them."

Tony Greenleigh was holding his arms over his head shielding himself. He was yelling as if in pain, babbling what seemed to be random words. Hally actually felt like giggling. She couldn't see Dana but guessed she was venting pent up anger.

"Call the police dad. He needs locking up."

Hally said as Greenleigh shrieked and writhed.

★★★★

There's Hally on the bed and she's alive. I don't think she can see me here but he can, his eyes are big and scared. Now let me see how he likes it being terrified and helpless. I wonder if he can hear me too. Oh yes he can. He's screaming and crying, begging me to stop. But I won't. I'll keep on to him until he agrees to confess to my murder. His eyes are big and scared. I feel like I'm expanding, growing, as I tell him over and over *confess.* He's backed into a corner, nowhere to go, cowering with his arms over his head.

Now he's babbling and gabbling that he will, and tell all about all of them. So there are more girls. Has he killed any more of them or just me? I thought I was special, the only one. How stupid I was. There, he doesn't like that. He doesn't like being shouted at and threatened. He doesn't like that I'm angry and can hurt him. He was so big and powerful. He had me completely in his control. Now it's my turn and it feels so good. I feel free.

Chapter 20

Everyone who loved her was nearby. Mum and dad were on one side of the hospital bed, Wes on the other. Granddad sat in a chair by the window with Nathan on his lap and Corrinne and Clia stood next to him. They all looked worried but she felt fine. At least she did now she was safe and comfortable.

She knew there would be questions, tons of questions but for now the police had left her alone to be checked over and to rest. She didn't want to rest. She wanted to talk but she still wasn't sure what to say. She had a lot to try and explain to her family, and Mr Austin would want an explanation too. He had come to her home without question to support her mum, brother and friends. He deserved the truth, and somehow she knew he would believe it too. But the police, that was a different story. Somehow she had to give them what they wanted without the ghostly stuff, they would never believe that.

"Hally do you want a drink?"
Mum asked in her most soft and motherly voice breaking into her thoughts. Hally pulled herself into a sitting position.

"Please, but mostly I want to go home. I'm ok. Most of the shock has worn off and nothing physical happened to me. Except of course being tied up."
She whispered the last part so Nathan wouldn't hear. Dad gave her a tiny smile and patted her hand.

"Soon my angel."
He told her.

Soon was actually right as a doctor came in then and told them all he was discharging her. Hally all but leapt out of the bed. Mum pulled the curtain around her so she could dress in the fresh clothes she, mum had brought to the hospital. What Hally had been wearing when Greenleigh abducted her was now in police evidence bags, along with the chemise.

At home mum made her usual hot chocolate for everyone and settled Hally on the sofa, a soft throw wrapped around her. Nathan had been coaxed to bed assured his sister was safe and sound. They had kept most of it from him. He knew Hally had been taken by someone bad but not the details, and that the police now had the bad person. He was young enough to accept that.

Now all eyes were on her for the expected explanation.

"Um, before I tell you can I have a word with Wes and the girls?"
She asked. Her parents agreed and together with granddad left them to it. As soon as they were alone Hally turned to them.

"How did you know?"
She spurted out. Corrinne and Clia looked at Wes. He took a deep breath and told them all everything that had happened in Hally's room. Hally grinned.

"She did it then. She found a way like she said she would. She was there you know. That's why Greenleigh was going mental."

Wes nodded but the girls looking at her questioningly. So Hally launched into a full description of the last minutes in Greenleigh's house. When she finished they all looked a lot happier.

"So what next Hally?"
Clia asked. Hally shrugged.

"I tell mum, dad and granddad everything. I think they'll believe me."

"I'll tell them what I saw too. Then they're sure to." Wes said pulling her close to him. Hally called her family back into the room.

"Best get comfy. This is going to take a while." She said as she began the story from the first dream.

Hally stayed home from college the next day. She expected word to get around quickly, and needed time to adjust before being bombarded with questions from her fellow students. Wes had stayed the night, holding her like he would never let her go. He dashed off home first thing but soon came back, taking the day off college too. Corrinne and Clia took time off as well and came to her house to sit with her, just as they had done after they all found out about Dana's death the year before.

Colin had been given compassionate leave from work, and after he had taken a protesting Nathan to school, picked granddad up and brought him home. They were all waiting for the visit from the police they knew was coming.

Detective Inspector Sheila Anderson and Detective Constable Andrea Shorley arrived just after lunchtime. They gathered the family in the sitting room but Hally insisted Wes, Corrinne and Clia be there too. So once they were all crammed in and settled, Detective Anderson told them what they needed to know.

Tony Greenleigh had been arrested and charged with Hally's abduction and confinement. He had gone willingly. During interview he had made a statement confessing to the murder of Dana, giving details of what he did to her so adding to the charges.

He then went on to admit he had groomed and raped a number of girls under sixteen. All of them had been students at Hally's old school. All of them had been girls from difficult backgrounds, struggled with school and were susceptible to his charms. Dana had been one of those girls. But she had also been the first, beginning as soon as she started secondary school. He had held onto her the longest. The other girls were fourteen and fifteen years old, and as they neared sixteen he would simply stop, dump them like a tired boyfriend. He made them feel worthless, reduced their self-esteem to zero and cajoled them into keeping quiet. He made them believe that no one would believe them if they reported him.

The detectives told them all of this came directly from him. Apparently he had sat in the interview room trembling and afraid. He wouldn't tell them what he feared, only that *she* would hurt him again if he didn't tell them everything, and he wouldn't explain who *she* was. Hally got the impression they thought it might be her. She knew otherwise.

Luckily Hally didn't have to give too many details herself as Tony Greenleigh had done most of the work for her. There was one sticky moment when Detective Anderson asked how Wes knew where she was. Before he could answer, Hally quickly stepped in. She said she had thought about the man on the station and put a name to his face. That she was afraid he had been following her and watching her, and had jotted her fears down in her notebook. Detective Anderson gave her a quizzical look but didn't question her explanation. Hally sighed inwardly, no way would the detective believe the truth.

Finally, the detectives left them in peace. They all knew it wasn't entirely over as the police had a lot of work to do. But for Hally it felt as if it was over. Sighing, she leaned back into the sofa with her knees drawn up, and felt more relaxed than she had in the last week and a half. Such a short time, it had seemed so much longer.

"Penny for them?"

Wes whispered in her ear. She smiled at him, at her two closest friends.

"Just glad it's over."

Wes pulled her into his arms and leaned his head on hers. Corrinne and Clia sat on the floor their backs up against the sofa.

"The boys are coming 'round in a bit. Is that ok Hals?"

Corrinne said tilting her head back so she could see Hally.

"Of course. We all need to get back to normal."

Hally replied with her eyes closed. Corrinne gave Wes a tiny wink and he grinned back.

Gregg and Rhys got to Hally's just after five. Mum, knowing they were coming had prepared a large buffet dinner. She laid the food out on the kitchen table and told everyone to tuck in. Both boys had very nearly squashed Hally when they hugged her, and she knew they had been just as concerned as their girlfriends.

The food was delicious as was the company. Hally was enjoying herself. Nathan was buzzing, partly because he had been the centre of attention at school as he imparted what he knew to his friends, and also because mum was letting him eat anything he wanted. Granddad was happily chatting to Gregg and Rhys about their jobs, they both worked for Wes' dad who was a builder. Colin had his arm around May who watched her daughter. She hadn't yet got over nearly losing her. Corrinne and Clia were whispering conspiratorially by the sink and Wes was fidgeting.

"You ok?"

Hally asked with a cheeky grin. Wes nodded.

"Um, I'm fine."

But he seemed nervous. He took her hand in his and kissed her fingers. Then he looked around the room.

"Um, could I...um, say something please?"
He called out, blushing. A little hush settled over the kitchen as all eyes turned towards him. Corrinne and Clia were grinning like the cat that got the cream. Wes pulled Hally to his side.

"I don't think I've ever been so afraid as when Hally was missing. And I don't think I've ever felt so relieved or grateful when we got her back. But the one thing I know above all else is that I love her so much, and I never want to be away from her again. So..." he paused, turned to face Hally and dropped to one knee. "Hally, will you please marry me?"

Hally gasped in delighted shock. She flicked her eyes to her mother and saw tears of joy streaming down her cheeks. She looked down at Wes. He was holding a little velvet box open in front of her. Inside nestled on a satin cushion was a delicate ring with a perfect little diamond at its heart. Hally, tears glistening on her cheeks stretched out her left hand. Wes lifted the ring and slid it onto her finger.

"Yes oh yes Wes. Of course I'll marry you."

Wes stood up and swung her into his arms kissing her smiling lips. There was a round of applause, and a very loud "Yuck" from Nathan. As Wes turned her in a circle, she saw his parents and Ellie standing just inside the back door. They had arrived in time to witness their son's proposal.

"So did you all know?"
Hally squealed. There were nods and yesses from everyone. Colin reached into the fridge and Hally heard the pop from a champagne cork. Wes lowered her to the ground but held onto her hand. May handed each of them a glass of golden champagne and took her daughter's face between her palms.

"Congratulations angel. Be happy. I know you will be happy, like your dad and me."

Hally kissed her mum, then everyone else. Nathan as usual groaned and wiped at his cheek, but Hally could see he didn't really mind. Granddad came over and held her in his arms.

"Your gran would have loved this. That's her ring, she wanted you to have it. I know you're young my darling girl, but so were we, your parents too. But I also know it doesn't matter. You and Wes, you love each other, that's all that matters."

He whispered to her hugging her tight. Hally felt the tiny prickle of tears, wishing her gran was with them, knowing she very probably was.

Finally, the party had ended and her friends had gone home. Wes was walking back with his parents to put Ellie to bed then he was coming back to be with her. Her room seemed strangely quiet after everything that had gone on before.

Dressed in pyjamas and dressing gown, Hally sat on the edge of her bed with her book of poems between her hands. Wes had explained how after reading the last two poems, Dana had taken the book from him and written the name of her captor on one of the pages. Hally found the page and tore it out. The book was for love poems to Wes, she didn't want Tony Greenleigh's name in it anywhere. Besides, she could truthfully tell the police she had done this, if they ever asked to see what she had supposedly written about him.

She pondered over everything for a moment. When she had told her family about Dana, she saw some scepticism across their faces for just a little while. But then she saw belief. They knew her well enough to know she didn't make things up, and besides there was no other explanation.

She sighed and looked up towards her desk.

"Where are you Dana? Are you at peace?"

She whispered to herself. She closed her eyes. A tiny breeze ruffled her hair, and she thought her mum must have opened the window to let in a little fresh air. It came again, a bit stronger. Hally opened her eyes and smiled. Dana was hovering next to her.

"Are you all right?"

The apparition said softly. Hally nodded. Dana was bright and her voice was clear.

"You...you're stronger."

Hally murmured.

"Yes I am. I can go wherever I want to now and that's down to you. Thank you Hally. I was terrible to you when I was alive and for that I will be forever sorry. And I will be forever grateful that you helped me find myself and him. I know I'm dead, but now he's been caught and will be punished I'm not sad anymore, or lonely. It's strange this world I exist in. There are others here. We keep each other company, guide one another when one is lost or needs help. I think maybe they were there guiding me, but I'm not sure. There's still so much for me to learn. What I am sure of though is there is life after death. Hally, I'm leaving now but I won't be gone. If you ever need me I will know and I will return to help you. Once again Hally thank you. Goodbye."

Dana leaned her ghostly head towards Hally and pressed her silver lips to Hally's cheek. Hally felt the soft warm mist for a moment then it was gone, so was Dana.

Hally pulled back her duvet and slipped into bed. She rested against the pillows, a small smile of contentment across her face. She raised her left hand and kissed the little ring and its precious diamond. As she waited for Wes, her fiancé, to return she glanced up at the picture of the baby and the angels. Her smile spread, secure now in the knowledge that the angels were real, and knowing she was loved and was being looked after from down here and from up above.

ABOUT THE AUTHOR

Stephanie M Turner has been writing since she could put pen to paper. She has a Bachelor of Education degree and is a qualified teacher. She is married with four children and is also a grandmother.

Other titles by Stephanie M Turner

Fifteen Going On Grown Up

Out Of The Grey

Caramel Cupcakes

Ripples In The Silk